The Devil's Bounty

The Devil's Bounty

A Ryan Lock Thriller

SEAN BLACK

First published in Great Britain
in 2012 by Bantam Press
an imprint of Transworld Publishers

This edition published in the United
States and Canada by Sean Black
Digital

ISBN: 9781909062108

For Gordon Gray, a true Trojan

Prologue

Santa Barbara, California

It was eight o'clock on Friday evening and the bars and clubs that ran the length of State Street were already filling up. Three frat boys wove an unsteady path out of the James Joyce Irish bar, before collapsing in a good-natured heap on the sidewalk where one of them grabbed his two buddies in a fraternal headlock. Outside the Velvet Jones nightclub, a bouncer carded two young co-eds, making a big show of examining their no doubt fake IDs before unclipping the red rope and letting them inside. He watched as they wiggled past him and into the club.

Up and down the town's main party drag, the same scenes of mostly good-natured youthful debauchery played themselves out, as they had done every year for about as long as anyone in the wealthy California beach community could remember.

Charlie Mendez stood on the corner of State and West Haley and surveyed the scene. He plucked a fresh cigarette from the pack of Marlboro Reds tucked into the rolled-up sleeve of his

T-shirt, dug out a Cartier lighter from the front pocket of his jeans and lit up. He pulled the smoke deep into his lungs as he continued to scan the street. A crowd of girls passed, one, a long-legged brunette, turning to smile at him. Charlie gave her his best California-surf-bum smile in return and ran a hand through his thick mop of blond curls. She giggled and looked as if she was about to say something to him, but her friend grabbed her elbow and pulled her back along the street.

Charlie took out the small digital camera he always carried with him for just such opportunities and called after her, 'Hey, beautiful! Smile!'

The cheesy line and the picture-taking would have earned most men of Charlie's age a raised middle finger or a look of disgust, but Charlie wasn't most men. In his late teens and twenties, he had been good enough to work for a time as a model in New York, and despite his lifestyle, his looks were still merely faded rather than entirely departed. His hair and teeth were perfect, and his face, beaten by sun, sand and surf, was rugged.

The girl blushed, whispering something to her friend, then walked on with the rest of her group.

He gazed at the image on the screen. She must have been startled by the tiny flash because her eyes were closed. It gave him a shiver of anticipation for what might come later.

These were the nights he lived for. There were many things he loved about the town where he had grown up, but perhaps none was greater than the opportunities it afforded a man like him. Every year the seniors left, and every year the freshmen arrived. The town was in a state of constant transfusion and replenishment. But Charlie remained constant. Watching. Waiting. Choosing his moment. Always ready to add to his collection.

He glanced at his wristwatch, a very un-surferlike five-thousand-dollar Rolex Oyster Submariner. The night was young. He would go home and get things ready. Then, around eleven, he would return to see what the rest of the evening held for him. Tomorrow the students would begin to drift away, and over the following few days Santa Barbara would shift from college town to tourist town. The people who lived in LA or San Francisco but kept summer homes in the area would arrive. Couples. Families. None of them any use to him. They would crowd the beach he surfed every morning and generally make his life miserable.

That meant he had to make tonight count. He had to make it special. Tonight would have to sustain him through the long, lonely months of summer before fall semester when fresh meat arrived.

He turned and walked back to his car, a low-slung red Aston Martin convertible. He jumped into the driver's seat, gunned the engine and took off, heading northwards up the coast, eager to set the scene for what lay ahead.

Part One

One

Sixteen Months Later

Los Angeles, California

Heart pounding, Melissa Warner pushed her way through the crush of bodies towards the front of the stage. Almost directly above her, a sweet-faced black kid, dressed in baggy jeans and an LA Lakers top, was singing about *bitches* and *hoes* while two similarly attired DJs worked the decks behind him. Either side of the rapper, a dozen female dancers, in bondage gear and lingerie, gyrated in apparent ecstasy as the words poured forth.

> *Y'all know that hoes and bitches,*
> *They only after one thing.*

Two spotlights zigzagged across the mass of bodies filling the arena. The bass pounded so hard from the speakers that Melissa could feel the floor beneath her moving in time with it. The rapper grabbed his crotch with one hand, and waved a roll of dollar bills in the other. The crowd of mostly white suburban teenagers screamed and hollered their endorsement of the lyrics. *Lyrics that reduced their sisters and mothers and girlfriends to what exactly? To prostitutes. To people who served only one function. To pieces of meat.* Stay focused, she told herself.

Remember why you're here. To find him.

Not that he had been an easy man to locate. Far from it. But she had stayed doggedly on his trail, ignoring everyone around her who had told her it would be best if she let it go. And now her persistence was about to pay off. He was close by. The man who would bring her justice and, with it, the chance finally to move on with her life.

She scanned the barrier, and the line of muscular, T-shirted security guards. There was no sign of the man she was looking for. She pushed her way to the side of the stage, ducking under flying elbows and pushing her arms out, like a swimmer, to create gaps in the wall of flesh that surrounded her.

The press of bodies against her made her feel sick and light-headed. She was gasping for breath, but the air seemed to hold heat and moisture rather than oxygen. Then, just as she was starting to worry that she might pass out, she found a space and she was out of the crowd.

A lone security guard, wearing a Triple-C tour shirt (it stood for Compton Clown Crew) and a laminated picture ID hooked to a black silk lanyard, stood next to the crush barrier. Beyond him, a wooden black ramp led towards the backstage area. Melissa dug out her cell phone and pulled up the only picture she had been able to find of the man. She showed it to the security guard. He looked at it and shrugged.

'Don't know that dude,' he said.

'But you must,' she pressed. 'He's in charge of security.'

'Not here, he ain't.'

'No, I mean security for the band.'

He gave another shrug. 'I don't know nothing about that.'

She stood on tiptoe and tried to get a glimpse of the backstage area. The security guard shifted his position, blocking her view. He had damp patches of sweat blossoming under his arms. She caught a whiff of body odor and her stomach churned.

'You want to get backstage, huh? I can arrange it. Get you in to see the artists too,' he said, with a nod towards the stage. 'Gonna cost you, though,' he said, staring at her breasts.

She took a step back and closed her eyes, trying desperately not to cry. If only he knew, she thought. If only he knew what his leering was doing to her. If only he could experience a tenth of the pain she felt.

She opened her eyes, but his attention was elsewhere now. He was on a walkie-talkie, barking instructions and staring at the crowd.

She turned to see people scattering in all directions. Music was still pouring from the speakers but the rapper had stopped rapping and now he was at the edge of the stage, one hand raised as if to calm the crowd. 'Be cool, people. Be cool out there.'

Following the security guard's gaze, Melissa could see panic taking hold as clusters of concertgoers scrambled in all directions, a shoal of fish parting at the approach of a predator.

She strained to get a better view.

There must have been a half-dozen of them: young, male and Hispanic, they wore blue hats and bandannas – gang members. They pushed through the crowd, throwing punches and kicking out at anyone within striking distance. A kid, no more than seventeen, took a fist to the face and went down. Three of the gang members swarmed him, kicking him in the head and body, grabbing other people in the crowd to steady themselves and give their blows more purchase.

At the edge of the group, a lone gang member stood perfectly still and watched the beating with cold detachment. He was smaller than the rest but he seemed the most in control. He called to the three delivering the beating and they stopped.

He raised his head and, as he did, Melissa saw that it wasn't a male after all. A young girl had been leading the rampage. She looked around, perfectly calm in the middle of the mêlée as, on stage, the group made its retreat into the wings and security guards poured over the barrier in a futile attempt to restore order.

The gang leader glanced at the stage. Her gaze settled on Melissa and their eyes met. She raised a hand and extended her index finger, pointing Melissa out to the others.

In that moment, Melissa knew this was no random event. They were here for a reason. As she was here looking for him, so they were here looking for her. She began to edge away until she felt the cold metal of the crush barrier at her back.

Now the gang members were shrugging off whatever resistance they were meeting, and starting to move in her direction. Melissa felt a wave of terror wash over her as the girl leading the gang lifted her T-shirt to reveal the dull black handle of a gun.

The sight of it snapped Melissa back to the present. She looked around for an escape route. Twenty yards away, she saw it – a single-door fire exit.

She sprinted towards it, not daring to look back. If she could get through the door, she could reach the parking lot. If she could make it that far, she could jump into her car, and get away.

Her quest abandoned, Melissa Warner burst through the door and out into the warm Los Angeles night. She had to stay alive long enough to find him. What happened to her after that didn't matter.

Two

In his line of work, Ryan Lock was constantly vigilant for two things. The first was the absence of the normal: a security guard missing from his post, a blank corner of an office, which had previously housed a security camera, a silent junkyard normally patrolled by a bad-tempered Doberman. The second was the presence of the abnormal, something strange and out of place: an unfamiliar car appearing outside a school at pick-up time or a newly installed manhole cover on a parade route.

That evening, as he scanned the crowded hotel lobby, which was filled with revelers attending the after-show party for his latest clients, a double-platinum rap group called Triple-C, Lock spotted something that fell, most definitely, into the second category. Unnoticed by the rest of the partygoers, a young woman stepped gingerly from the barrel of the gleaming gold revolving door into the hotel lobby, and stopped, eyes darting around, searching someone out.

In and of itself, her arrival was hardly worthy of note. The defining feature of Triple-C's after-parties was the number of young women in attendance. They tended, he had noted, to out-number the men by at least six to one. But no one looked even vaguely like the young woman walking through the press of bodies towards him.

For a start, their hair was perfectly coiffed instead of damp and matted on their foreheads. Their eyes sparkled with life, or excite-ment, or too much alcohol, while this young woman's were like a doll's: black and lifeless. And none of the other young women crowding the lobby had blood pouring from her abdomen, running down her legs and splashing, like thick scarlet raindrops, on to the hotel's white marble floor.

As she staggered across the lobby, people fell silent. Cocktail glasses and champagne flutes hung in suspended animation inches from lips. Eyes widened in disbelief and horror. People stepped back, unconsciously clearing a path, as the blood continued to pour from her belly, leaving a trail on the marble.

As the silence washed behind her, the only person to react was Lock. Taking off his jacket, he half turned towards his best friend and business partner, the six-foot-two African American marine Ty Johnson. 'Get the guys upstairs into the suite.'

There had been a disturbance at that night's concert, a series of brawls among the crowd, possibly gang-related, and he was taking no chances. Ty did as he was told, quickly marshaling the rap group and their management towards a bank of elevators. Their movement punctured the silence, and a babble of incompre- hension filled the void as Lock went quickly to the young woman, reaching her in four long strides.

Her shoulders were hunched and she was shivering. She flinched visibly as Lock reached out to her. He could see the pain pinching her face as he sat her on a nearby couch as gently as he could, hushing her whimpers with words of reassurance.

Blood was oozing through a hole in her shirt and he could see where the fabric had charred. A gunshot wound – clear as day. Just the one by the look of it. He balled up his jacket and pushed it hard against the wound. She screamed as he pressed, talking to her while he tried to staunch the bleeding.

A male receptionist had made his way over to them, lips puckered in apparent displeasure at the sight of so much blood on his formerly pristine marble floor – and now the designer couch. He nodded from the girl to the door, indicating, Lock assumed, that she belonged outside. He met the man's eyes with a level gaze.

That was all it took. Lock's stare was frightening. He had blue eyes that burned with rage at lives lost or taken.

The receptionist flushed bright red.

'Call nine one one,' Lock told him. 'Tell them we have a gun-shot victim and she's bleeding out.'

As the receptionist ran, Lock looked around the lobby at the last of the stragglers. There was a knot of glamorous party girls in their twenties who had backed against a wall. He shouted across the lobby, 'Ladies, check your bags and see if you can find me a tampon or a sanitary towel.'

They stared at him, horrified.

'Check your purses, goddamnit,' he repeated, raising his voice.

A willowy blonde in a black cocktail dress pulled out a pack of tampons. 'Will these do?'

'Perfect. Bring them here,' he said, waving her over with his free hand.

She tottered towards him on high heels, holding a still-wrapped tampon at arm's length between thumb and forefinger.

'Take the wrapper off,' Lock barked, 'and see if you can find me some hand sanitizer.'

An Asian girl with the group piped up, 'I have some.'

'Good. Let me have it.'

Lock turned back to the victim. 'Okay. I'm going to take the jacket away, and then I'm going to have to take off your shirt so I can pack the wound. I'll be as gentle as I can but it'll hurt.'

She looked up at him, her eyes tracing the contours of his face, like a finger running over a road map. Her pupils widened a fraction and life seemed to return to them.

Up close, he could tell that she was younger than she had first appeared. Nineteen. Maybe twenty at a push. Her skin was pale and sallow. She had small, delicate features, and bright green eyes. Her hair was a deep chestnut brown, almost auburn.

Finally she nodded. He looked at the blonde who had given him the tampon. 'What's your name?' he asked.

'Ashley,' said the blonde.

'Okay, Ashley, I'm going to need you to hold her jacket where it is for a moment.'

'But I . . . the blood . . . What if she, like, *has* something?' Ashley protested.

Lock fixed her with the same gaze he'd used on the reception-ist. 'If we don't do this, she is going to die right here in front of us. So, please, just do as I asked.'

She complied. He cupped his hands and the Asian girl pumped four squirts of sanitizer into them. He rubbed it in. 'Okay, Ashley, you can move the jacket away now and give me that tampon.'

She did as she was told and Lock began to peel away the cotton shirt from the edge of the wound. It was maybe a half-inch in diameter, bad but not the worst he'd seen. It looked as if the bullet had stayed inside – better than there being an exit wound and two places to lose blood. He pulled out the blue cord of the tampon and pressed the other end into the wound. Almost immediately it began to expand as it absorbed the blood, puffing out and filling the hole in the girl's stomach. Blood seeped from the edges of the wound but just moments before it had been pouring out.

He glanced at the desk. The receptionist had the phone at his ear. 'They're on their way,' he called.

'How long?' Lock asked.

The receptionist went back to the phone.

Lock worked the numbers. Where had the girl been when she was shot and how long ago? Life or death would be separated by seconds rather than minutes.

'Mr Lock?' she said, tears welling in her eyes.

She knew his name. He tried to place her. Had he met her before? He didn't think so, but something about her was familiar. Had she been at the concert earlier, maybe at the stage door? Over the last month he had seen some pretty elaborate stunts to grab Triple-C's attention, not to mention that evening's near-riot.

'You were looking for *me*?' he asked her.

Her chin fell on to her chest. 'They tried to stop me,' she stuttered.

'Who? Who tried to stop you?'

'He sent them. He wants me to stop looking for him. But I won't.'

The hairs rose at the back of Lock's neck. He scanned the crowd, which was slowly drifting away, their backward glances a mix of disgust and curiosity. No one stood out. No one appeared to be a threat.

'Who?' he asked her gently. 'Who does?'

Her lips started to form a name but no sound came.

'Is this person after you?'

She shook her head, the deadness settling back in her eyes. 'You have to catch him.'

Lock's patience was fraying. 'Whoever you are, whatever this is about, I'm not a cop. I don't catch people, I keep them safe.'

'That's why it has to be you,' she said.

'Why what has to be me?' he asked.

'The one who brings him back.'

She was talking in riddles. Every answer she gave led to more questions. 'Bring who back?'

'Joe tried. But they killed him.'

'Joe? Is that the name of the man you want me to find?'

'It's not fair. He should be in prison for what he did.'

'Who?'

She stared at Lock and a sudden intensity flared in her eyes, like the last burst of a candle flame before the wind snuffs it out. 'You're my last chance. If you don't catch him and bring him back, they're going to kill me.'

Lock kept the pressure on her wound as best he could. The fire was dying down. She was blinking. If he didn't keep her conscious, he would lose her before they made it to a hospital. He had to keep her awake, and the best way of doing that was to keep her talking. 'Listen, let's start over, okay? Can you tell me your name?'

Her eyes focused. That was good. 'Melissa,' she said.

A tiny victory. 'Okay, Melissa,' he said. 'I'm going to come with you to the hospital, and on the way, I want you to tell me everything. But start at the beginning. Can you do that for me, Melissa? Can you tell me your story all the way through? If you do that, and I feel I can help you, then I promise I will. Do we have a deal?'

'Deal.'

Lock turned back to the receptionist. 'ETA?'

The man looked at him blankly.

'How long until they get here?'

'They said ten minutes.'

Lock did the math. If the EMS ambulance had deployed from the hospital, that would mean at least another ten minutes. In twenty she'd be dead.

He scooped the girl into his arms and ran for the door, struggling to stay on his feet as his shoes slipped on the bloodied floor.

Three

Lock placed her in the front passenger seat as gently as he could. Even the smallest movement made her moan. He closed himself off from the sound. If she was going to live, he had to concentrate on getting her to hospital and block out everything else.

He was already one small step ahead. As part of his security preparation for Triple-C, he knew the location of the closest emergency room – at the UCLA Medical Center – as well as the fastest route there from the hotel. He gunned the engine of his car, a black Audi A6, and roared out on to Wilshire Boulevard. He cut in ahead of a slow-moving Lexus, muscling into the left-hand lane, and buried the gas pedal.

The lights at the intersection of Wilshire and Beverly Glen flicked from red to green. He blew through the junction at speed. Ahead, both lanes of traffic were at a standstill. He moved into the turn lane to go round it, then as the next rack of lights turned green, cut up the cars at the front.

A couple of drivers behind him honked their horns but he kept moving, eyes sweeping the road ahead. It was clear now. He slowed a little to make the turn on to Westwood Boulevard.

The girl shifted in her seat and groaned. 'Stay with me, Melissa, okay?'

'It hurts so much.'

He shifted up a gear and reached a hand over. 'You're doing really good.'

She grabbed at his hand and squeezed it. 'Cesar Mendez,' she said.

The name had come from nowhere. She was beyond pale now – even her lips had lost their color: a bad sign.

'What was that?' he asked.

'Cesar Mendez. They call him Charlie,' she said. 'That's who I want you to find for me. Find him and bring him back.'

Lock must have taken his eyes off the road for a split second because the Audi's front right wheel hit a pot-hole. The car bounced, prompting a scream from Melissa. She grabbed at Lock's forearm, digging her nails into his flesh.

'You do what you have to do,' said Lock, ignoring the pain as he felt her break the skin. 'Charlie? He shot you?'

There was no reply. He felt her grip on his arm relax and his heart flipped. He could see the hospital entrance, maybe a half-block further on the right.

He snuck another look. Her eyes were fluttering closed. He hit the button to lower the window next to her and let in some air.

'Melissa? Can you hear me? Don't go to sleep, okay. We're almost there now.'

He raced towards the hospital, his eyes flicking to and from the girl. She was fighting to stay conscious.

With a screech of brakes he pulled into the no-parking zone at the main entrance. A security guard appeared from nowhere and hollered at him to move the car. He ignored the guy, got out of the car and ran around to the passenger side. He leaned in, unclipped the seatbelt and struggled in the confined space to lift her out.

Oblivious to everything and everyone around him, he ran with her into the emergency-room reception area. Her eyes were closed and she had stopped breathing.

Four

With Melissa in surgery, two detectives from the LAPD's Robbery Homicide Division swung by to take an informal witness statement from Lock. When he asked whether they would provide any form of police protection, they answered, as he had known they would, in the negative. They left, but he stayed to pace the corridor.

He checked in with Ty, sharing what little information he had. Everything at the hotel was quiet.

The hours passed and Lock waited. After years in close protection it was one thing he had become expert at. If it had been an Olympic event, he would have been looking at a gold medal. Eventually Melissa was moved into a private room on the fourth floor. The surgeon wouldn't speak to him but he gleaned a little information from a nurse, who, in breach of official policy, allowed him to stand guard when he explained that the person or persons who had shot the girl might return to finish the job.

In the room, he grabbed a metal-backed folding chair from

beside the bed and set it in the corner nearest to the door so that he would see anyone coming into the room before they spotted him. Someone looking to kill her most likely wouldn't risk shooting her from the doorway, not after they had screwed up their first attempt. They'd want to be close. Pillow over the head, gun pressed in tight to dampen the sound, then squeeze the trigger. Or they'd smother her: the heart monitor would tell them when she was dead.

His shirt and trousers were caked with dried blood, he noticed. He got up and crossed to the sink mounted against the far wall. He washed his hands and face, then crossed to the bed and picked up the chart hanging from the bed rail. At the very top it had the girl's full name – Melissa Warner – and her date of birth. The medical staff must have found some form of ID on her when they cut off her clothing.

She was lying on her side, chestnut hair fanned out over the crisp white pillow.

Melissa Warner. Charlie Mendez.

Something about the two names resonated. He had heard them before, but where? He sat down again and texted Ty with an update, then asked him to find out what he could. A few seconds later Ty was back to say he'd do some digging.

He looked across at the sleeping girl as the monitor sketched her heartbeat with a green glow. The tension in her face had slowly released as she slept but she was in the fetal position, knees pulled up to her chest. Lock had often thought that you could trace a person's journey in the world by their sleep pattern. Little kids stretched out like starfish, open and unafraid. But that stage soon passed. If things got bad enough, you rarely slept at all, like Lock. It made his job easier. He could get by on three hours a night. But it made his life hell. He knew why he couldn't sleep but he didn't know the cure. He just hoped that in time it would pass.

He went back to the chair but didn't sit down, preferring to lean against the wall. Even with his insomnia, he was worried about falling asleep. Eyes open, alert to every sound from the corridor, he stood vigil, as he had done so many times before, ready to protect the girl who had stepped from nowhere into his life.

It was a full two hours later that he saw the door handle move a fraction. Nurses had been in twice to check on Melissa but they had come straight in, as innocent people do. They pressed down the handle, opened the door and walked in.

The handle moved another fraction. Then another. Lock tensed and moved softly along the wall so that he was closer to the door.

There was a soft click as the latch cleared its slot. Lock kept inching along with his back to the wall.

The door edged open. Lock stood perfectly still as a figure stepped into the room, closing the door. It was too dark to get a clear view but the person was short, maybe five two. They wore baggy jeans, a baseball cap and an oversized jacket. A shaft of moonlight slid across the floor and he saw a long, thin steel blade in the figure's right hand. Whoever it was walked towards the sleeping girl, the knife raised.

Five

Ty sat alone in the hotel room and pecked away with two long index fingers at his laptop. He ran a simple Google search for Cesar 'Charlie' Mendez, then another for Melissa Warner. As he read them, he wished he could blot out the unhelpful soundtrack from the next room where one of the rappers from Triple-C was involved in a prolonged but apparently intimate party with two young women from the lobby. The sounds of hotel-room sex made what was already uncomfortable reading even more so.

As he sifted through the web pages, the story fell into place. There was no great mystery as to why Melissa had sought out Lock. It was all right there on the screen. The more he read, the more worried he became. Lock was one of the few people who could help her and, worryingly for Ty, he was psychologically primed for the mission because of what had happened to him in the recent past.

While he and Ty had been protecting a young female porn star, Raven Lane, from a murderous stalker, Lock's fiancée, Carrie, had been kidnapped. She had escaped but, in a cruel twist of Fate, had run out in front of the vehicle he and Lock had been driving as they raced to rescue her. Lock hadn't been able to save the woman he loved, and the guilt weighed heavily on both of them. It had left Ty's friend bereft. But under the grief lay a deep seam of anger.

Knowing this, the prospect of what Lock might do if he took on Melissa's case made Ty feel sick, but he went on cutting the relevant sections from the news stories and blog posts, then pasting them into a single Word document. In the end, he reflected, it could have been summarized in four lines.

A crime.

A trial.

An escape.

And a whole bunch of dead bodies – with a lot more to come.

When he was finished, he checked it over, saved the document on to a memory stick and headed downstairs to get it printed out in the hotel's business centre. As he stepped out of the lobby, he saw that the blood had been cleaned from the marble floor and the couch where Lock had tended Melissa had been removed. No one could have guessed that, only a few hours ago, a girl had been bleeding to death there.

If only that was the end of it.

Six

'Lemme go, you old pervert.'

As the would-be assassin twisted around to spit in his face, Lock saw she was a teenager. He had her pinned to the floor in the corridor. The knife was already tucked away safely in his jacket. His right knee was pressed into the base of her spine, and he was holding her right hand at the wrist, ready to bend it back on itself if she didn't stop struggling.

'Hey,' said Lock sharply. 'Less of the "old".' He relaxed his grip a little and she drove her elbow back, catching the side of his face. He grabbed her wrist again as she tried to wriggle out from under him.

She couldn't have weighed more than a hundred pounds but that was only making it harder for him to keep her still. He heard footsteps and looked up: a security guard was marching down the corridor, with two patrol cops in tow. Whatever information Lock was going to get, he had a very short window in which to secure it. Direct questions were hardly likely to yield much. The kid was a hood rat, and almost certainly a gang member. LA gangs often used younger members to do their dirty work because the criminal justice system treated them with relative lenience. And if it didn't they were expendable.

'Who do you run with?' Lock asked her. 'Who's your click?'

She smirked. 'You like being on top of me, huh? I can feel your jimmy digging into me.'

Lock rolled up the sleeve of her jacket, and shifted his weight so he could get a look at her tattoos. The first he glimpsed was a boy's name, Ramón – it ran in blue script from wrist to elbow. *A boyfriend? A pimp? A gang leader?*

'Who's Ramón?' he asked her.

'The guy who's gonna cap your ass, bitch.'

Well, thought Lock, at least she's stopped calling me 'old'. He checked the other arm. That was clean. 'What do you want with Melissa?'

There was a snarl. 'What you think? Bitch needs some killing is all.'

'Ramón tell you that?'

She lapsed into a sullen silence. He was going to get no more from her and they both knew it.

The security guard and the two cops were almost upon him. Lock got to his feet, and hauled her upright. He pulled down the hood of her sweatshirt to reveal a tangle of black hair, which he pushed off the nape of her neck. There, scrawled in black ink, was what he had been looking for: two words and a number – *Loco Diablo 13*. *Loco*: crazy. *Diablo*: the devil. *13* stood for the thirteenth letter of the alphabet, M, which stood in turn for 'Mexican Mafia', or La Eme.

Seven

Melissa's eyes were still closed when Ty arrived a little after eight o'clock with orange juice and bagels – the west coast equivalent of coffee and doughnuts. He handed Lock a small carton of juice and put the brown-paper bag on the slide-in table at the foot of the bed, along with some low-fat cream cheese and paper napkins.

'You want to head back to the hotel and get some shut-eye?' he asked.

Lock shook his head, then nodded to the manila folder Ty was holding. 'What you got?'

Ty sighed. 'It's pretty messed up. In fact, it's about as messed up as it gets.' He put the folder on the table beside the bagels, then looked at Melissa. 'You sure she can't hear us?'

Lock crossed to the bed. Her face was tight and troubled, three parallel lines furrowing her brow. He lifted her right hand and ran his fingers over the back. 'She's still pretty far gone from the anesthetic.'

Ty shrugged. 'Melissa's a student up at the University of

California in Santa Barbara. Regular kid, middle-class family, Mom and an older sister, Dad either dead or gone, not sure which. She's working as a hostess in a restaurant but keeping her grades up. So, it's the last day of her first year. She goes out with a couple of friends. There's a fight at a club between one of her male friends and some football player. This guy Charlie Mendez intervenes, saves the friend from getting his ass kicked.'

'Who is Mendez?' Lock asked.

Ty raised an open palm. 'Kind of a good question, but I'll get to that. Anyway, he invites Melissa and her friends back to his place on the beach. Serious piece of real estate worth a couple of million. More drinks. They all end up in the hot tub. He tells them they can stay over. She starts feeling groggy, heads to bed. Next morning she wakes up next to him *and* they're both naked.'

'He drugged her?'

'No way of knowing for sure. Could've been a date-rape drug or all that booze. Lot of times girls think a drink's been drugged when it's just that someone's dumped a bunch of extra alcohol in there. Anyway, it don't matter because whatever it was she wasn't in any fit state to consent and she'd definitely had sex.' Ty lowered his voice. 'A lot of sex, if you know what I mean.'

'Let's finish this outside.' Lock felt uncomfortable – out cold or not, the girl was still within earshot. They picked up their breakfast and the papers, then walked into the corridor. Lock stood with his back to the half-open door, still vigilant. 'What then?'

'Okay,' Ty continued. 'She gets out of there as fast as she can, and goes to the cops. They do a medical exam. Bingo. There's DNA from this Mendez cat up inside her.'

'He was already on the database?'

'Drug possession. Minor shit. But they get a hit. So they set up a pretext call. You know, she calls him, asks what he did, and the asshole is dumb enough to laugh about it.'

'He copped to it?'

Ty gave a rueful smile. 'Guy isn't the brightest star in the sky, plus he's got an ego the size of a planet. Young rich asshole, know what I'm saying? Cops pick him up, he makes out like he was joking when she called, and he has money, right? Or, rather, his family does. They hire themselves a whole bunch of expensive lawyers. And this is where it gets really fucked up. Those lawyers, they persuade the judge to bail him.'

Lock felt his blood run cold. 'Bail?'

'Two million dollars and he has to surrender his passport,' said Ty. 'But he's out.'

'Where'd he get two million bucks?'

'Don't let the name fool you. The family got serious coin – deep roots in Santa Barbara too.'

The next part of the story Lock could guess. 'So he's bailed and runs?'

'Not right away, no. He turns up every morning, like a good boy, just long enough to realize that he's shit out of luck. His fancy lawyers rip her story to shreds in the courtroom but she stands firm. Plus they messed up with the jury selection. Got rid of as many women as they could, but a lot of fathers are sitting there, listening to this.' Ty paused for a moment. 'Fathers with young daughters. He's going to prison and you and me both know how much they love rapists in somewhere like the Bay. The next day, he's a no-show. The US Marshals go looking but he's long gone. Defense lawyers try to get a delay but the trial goes on with an empty chair. Unanimous guilty verdict and a judge who's been made to look like a complete asshole.'

Based on what he knew about the vagaries of the American justice system, in which property was more valued than people, Lock guessed at the sentence: 'Six to ten?'

'Might have been, if the lead investigator hadn't turned up a whole bunch of video tapes of other girls he'd raped. All of 'em drugged. The judge was so pissed that when the jury came back with a guilty verdict he gave Mendez life without.'

That meant he'd die in prison. No chance of parole, even if he found Jesus. It was a rare sentence for a man like Mendez but the crimes had been particularly venal and, as Ty had just said, he'd ruined the judge's career.

Ty gave a wry smile. 'Pretty awesome incentive to stay wherever he is, right?'

'And to make sure that Melissa doesn't complain too loudly,' said Lock, pulling the door closed, but leaving enough of a gap that he could still see her.

Ty had a sip of orange juice, then opened the folder, took from it a bunch of printouts and handed them to Lock. 'This dude Joe Brady was a bondsman working out of an office north of LA. Melissa talked him into going after our boy. Not that he needed much persuading. Two million bond means a bondsman gets two hundred grand for his safe return. He found our boy Charlie down in Chihuahua, Mexico.'

Lock started to flick through the printouts. They were mostly new stories from the wires. Any number of bail bondsmen and bounty hunters had ventured south of the border to find Mendez, bring him back and claim their share of the bond. Most had expended considerable resources, only to fetch up at a series of dead ends. Just one had come close to finding him. That was Joe Brady – the Joe, he guessed, that Melissa had mentioned.

Joe tried.

According to what was in front of him, Brady had gone to Mexico with a posse of men and a camera crew to capture the moment for posterity. But whoever was looking after Mendez had not taken well to Brady's avowed desire to repatriate him. In the middle of the night, while Brady, his team and the camera crew had slept in a small hotel, a group of paramilitaries had arrived. They had taken the Americans and an Aussie sound man hostage. The following morning their bodies, including Joe Brady's, were found hanging from a bridge in Santa Maria, the border town notorious for more homicides per head of population than any- where else in the world, Afghanistan and Somalia included.

Lock handed the printouts back to Ty. 'And now she wants me to go and get him,' he said.

A silence settled between them. Ty broke it: 'And what do you think?'

Lock looked again at Melissa. 'I don't know. I need some more information. And we have the small matter of someone out there wanting to kill her.'

Ty tilted his head back and sighed. 'Maybe we could cut a deal. She drops it and so do they.'

'These aren't the kind of people who make deals, Ty. The kid I caught sneaking in here with a knife, she had some pretty heavy ink.' He reached up to rub the back of his neck. 'Right here. Gang name and the number thirteen.'

'La Eme?'

'You got it.'

A stint in Pelican Bay Supermax Prison as an undercover operative had given Lock a better working knowledge of prison gangs, and their outside support structures, than most law-enforcement officers would accumulate in a lifetime. The Pelican Bay administration enforced a policy of strict racial segregation. The Secure Housing Unit, which held a third of the institution's three and a half thousand inmates, essentially served as corporate headquarters to the gangs. This was where their CEOs and boards of directors were held, and from where they ran multi-million- and, in the case of the Mexican Mafia, multi-billion-dollar criminal enterprises.

On the exercise yards, the Hispanic inmates divided into *norteños* (northern Hispanics), *sureños* (southern Hispanics) and the so-called Border Brothers (who hailed from south of the US–Mexico border), but the overarching organization that ruled the factions was the Mexican Mafia. Capable of devastating violence, both within and outside the prison's walls, what set it apart from the other gangs was its businesslike approach. It was run with the same efficiency and lack of sentiment as any Fortune 500 company.

If a Mexican Mafia member was coming after Melissa, she had been marked for assassination.

'This Mendez guy,' Ty said, fanning the printouts, 'you think he's connected?'

'I don't know,' Lock said. 'And I plan on finding out. But if I'm going down there to get the asshole, I want to know what I'm walking into. Can you stay with her?'

Ty put out a giant fist and they bumped. 'You got it. Already spoke to Triple-C's management. They know what time it is. Got them another company coming in. Where you headed, anyway?'

'Santa Barbara. See if I can't lift a few rocks and figure out what's really going on here.' He glanced at Melissa, still pale and fragile.

'Then we heading down to Mexico to go get him?'

'If he's still there.'

'You think he might have skipped?'

Lock shrugged. 'I don't know. And going down there without knowing . . .' He trailed off. 'You saw what happened to the last couple of people who went down there looking for him.'

Ty grunted. 'Wasn't nothing pretty.'

Eight

Lock pulled up his Audi beside the hotel's valet-parking stand and got out, still clad in his blood-stained clothes from the previous evening. A well-dressed Beverly Hills couple waiting for their car stared at him, open-mouthed, as he handed the keys to one of the hotel valets with twenty dollars. 'Sorry, the interior's kind of a mess.' The kid peered inside and gulped. 'Good job I went for leather seats, right?'

He pivoted away and headed for the lobby. The receptionist from the evening before gave him a shit-eating grin and a chirpy 'Good morning' as he headed to the bank of elevators that would take him up to his room.

Back in his room, he took a shower, changed into fresh clothes and dumped the others in the trash. He packed the rest of his gear into a bag, placed his laptop in its case and, forty-five minutes later, walked into the corridor leaving the door to close behind him. As he was in Los Angeles, where permits for private security consultants were next to impossible to come by (which was not necessarily a bad thing, given the number of cowboys in the business), he wasn't carrying a gun. That would have to change if he and Ty went to Mexico. Maybe sooner.

The drive from Los Angeles to Santa Barbara along the Pacific Coast Highway was one of rare beauty. There weren't many stretches of highway that people travelled from all over the globe to experience but this was one of them. For Lock, though, as he passed the turn to Topanga Canyon and ventured beyond into Malibu, it was a road of demons and ghosts.

Malibu was where Carrie had been abducted by Reardon Galt, the house she and Lock had been living in burned down to cover the kidnapper's tracks. As he passed the site he slowed a little. The old structure had already been torn down and a new gleaming, post-modern home erected in its place. He jabbed at the gas pedal to make the lights at Big Rock before they turned red, and was stuck staring at his past.

He stopped at the mall at Cross Creek to get gas and some water. Then he was out of Malibu, driving through Trancas, a weight lifting from his shoulders with every mile. It wasn't a long drive to Santa Barbara but it afforded him time to think. On the face of it, the Mendez case was logical. Rich kid gets charged with rape. When he realizes he's not going to beat the rap, he uses a gullible judge and his money to get the hell out of Dodge. Once he's south of the border he pays some heavyweight Mexican muscle to ensure that he stays there.

The only thing Mendez hadn't reckoned with was Melissa Warner. The tapes in court had shown that she had been one of many victims but she alone had encouraged those with a financial interest to pursue him. That had pushed him into going after her

– albeit by proxy. But it was also drawing the heat on to him. And that was stupid. At some point the Department of Justice would get tired of him thumbing his nose at them and put some pressure on the Mexican government to catch him. It also raised another question. Who was looking after him down there? And, more crucially, why? Sure, he had money, but the execution of the bounty hunter had all the hallmarks of one of Mexico's notorious drug cartels, and they weren't short of cash. The downside to them protecting Mendez was extra media and government attention, which would far outweigh the financial boost he provided.

Something didn't add up.

Nine

The desk sergeant at the Santa Barbara Police Department was pleasant enough, while simultaneously managing to be entirely unhelpful. Santa Barbara was that kind of town and Lock understood his reticence. As far as the Santa Barbara PD was concerned, they had apprehended Charlie Mendez and gathered sufficient evidence to get a conviction. The fact that a judge had screwed up hadn't been down to them. Lock sympathized, but he wasn't about to go away.

After he waited for two hours, a young patrol officer, Ken Fossum, came to talk to him. He was on his way out to begin a fresh shift. 'And if I could ask what your connection to the case is?' was his opener.

'Yesterday evening someone tried to kill Melissa Warner. I believe they were connected to Charlie Mendez.'

The patrol officer looked ruffled. 'Here in Santa Barbara?'

'LA.'

'Well, I'm not sure why you're talking to us, Mr Lock. That's a matter for the LAPD.'

Lock choked back a sarcastic reply. 'I realize that, Officer. But I was hoping to speak to the lead detective on the original case.'

Fossum assumed a pained expression. 'She's retired. Went a few months back.'

'You know where I could find her?'

'I do, but I can't tell you. I'm sure a man in your line of work is aware of how that goes.'

Lock did. 'In that case could someone pass a message along that I'd like to speak with her?'

'I can do that. Doesn't mean she'll want to talk to you, though.'

Lock went back to his car, got in and called Ty. The news from the hospital was the same: Melissa was critical but stable. He finished the call, and looked at the empty passenger seat. *Raped and then shot for her trouble. Just when you think the world can't get any more messed up something comes along to surprise you.*

He started the engine and pulled out into the traffic. He had an address for the beach house where the attack had taken place. He didn't think it would yield anything, but he wanted to go there and see the place for himself. If nothing else it might give him a sense of who Charlie Mendez really was. If Lock was going after him, he would need that. Mendez would become Lock's prey, and the better you knew your prey, the easier it was to catch.

The drive took about fifteen minutes. It was a pleasant afternoon. He guessed that most afternoons in Santa Barbara were. It was the kind of place where a young college student would find it easy to lower her guard.

He turned into the road where the house was and scanned the numbers until he found it. It had been sold during the run-up to the trial. No doubt the proceeds had gone towards the two million dollars cash that Mendez had had to raise as bail to secure his freedom.

Lock got out of the car and stared up at the outside of the house. He thought about ringing the bell but decided against it. Instead he walked down the road until he found a flight of steps that led to the beach. At the bottom, he took off his shoes and socks and walked along the sand.

The glass-fronted house was very similar to the one he'd shared with Carrie. In fact the resemblance was eerie. He scanned the decks but no one was sitting on them and all the doors and windows were shut. There had been no cars parked outside either. The new owner must be using it as a weekend getaway or vacation home.

Steps led up to a small wooden gate and the house. He climbed them, hopped over the gate and walked up to a side window. Inside, the house seemed cold and antiseptic. It told him everything and nothing about Mendez.

His cell phone rang. He clicked the answer button.

'Mr Lock?' said a woman's voice.

'Yes.'

'I got a message that you wanted to speak to me.'

Ten

Marcie Braun's retirement hadn't taken her very far. She lived a shade off the beaten track, about thirty miles inland from Santa Barbara in a small Cape Cod-style house with stables and a paddock.

Lock found her clearing out a horse stall with a pitchfork. She was wearing a T-shirt and shorts, and her hair was tied back in a ponytail. She straightened when she saw him, one hand moving to massage the small of her back. 'So, you want to go get Charlie Mendez, huh?' she said, with a smile, after he had apologized for disturbing her. 'You do know what happened to the other guy who went looking for him, right?'

Lock nodded.

'But you still think it's a good idea?'

'I don't know if it is or not, Detective Braun, but a girl is lying in a hospital bed in Los Angeles and she asked me to help her.'

Marcie Braun seemed unsure what to make of him. A long

moment of silence passed. 'Call me Marcie.' She nodded to
the horse manure. 'I'll finish up, then why don't you come into the
house and we can talk?'

Lock sipped coffee as the retired detective settled at the big pine
kitchen table and spread out a thick folder. She sighed as she
flicked through the thick stack of papers inside. 'Funny, this was
the only case where I took a copy of the paperwork when I left the
job. Guess it was Mendez skipping bail like he did. Made
the whole thing feel unfinished.'

'How long were you with the job?' he asked her.

'Too long. I thought coming to work in Santa Barbara would
be a nice way of making the transition to retirement after the
LAPD.'

'It wasn't?' he probed.

'I guess it was until the Mendez case. Lot of good cops in the
department. Good people to take care of too. But you didn't
come out here to listen to me reminisce, did you now?'

'Did you know Mendez before it went down?'

Marcie threw back her head and laughed. 'Every cop in Santa
Barbara knew Charlie and everyone in Santa Barbara knows the
Mendez family. They've been here for a long time, lot longer than
I have.'

'The judge know them?' he prompted, even though he knew the
question was taking him on to dangerous ground.

Marcie's easy smile fell away. 'If you're suggesting what I think
you are then all I'd say is that's a pretty serious charge to lay
against a judge.'

'So why'd he bail him?'

Marcie shrugged. 'If you're asking whether Charlie being from that family helped him, then of course it did. It would be naïve to think anything else. This is America, right? Land of equal opportunity, but having big bucks makes you that little bit more equal. I'm sure you know how it goes, Mr Lock. If you're rich in this country you'll be treated a little differently from the rest of us. Not because you're rich – hell, with a jury that might work against you – but because you can pay for a better defense. Charlie had really good lawyers. The kind of people who could persuade someone that black was white and two plus two makes five. I mean, that's why they cost a lot of money, right?'

'And the judge?' said Lock.

Marcie blew on her coffee. 'There you go again. Why don't you ask me straight out? Do I think the judge was bribed or someone called in a favor? No, I don't. I think he was talked into making a mistake. There's no small-town conspiracy here, if that's what you're thinking.'

He decided to let it go. He believed her and he wanted to get back to Charlie.

'But the Police Department had come into contact with Charlie Mendez before?'

Marcie made a face. 'Sure, when he was younger. He was a kid with everything handed to him on a silver platter. A player. He got into some scrapes. Nothing serious, though.'

'What kind of "nothing serious"?' he prompted.

'Being drunk in public. Shooting off his mouth. A couple of assaults. Always kids smaller than him or when he was with his buddies. Never liked the look of a fight he might lose.'

'Anything of a sexual nature?'

Marcie took a sip of coffee. 'That was what was weird when his name came up. I mean, like I said, he was a player, had an eye for the ladies, but he was good-looking, rich. You wouldn't think he'd've had to drug someone, although in my experience rape isn't usually about the sex.'

'So why do you think he did it? Some kind of power trip?' Lock asked.

'I've seen a lot of crazy stuff, being a cop. And you want to know what all those years on the job taught me?'

He nodded.

'When it comes down to the really bad shit, some people are just fucked up.' She got up and emptied the dregs of her coffee into an old white ceramic sink, then turned on the faucet. Her eyes fell to the folder she had passed to Lock. 'There's some more recent material in the back.'

'Concerning?'

'Stuff that makes no sense to me.'

'Such as?'

'Such as the last place he's been seen.' Marcie sighed. 'I mean, if you skip bail, and you have more than money than God, why not pick a country that has no extradition treaty with the United States?'

Lock decided to play devil's advocate. 'Not many of those left, and Mexico has worked out pretty well for him so far. Whoever he's paying to take care of him down there seems to be doing a pretty good job.'

'If he's still there,' said Marcie.

'You think he might have left?'

'I know I would have.'

He thought about it. If Charlie Mendez hadn't been spooked enough by the first bounty hunter to relocate, he must have a good reason for staying where he was. Obviously he felt safe down there. 'What about the family?' he asked. 'They have any ties to Mexico? Business interests?'

'Apart from the name, none that anyone in the department knew about, although with old money like that it's difficult to be sure. There are shell corporations and trusts and a bazillion layers you have to get through. Everything they have is privately held.'

'You have any idea who's looking after him?'

Marcie pursed her lips. 'Well, from the way they dealt with Brady, it looks like narco-traffickers. But you probably guessed that. The girl you caught at the hospital was a Latina gang member?'

Lock wondered how she knew that, but not for long.

'I made some calls when I heard Melissa had been shot,' Marcie said.

'Gang ink.'

Marcie picked up the folder and passed it to him. 'A lot of people have been hustling to get Mendez returned. But you know how it goes – the more time passes, the more likely it is they've moved on to other things. We have a lot of border issues and, with everything that's going on down there, Mendez is hardly a priority.'

The folder felt heavy in his hand. 'Thanks for everything.'

Marcie smiled. 'I sure hope you bring him back. He's a dangerous man to have running around.'

Eleven

At his hotel opposite the Greyhound bus terminal in the centre of Santa Barbara, Lock ordered a club sandwich and some mineral water while he worked methodically in his room through the witness statements in the file Marcie Braun had given him. There was nothing new, although reading it in detail made what had happened seem more real – in a way that urged him to cause serious physical harm not only to Charlie Mendez but to his smarmy high-powered defense lawyers.

Halfway through, he found that he had lost his appetite. He put the sandwich on the tray outside the door, then returned to his work. With the file exhausted, he got out his laptop and opened up the web browser. He threw Charlie Mendez's name into Google and waited.

On the second page of search results there was a link to a video clip from a local news channel. The heading read: 'Mendez Bail Outrage'. He clicked on the link and a separate window opened. He hit Play. It was only when the footage rolled that he realized he had no idea what Mendez looked like. Although he had read several thousand words about the man, the file had contained no photographs.

On screen, dressed in a smart but obviously off-the-rack suit – probably chosen by his multi-million-dollar legal team to down-play his wealth – Charlie Mendez stood on the courthouse steps. He was about five feet ten inches tall, slim, with sandy blond hair, brown eyes and broad, handsome features. He had the healthy glow typical of those who had grown up wealthy.

To his left, with one hand resting on his shoulder, was his mother, Miriam, a pinch-faced WASP dressed in a twin-set and pearls. Her hair was blonde and perfectly coiffed. Charlie's lead counsel was on his right: Tony Medina, a handsome, but prematurely greying middle-aged Hispanic, with serious political ambitions. Although the Mendez family were about as Hispanic as Ronald McDonald, Medina had done his best to introduce a racial element into the case, arguing that police and prosecution fervor had been heightened because the victim was a young white woman and his client was, at least in name, a member of a minority group.

Needless to say, painting the playboy heir to a multi-billion-dollar fortune as a victim was a tough sell in a country still reeling from a bitter recession. But, like any attorney, Medina was work-ing with what he had: very little.

As a forest of microphones bunched around him, Charlie Mendez read from a prepared statement. His delivery was flat and almost entirely devoid of emotion. 'I would like to thank my family, particularly my mother, for standing by me during this dif-ficult time. I would also like to thank my attorney, Anthony Medina, and the other members of my legal team,' Medina squeezed Charlie's shoulder paternally, 'for their hard work and dedication so far. I am also grateful to the judge for allowing me to return to my family for the remainder of this process.'

'No kidding,' Lock muttered, under his breath, and paused the clip. Less than two weeks later, Mendez had fled. A rapist and a coward.

The phone rang on his desk. It was a local number. He picked it up. 'Marcie?'

'Mr Lock,' said a perky-sounding young woman, 'I work for Mrs Miriam Mendez, the mother of Charlie Mendez. Mrs Mendez would like to speak with you. Do you have a pen so you can take down the address?'

Twelve

Twelve-foot-high black security gates slid open and Lock's Audi nudged its way through. Next to him on the front passenger seat was Marcie Braun's case folder. As he crested a rise leading up to the Mendez compound, he glimpsed Montecito laid out beneath him, the upscale part of already upscale Santa Barbara. A deep blue Pacific shimmered in the distance.

He wondered how the matriarch of the Mendez family had known he was in town. Not that it was much of a jump: the Santa Barbara Police Department was a small force. Santa Barbara, at the higher end, was probably a pretty tight-knit community. Word would have got round.

A minute and a half later he pulled his Audi on to a large motor court, which fronted the main house: a 1930s colonial mansion. To one side, Lock could see two tennis courts, one grass and one clay. Beyond them lay an Olympic-sized swimming pool with separate ten-person hot tubs at either end. A pool boy was fishing out a couple of rogue leaves with a large net.

He pulled into a space between a special-edition Aston Martin
V12 Vantage Carbon Black and a Bentley Flying Spur and got
out. He took a moment to check out the two automobiles. Neither
looked as if they had ever been driven: they were showroom new.
There was money, he thought, and then there was Montecito
money.

Sunlight filtered through the sycamores at the edge of the
house, dappling the steps leading up to the vast front door. Lock
rang the bell and settled in to wait. His invitation was for four
p.m. It was one minute past. He had no idea if that counted as
fashionably late.

The front door opened and a maid ushered him inside. She
offered to take his jacket but he declined. 'Mrs Mendez is in the
drawing room,' she said.

He followed her down a long corridor, their footsteps echoing
on the dark mahogany floor. Lock didn't know much about art
but he could pick out one or two names from the pictures on the
wall. Carrie had dragged him around the Museum of Modern Art
in New York a couple of times. There was a Klimt and what
looked to him, from the angular face staring at him, like a Picasso.
He doubted they were prints.

Glancing up, he saw the red orb of a camera tracking their
progress. You didn't spend that kind of money on an art
collection without an efficient security system to protect it. He
wondered what the cameras had witnessed, whether they had
observed Charlie Mendez saying a final goodbye to his mother
before he had taken off.

'Mr Lock. Thank you for agreeing to meet with me.'

The corridor opened into a large sunny room, dominated by a
vast marble fireplace. Miriam Mendez was standing by a set of

french windows, which opened on to the azure swimming pool. Whatever Lock's preconceived notions had been, she was not the woman he had been expecting. For a start, the perfectly coiffed blonde curls of a wealthy Santa Barbara matron were gone, reduced to a few wispy clumps at the side of her head. Her face was gaunt, cheekbones jutting, not unlike those in the Picasso he had passed. She was skeletal and drawn.

'Cancer,' she said, by way of explanation. 'Terminal. If there was a cure then, believe me, I would have found it – I have the money and access to the finest doctors in the world. Sadly, there are certain things that money can't buy. Please, sit down.'

Lock eased himself into a club chair.

'You're looking for my son, I believe,' she said, after a long pause.

Lock cleared his throat. 'Like many people. The only difference is that I'm going to find him and bring him back to serve his sentence.'

Miriam Mendez smiled. It was a warm, open smile, which wrong-footed Lock. It wasn't the reaction he had been expecting. 'Good. I hope you do. I mean that. Charlie has brought nothing but shame to our family. Of course I don't wish anything terrible to happen to him but it's right that he should take his punishment like a man.'

'So will you help me find him, Mrs Mendez?' Lock asked.

'You don't know where he is?' she asked, innocence personified.

Lock smiled. 'I have no idea.'

'Well, Mr Lock, if I knew where he was, I would fly down there myself and tell him to put an end to all of this nonsense. All the family knows is that he's in Mexico somewhere, and even that's a guess. He may have moved on from there for all we know.'

'So if you don't know where he is, why did you want to see me?'

'You heard what happened to the other men who tried to find him?' She allowed the question to hang in the air. 'Charlie has obviously got in with a bad crowd.'

Lock bit back a smirk. 'Bad crowd' suggested kids who hung out late smoking dope and drinking beer, rather than narco-trafficking paramilitaries who butchered people in cold blood. 'You think I shouldn't go?' he asked.

She did her best to look puzzled. 'I'm certainly not trying to dissuade you, but at the same time I hope there's no more sense-less loss of life.'

'Before he left, did your son give any indication that he was going to flee, Mrs Mendez?'

Miriam Mendez sighed. 'If he did, I'd hardly make it public. But, no, Mr Lock, he didn't. I think he just panicked.'

Yeah, right, thought Lock. 'Is there anything else, Mrs Mendez?'

Her hand fell into her pocket and she pulled out a cream envelope. 'I was hoping that if you find Charlie you might give him this for me. My time is limited and I'm not sure I'll have the chance to see him before . . .'

Lock stood up, walked over to her and took the envelope. It was thick, maybe three or four sheets of heavy old-fashioned writing paper inside. On the front, in neat, cursive handwriting, was her son's name. 'I'll make sure to pass it on,' he said.

She clasped his hand. Her grip was surprisingly strong. 'I know you will, Mr Lock. And, because I'm counting the days rather than the months, can you let me know as soon as you have? I mean, the very moment. It would give me such peace to know he had it before I depart this earth. Will you promise me?'

'I promise you'll be the first to know,' said Lock.

Before he had made the trip to the Mendez estate to see the family matriarch, he had done a little more research. Miriam Mendez did have cancer, and any kind of cancer was a terrible thing, but the type she had wasn't usually fatal. In fact, she was in remission. She had lost her hair but she was almost certainly going to be fine. There was only one reason she could have for asking Lock to make sure he contacted her first and that was to stop him delivering her son to the authorities.

'Thank you, Mr Lock. You're a good man,' she said, with a wan smile

'I'll see myself out, Mrs Mendez.'

As he left the room, he stopped in the doorway and turned. She was still in the same pose.

'Yes, Mr Lock?'

'I was just thinking, Mrs Mendez. If by some chance you hear from your son before I do, could you give him a message from me?'

Her eyes widened, and he detected anger simmering just beneath the surface.

'Tell him that no amount of money or muscle is going to stop me putting him behind bars with all the other animals.'

A hardness settled in her eyes but her smile didn't fade. 'Just be careful, Mr Lock. No one wants to see anyone else suffer.'

Outside, the all-American pool boy had been replaced by a thick-set Hispanic man, whose girth suggested he might have eaten the job's previous incumbent. *Presence of the abnormal*, thought Lock. The man watched his every move as he got back into his car.

Lock tossed the letter on to the passenger seat. He started the engine, and headed down the driveway. The gates opened as he approached and he left the Mendez estate. About a half-mile down the road he pulled over. He stared at the letter, debating the morality of opening it. He picked it up, ripped open the envelope and pulled out three thick sheets of cream writing-paper.

They were blank.

Thirteen

Back at the hotel, Lock drove past the valet stand to a far corner of the hotel parking lot. He pulled in between two oversized SUVs. The nose of the Audi was facing a brick wall so the only view of the car for anyone watching him was from behind. He was pretty sure he hadn't been followed from the Mendez estate but he wanted to ensure that he wasn't observed in what he was about to do.

He got out of the car, and walked slowly around it. On the second circuit, he checked the inside of the wheel arches using his fingertips. Next he clambered under the car to inspect it. Satisfied, he wriggled out, then opened both doors, searched the interior, and ran his fingertips over every inch of the trunk.

He found what he was looking for hidden at the very back, a black box the size of a pack of cigarettes. He went back into the car, pulled out his Maglite and shone it into the dark recess. Using his Gerber, he levered the box out of position, and turned it over in his hand.

It was a Real-Time Asset GPS tracking device. They were commercially available and retailed at around five hundred bucks. He knew the price because he had recommended this very gizmo a while back to a trucking company: they had been concerned about a couple of their drivers, who were losing a lot of cargo.

Lock guessed the device had been placed inside his car while he had been inside the house, talking to Miriam Mendez. He had suspected something was going down when he had come back out to find the pool boy replaced by the older Hispanic man. The change of personnel had jarred, and anything that jarred was worth checking out.

He looked around the parking lot. He thought about planting the device on one of the cars with out-of-state plates, but dismissed the idea. If someone was prepared to send gang members out to kill a teenage rape victim, who was to say they wouldn't cap a couple of hapless vacationers from Oregon? For now, the tracking device could stay put. If they wanted to know where he was, they could – for now.

Back in his room, he put Miriam Mendez's blank pages into Marcie Braun's case file and texted Ty for a situation report.

A few seconds later his cell phone chirped.

'How is she?' Lock asked.

'She's conscious but they kicked me out of the room,' Ty said. 'Don't worry, I'm sitting right outside.'

'You had a chance to speak to her yet?'

'I tried but she wants to see you.'

Lock glanced out of the window to the Greyhound bus terminal. 'I have a couple of people still to talk to. The cops been back yet?'

'Doctor's holding them off. He wants her to rest some more before she talks to them.'

'He tell you anything?'

'Sorry, brother, I tried to ask him about her condition but I can't fake being a relative, if you know what I mean.'

'Speaking of which, any of her family show up yet?'

'Her mom's on the way. Should be here any minute,' said Ty.

'Okay, talk to her for me.'

'You got it. Oh, and, Ryan, I do have one piece of news but you ain't gonna like it.'

'What is it?'

'That kid you caught with the knife?'

'Yeah?' Lock asked, although he already had a pretty good idea what was coming.

'She got bailed.'

'She could have pulled the trigger, for all they know.'

'Oh, it gets better. Want to take a wild guess at who she had representing her when she was arraigned?'

'Johnnie Cochran?'

'Where you been? Johnnie died back in 'oh-five, brother.'

'Must have missed the obituary. So, who did she have in court?'

'Junior attorney from Tony Medina's office.'

'You get their name?'

'Working on it. I'll email it.'

Lock could add another person to the list of people he'd like to speak to. While he couldn't imagine getting anything out of a shyster like Medina, a new attorney in his office might give something away about who was paying the legal bill for a teenage gang-banger. Of course, it could be that the gang was paying, and that she and Charlie Mendez sharing a law firm was a coincidence. But as far as Lock was concerned coincidences were up there with the Tooth Fairy and Santa Claus. Believing in them might make you feel good, but that was about it.

'So when you heading back?' Ty asked.

'Got one more call to make up here first.'

'Okay, brother, but, hey?'

'Yeah?'

'Be safe.'

Fourteen

Her nose bisected by a sliver of brass safety chain, Joe Brady's widow, Sarah, stared at Lock through the gap between front door and frame. It was a little more than three months since her husband had been butchered in Mexico. Lock knew from bitter recent experience that the first three months after the loss of a loved one were some of the toughest.

Your heart was put through a mincer. You didn't sleep. Your brain tricked you: something would happen, and Lock would be about to share it with Carrie, then remember that she was gone. His gut churned even to think of it.

'Mrs Brady?' Lock asked, observing the social niceties. 'My name's Ryan Lock. I'm a friend of Melissa Warner. I'm here to speak to you about your husband.'

The door closed. He waited. He was hardly going to make her speak to him, not after what she'd been through.

There was the rattle of the chain being removed, and then it opened again, wider this time. 'You'd better come in.'

He followed her into a living room. There was a couch, a television and a playpen in which a little girl was busy trying to find out if a wooden building block would fit inside her nostril. Sarah Brady motioned for him to sit down. 'Can I get you something?' she asked.

'No, thank you.'

She remained standing. 'I have work in a half-hour, and I have to drop her at my mom's, so if you could ask what you want to ask – I don't mean to be rude but . . .'

Lock cleared his throat. A visit from someone like him was probably the last thing this woman needed but now he was here he would press on. 'Mrs Brady,' he began.

'You can call me Sarah. Mrs Brady makes me sound old, and I already feel like a million,' she said.

'Sarah, Melissa Warner has asked me to find Charlie Mendez for her.'

Sarah bent over the playpen and picked up her daughter. 'Two hundred grand is a lot of money, huh? But it's no good to you if you're not around to spend it.'

Lock guessed he had better get used to hearing that line. 'This isn't about money, I can assure you.'

She shot him a look of sheer skepticism. 'Sure it's not.'

'I believe your husband had caught up with Mendez before he was killed.'

The little girl chewed at the building block and stared at him with wide blue eyes. Sarah tried to take it from her. She bunched chubby fingers tightly around it, refusing to give it up.

'He had him in his vehicle. But they were pulled over by the cops and arrested before they got to the border,' Sarah said.

'Twenty miles short. Twenty miles further on and he would still be here.'

This was news to Lock. 'I thought he and the people he was with were abducted by narco-traffickers.'

'Boy, you really don't know too much about how things work down there, do you? Cops, gangsters. A lot of the time they're the same thing.'

She was wrong in one regard. He wasn't wholly naïve about police corruption in Mexico. It was rife. That was all you needed to know. 'You think the police killed your husband?'

She bounced the little girl in her arms and kissed her cheek. Distracted, the the child dropped the block, then struggled to get down, wanting to retrieve it.

'They might have killed him themselves. They might have handed him over to the people who did. Either way, he's still gone.' She looked around the grubby apartment. 'I begged him not to go down there but all he could talk about was what we could do with that money. Listen, I really do have to get ready for work.'

He raised a hand. 'Did your husband leave any papers, any notes about Mendez?'

Sarah shrugged. 'If he did they wouldn't be here. He kept all that stuff at his office. I haven't been back there since he left. He always paid a year ahead so I have a few more months before I have to deal with it. Guess I'm not ready to face it yet.'

He took a breath. 'Would you mind if I did?'

'Come on, baby,' she said to her daughter, turning her back to him and walking through into the kitchen. She returned a few moments later with a set of keys, which she handed to him. 'The alarm code's written on the fob. Just drop them into the mailbox when you come back – I don't get home from work until late.'

Lock felt the weight of the keys in his hand. A thought flashed into his mind that he should hand them back. But he didn't. He thanked her, and promised to return them, then walked out of the dingy rooms into the mild California evening.

Fifteen

Bail-bond offices were generally grim, and Joe Brady's was no exception. The final unit in a greying strip mall off a narrow two-lane road, its dirt-streaked windows were covered with metal bars, and there was a dent in the front door where someone had kicked it. A sign announced the nature of the business conducted within.

Lock fumbled with the keys until he found the one that fitted. He opened the door, and stepped inside. The alarm panel was to his right. He plugged in the code written on the key fob and the box chirped briefly, then deactivated. The interior consisted of a small reception area and a larger back office, a toilet and a small kitchen.

Posters adorned Reception, including one advertising the company's services – 'Brady Bail Bonds – Because Jail Sucks.' A pen set, like the kind you find in banks, was secured to the long wooden reception desk with a couple of bolts, a reflection perhaps of the business's client base.

In the main office there was a desk, a leather swivel chair and two regular chairs on the other side. A smaller table stood to one side with a PC and a printer underneath. Both pieces of equipment were secured to the wall with thick metal ties. Brady might have bailed criminals but he sure as hell didn't trust them so he couldn't have been entirely stupid. Three four-drawer filing cabinets sat against the far wall.

Lock checked the toilet ('Employees Only'), then the kitchen. A solitary Brady Bail Bonds coffee mug stood next to the sink. There were more mugs in the cupboard, and a pint of milk had soured in the small refrigerator. He held his breath as he took it out, poured it into the sink and rinsed it away.

Back in the main office, he found the key to the filing cabinet and started sorting through the drawers. Clients' records were filed alphabetically. He flicked through a few, closed the cabinets and sat down on the swivel chair. On the desk in front of him he found a half-dozen glossy brochures, including one for a new housing development, Woodland Oaks. It showed large detached McMansions with dramatic entryways and sweeping staircases inhabited by the kind of smiling automatons only ever glimpsed in real-estate literature. He didn't see any woodland. Or any oaks. Presumably they'd all been chopped down to make way for the houses.

The other brochures on the desk were split between cars (Mercedes and BMW) and boats. Rather than focus on the task in hand, Brady'd been spending the money before he had left his office. It was an approach to life that all but guaranteed disappointment. Do the job, then worry about the pay-off, was how Lock approached his work, and it had served him well.

He put the brochures to one side and sorted through the other papers on the desk. There were bills and invoices. Nothing leaped out as significant. He eased back in the chair and closed his eyes. Surely Brady wouldn't have set off into the heart of narco-territory to find Mendez without some clue as to where the man was. For there to be nothing in the office relating to either Melissa or Mendez seemed remarkable.

The bills.

Opening his eyes, Lock grabbed the stack of papers and thumbed through them again. He looked for a phone bill but there was none. The most recent piece of paperwork dated back to a few weeks before Brady had left his office for the last time. There was no recent mail.

He got up from the desk and went to the front door. There was no mail slot and no mailbox immediately outside. There had been no fresh mail inside the door when he had walked in and none anywhere else.

Back in the office, he lifted the phone. Dial tone. It was still connected, and there was power, so the utilities hadn't been cancelled.

Something else on the desk caught his eye. Lying under the brochures was a *faux*-leather desk pad. He slid it out. The top sheet of white paper was a mass of doodles. Long, curving lines swooped down and around the edge of the paper where they settled into a series of maze-like lines. There were faces too: a line drawing of a young woman Lock recognized as Melissa Warner, and a black-ink rendering of Charlie Mendez. Settled between them was another face, a caricatured devil's face, complete with horns, demonic eyes and a neatly pointed goatee beard. Beneath the three faces inscribed in the centre of the paper there were three words. The handwriting matched Brady's signature on the couple of invoices Lock had glanced at.

THE DEVIL'S BOUNTY?

That was it. Lock used his fingernail to lift out the piece of paper from the pad, folded it and jammed it into his back pocket. Then he checked the paper underneath. It was blank.

Back outside, he stood on the narrow concrete walkway and looked around. The next unit housed a dry cleaner's. He pushed open the door and went in. A woman with grey hair and spectacles was sorting through a pile of freshly laundered shirts.

'Excuse me, ma'am?'

She looked up.

He thumbed in the direction of the bail-bond office. 'I'm helping Joe's wife Sarah tidy out his office and I was wondering if you knew where his mail had gone. I don't see a mailbox.'

'The mailboxes are out back,' she said, then shook her head. 'You know who's going to move into his office?'

'No idea. Like I said, I'm just clearing it out.'

'Well,' she sighed, 'he was a nice man but I hope it's not another bond company. Draws the wrong kind of people, if you know what I mean.'

Lock did. If he had been in her position he wouldn't have wanted a bail-bond company next door either. 'Did you know him well?' he asked.

'Just to say hello to. He never used us,' she said, a little sourly. 'Guess his wife took care of his laundry for him.'

'You haven't seen anyone else around his place over the past few weeks, have you?'

'Not apart from you,' she said, turning back to the shirts, the conversation apparently over.

Lock walked around the side of the unit. Next to an air-conditioner vent, he found a mailbox with 'Brady Bail Bonds' stenciled on it. He sifted through the keys and found a small one, which looked like it might open the box. It did. He grabbed the stack of envelopes and a couple of flyers, and quickly sorted through them. There were two letters from the phone company, thick enough to be bills. He put them on top of the stack, went back into the unit, reactivated the alarm, locked the door, got into his car and drove back to Sarah Brady's apartment.

She and her daughter had gone so he left the keys and the mail with a neighbor, who swallowed a full half-hour commiserating with him about Mrs Brady's predicament. He kept the phone bills.

Sitting inside the Audi, he switched on the engine, turned up the air-con to maximum, and ripped them open. He scanned the numbers Brady had called. Halfway down the second bill, he found what he was looking for: a number in Mexico. He used the browser on his cell phone to search the area code. It was for a city just over the border: Santa Maria.

Lock scrolled through the menus on his cell phone and selected the option to withhold his number. He keyed in the Santa Maria number and listened to the foreign pulse of the ring tone.

Sixteen

Hunkered down in the dust next to the body of the dead girl, Detective Rafaela Carcharon studied the glowing cell-phone display. Number withheld. She could make a good guess as to who it was, and now wasn't the time to deal with another of *those* calls. She hit the red button to kill the call, powered down her phone so that he couldn't call back, and returned to the task in hand – eager to be done.

She wanted to be quick for two reasons. The first and most obvious was that statistics and probability dictated that the next murder would be called in soon. The second was that, these days, crime scenes themselves were places of danger for certain police officers. The cartels, militias and death squads, the hundred and one fragmented groups, knew that a crime scene drew their adversaries. In the past weeks suspicion had risen that the innocent and the not-so-innocent were being targeted precisely to draw people like her into the open.

She swiped away the flies that had gathered to feast on the

young woman's face, and took a closer look. Dark skin, big brown eyes, pretty and young, just like all the others. Rafaela would have placed her in her late teens or perhaps early twenties. A woman, perhaps, rather than a girl, but barely.

Rafaela already knew her story, even though she had no idea of her name, because all the stories were the same. That was part of what made the procession of dead women so exhausting. She would have been from one of the poorer parts of town. She would have worked at a *maquiladora*, a factory. She would have been snatched on her way home from her shift. That part Rafaela could be sure of because no young woman went out alone after dark now. Not any more. Not here. Too much blood had flowed. Too many women hadn't made it home. Too many families had been broken.

But people had to go to work. They had to come home when they were done. And some of the shifts in the factories ended and began in darkness. The buses supplied by the factory owners weren't always reliable or perhaps they set people down close to home but not at their door. There was always some small distance between leaving the bus and sanctuary. And that was when the women were spirited away.

By the time Rafaela reached the edge of the *colonia* it was close to sunset. Up ahead, an old yellow American school bus disgorged its cargo of women who were returning home. Rafaela pulled her car over to the side of the road, watching as they broke up into little groups of two or three and began the last part of their journey home. They shuffled past her car, exhausted after their twelve-hour shift sewing clothes or assembling products for a fraction of the wage the companies would have had to pay an American.

The bus coughed its way past her car in a cloud of dirty fumes, and the women disappeared. Rafaela took a deep breath. She could see her destination a few hundred yards away – a wood and corrugated-iron shack, originally painted a gaudy yellow, which had faded over time to mustard.

Out of all the tasks that Rafaela Carcharon was called upon to perform in the course of her duties, this was the worst. Back at her office, a well-meaning uniformed officer – as far as Rafaela knew, he hadn't yet taken the cartel's money – had offered to escort her out here. He was tall and handsome, with a warm smile, and in a different time and different place, Rafaela might have welcomed his company. But she had declined. It was better that she did this by herself. She didn't want to give him the wrong idea. A relationship of any kind was out of the question.

Before she got out of the car, Rafaela checked her weapon. She was a woman alone in the *colonia* near dark. Walking to the house, she passed a *tiendita*, a tiny convenience store crammed from floor to ceiling with the kind of junk food you found in poor neighborhoods – lots of fat and sugar to fill an empty belly. This one, like many others, was simply a tiny spare room in a house, with a rectangular hole punched in the wall to create a storefront. An older man sat on a stool by the counter and watched her pass. She said good evening. He pretended not to hear and began sorting through a box of loose candy.

She stopped for a moment outside the house and took a deep breath. Then she knocked at the door and stepped back. A radio was playing somewhere nearby, a song by a band called Los Tigres del Norte. Rafaela liked them. They sang about regular life, and that included the narcos. Many of their songs celebrated the gangsters, and Rafaela understood their popularity. The old-time gangsters were patrons of their communities and of the people. The politicians were neither.

A woman's voice called from inside: 'Who is it?'

'Señora Valdez?'

The door opened a few inches and a middle-aged woman peered out, her face lined with fatigue.

'May I come in?' Rafaela asked her. 'I have news about your daughter.'

The door closed again, there was the rasp of a chain being removed and then it opened. Rafaela stepped into a low-ceilinged room. There was a sofa, a coffee-table and a television set, which was switched on with the volume turned down. Rafaela recognized a couple of popular soap-opera stars. Her eyes settled on a table behind the sofa. It was covered with framed photographs. Rafaela's heart sank as she saw that every picture was of the same young girl; only the settings and the age varied. There was one of her as a toddler, dressed in white for her confirmation; the most recent showed her in her late teens. An only child.

Señora Valdez's hands grasped Rafaela's arms. 'Tell me she's safe.'

In such circumstances there was a procedure to follow, a series of steps, a liturgy of words to mouth. Rafaela believed in none of this. When she had to arrest someone, or interrogate someone, or shoot someone, she was a cop. But at moments like this she was a woman.

Rafaela touched Señora Valdez's hands, feeling the calluses on her palms and the tips of her fingers, the result of all those hours in the factory. 'She's with the angels, Señora. I'm so sorry.'

The woman's body slumped, her chin falling on to her chest as she began to sob. Rafaela put her arms around her. They stayed like that for a long time. Rafaela spoke to her gently, as she would to a child. She had never known what it meant to cry your heart out until she had made the first of these calls. Then she had been brittle, detached, professional. Afterwards she had realized that there was no harm in showing her humanity. If nothing else, she reasoned, it must comfort the bereaved a little to know that one other human being cared.

Slowly, the woman's sobs ebbed away as, over her shoulder, the soap opera continued, with beautiful, wealthy people grieving over a missed promotion, perhaps, or an extra-marital affair. She peeled herself away from Rafaela, eyes puffy and glistening. She glanced at the photographs of her murdered daughter and something new came into her eyes, something far worse than the grief. Surrender. It disturbed Rafaela more than the blood and mayhem. Your daughter left the house. She never returned. And that was life in this city.

'Shall I take you to see her?' Rafaela asked.

The woman looked around the room, searching for her coat. Rafaela helped her put it on and then they walked out into the night.

Seventeen

Rosary beads clasped in her right hand, Melissa's mother, Jan, sat quietly by her daughter's bedside. Although her face was lined with worry and her eyes were pouched from lack of sleep, Ty could see where Melissa had got her looks from. Watching her vigil, he was glad that she had her faith to sustain her.

Part of him wished he believed more than he did. His mother was a churchgoer and, as a child, he had gone with her on Sunday, sitting there listening to the preacher, swinging his legs and counting the minutes until he could get home and change out of the suit she insisted he wear. He had never really taken to it.

A nurse flitted into the room to check on Melissa. She spoke to Jan, scratched some notes on the chart at the bottom of the bed and made for the door.

'How's she doing?' Ty asked her, as she left.

The nurse smiled. 'All her vital signs are stable and she's not bleeding now. That's all in her favor.'

'How long until she can leave?'

'It'll be a while,' the nurse said, heading past him and into the next room.

Ty rose from the chair and stretched his long, lean frame. He tapped gently on the door and Jan Warner glanced up from her prayers. 'If you need to take a break at any time just let me know,' he said.

She smiled, got up and walked to the door. 'Can I ask you something, Tyrone?'

Ty smiled. He probably only ever heard his full name from ladies who went to church, and Lock when he was being sarcastic. 'Sure.'

Jan's gaze fell away to the bed where her daughter lay sleeping. 'Why are you doing this for us?'

Ty could have given her some story about how he was happy to help, but he wanted to be honest. Much as he felt for Melissa, he hadn't welcomed her arrival in Lock's life. 'Because Ryan asked me to.'

Jan gave a tiny nod, apparently satisfied. 'You must be good friends.'

He shrugged. 'We've been through a lot together. Makes you close, I guess.'

'Not one of Melissa's college friends stayed in touch with her after what happened.' Ty noticed that Jan's eyes were moist. 'The damage that man did to her. She was such a beautiful young woman.'

'She still is,' Ty said. 'That don't change.'

Jan took a pack of tissues from her handbag, took one out and dabbed at her eyes. 'But it does. Not on the outside, maybe. But inside. She trusted people. She assumed they were good. He robbed her of that.'

'You know she wants us to go after him? She talk to you about finding Ryan?'

Jan nodded again. 'She thought he'd understand.'

'She tell you why she thought that?' Ty pressed.

'She said his fiancée had been killed by a man like Mendez. Is that right?'

Ty tilted his head so that he was staring at the ceiling. 'There was more to it but, yeah, I guess that's what it came down to. Ryan and I were looking after a woman who was being stalked. One of them kidnapped Ryan's fiancée as a way of getting him to back off. He didn't and she ended up dead.'

Jan Warner didn't say anything.

'We were out trying to find her,' Ty went on. 'It was dark and the weather was real bad. She'd escaped from where he was holding her. She ran out into the road in front of our vehicle. I was driving but Ryan still blames himself.'

'I'm so sorry,' said Jan.

Ty rubbed his face. 'I sometimes think that if she hadn't escaped, if the guy had killed her before she had the chance to get away, it might have been easier. Then I hate myself for thinking that.'

Jan reached out and touched his arm. 'Life doesn't always give us nice neat endings.'

'But that's what your daughter's looking for,' he said. 'An ending.'

'I suppose it is. She feels that until he's behind bars she can't move on with her life.'

'And what do you think?' Ty asked.

Jan blew her nose. 'I just want my baby back to the way she was before. I don't care about Mendez or what happens to him. I'm not interested in revenge. I only care about Melissa.'

Of course she did, thought Ty. She was a mom. But, sadly, the people who were hunting her daughter, who were seeking vengeance for her continued pursuit of Mendez, saw it differently. For whatever reason they believed that the only way of stopping the pursuit of Mendez was to murder his victim. Even if Melissa or Jan could speak to them directly and tell them that Melissa was scared enough to drop their crusade, Ty doubted it would have any effect. Once the word came down to street level that an individual was to be taken out, nothing else mattered. When you were marked, you were marked, not because the people giving the orders were unable to change their minds but because word came down and was difficult to reverse.

Ty was wary of Melissa overhearing them. He took Jan's elbow and moved her a little further down the corridor. 'You know these people aren't going to stop now.'

'But if I take her home with me . . .'

'The kid who came in here to finish the job, she was a gang member. They got gangs all over the country. Every city, every small town, there's no hiding-place if they want someone.'

'You're saying there's nothing we can do?'

Ty looked at her, his jaw tight. 'Nothing you can do. But we can find Mendez.'

'And Ryan? What does he think?'

'I think your daughter did her homework pretty well.'

Eighteen

The sun set low over the Pacific as Lock threaded his way back down the Pacific Coast Highway towards Los Angeles. His mood was lighter. He knew a lot more than he had before he left, and Ty had called with the news that Melissa had regained consciousness. She had been able to tell him a little of what had happened to her up to the night she'd been shot.

After months of trying to contact Lock and getting nowhere, she had seen a paparazzo picture of him escorting members of Triple-C into a West Hollywood restaurant. At first she had tried to get in touch with him via the group's management, who had given her the brush-off. When she had seen they were playing a gig in LA, she had bought a ticket.

At the concert, the gang members had begun to cause trouble. At first she had thought it was a random event. Gang problems or fights at rap concerts were hardly unique. Then she had realized that they were looking for her. She had fled to her car, been chased and got away. Or, at least, she'd thought she had.

She'd been on her way to the hotel where the after-party was taking place when she had stopped for gas. As she was getting back into her car, another car had pulled in front of her, blocking her in. The girl had got out and shot her through the driver's side window, leaving her for dead. But Melissa was alive. Delirious with pain, she had fixated on reaching the hotel and finding Lock.

The rest they knew.

Ty's voice echoed in the car from the speaker on Lock's cell phone. 'Cops are in with her now.'

'You ask them not to say anything to her about the girl being released?'

'I did,' said Ty. 'Don't know if they'll tell her or not. You find anything up there?'

'Some. Nothing that makes our job any easier. Think Brady had a contact in Mexico but they're not answering their phone.'

'Know who it is?'

'Nope. All I got so far is a number.' Lock drummed his fingers on the steering-wheel. 'Listen, can you talk to one of our data-mining guys and see what they can dredge up about the Mendez family's business interests?'

'Sure.'

'Especially anything related to business activities across the border in Mexico, subsidiary companies, suppliers, stock interests, business partnerships, anything of that nature.'

'You got it. So, are we going after this asshole or not?'

Lock sighed and glanced at a pale blue slab of ocean. 'Let's just see where this takes us, Ty. I'll be with you soon anyway.'

'Okay, brother.'

Lock killed the call and switched his focus back to the road. He tried the Mexican number he'd found on Brady's phone records one more time. This time he got a message in Spanish and English to say that the person was out of coverage area. He'd try again later.

He made one more call as he drove.

Sarah Brady answered on the second ring. He thanked her for her help and apologized for disturbing her at work.

'Did you find what you were looking for?' she asked.

He wouldn't tell her about the phone number until he knew whose it was. But something from the office had nagged away at him as he had snaked his way south. 'This might sound stupid, but Joe had scribbled some stuff on his desk pad. Nothing that seemed to mean anything but maybe you'd know. Did you ever hear him use the words "The Devil's Bounty"?'

There was a bitter laugh at the other end of the line. 'Yeah, I know what that means. It's just a shame Joe didn't take it to heart.'

'What does it mean, Mrs Brady?'

'It's dumb, really.' She paused, seeming to search for a way to put it into words. 'When Joe started out he worked for an old guy called Daniel Front. Front Bail Bonds. Danny had been in the job, like, for ever and it was one of his little phrases. I guess everyone thinks that bail bondsmen and skip tracers deal with bad asses all the time, but from what I know about it, it's mostly people who're just plain dumb or unlucky or a combination of the two. Anyway, from time to time they'd get someone who really was bad news. Joe would cut them some slack, but Danny had been around long enough that he'd send them to someone else because he knew they'd skip or they'd be too much trouble if he had to go after them. So, if he didn't want to deal with someone because he was a real bad guy who had a habit of skipping out, that was the phrase he'd use. He'd say that he didn't want to go after the Devil's Bounty. He was right too. If he'd still been around, there's no way he would have let Joe go after Mendez.'

The Devil's Bounty. Lock chewed it over. It made sense. He often turned down clients because he knew that they were going to be way more trouble than they were worth. And when he gave them the benefit of the doubt, it almost always ended in tears – and in his last major job, protecting Raven Lane, there had been an ocean of them.

'Is Danny still around?' he asked.

'He died ten years ago. Joe kept the name until he was established, then went with Brady Bail Bonds.'

'So, it was just an old-timer's phrase?'

'Pretty much. Good advice, though.'

As Lock thanked Joe's widow for her help and wound up the call, he glanced across at the tracking device. He had moved it from the trunk to the front passenger seat as a reminder that someone, somewhere, perhaps at the Mendez estate, perhaps in Santa Maria, was tracking his every move in front of a computer screen, watching the little dot that represented his car crawling across a map. He was glad of that. They thought they had the upper hand. Right now, that suited him just fine.

Nineteen

It was dark when Lock reached the UCLA Medical Center. This time he parked in the structure that was officially designated for visitors. He took the elevator up to the ICU and got out, hearing the shouts of a medical team, a doctor barking orders, nurses yelling back. He shrugged it off. It was Intensive Care: medical emergencies were hardly a rarity.

He walked down the long corridor. Unless she had been moved, Melissa's room was the sixth door on the left. He had counted before, not just the room but the steps to it from the elevator – an old habit acquired over years of close-protection work. Any time he found himself in a location that was unfamiliar to him, he would work out exit and entry points so that he would know exactly how long it would take him to reach them if there was a fire or a power outage.

Up ahead, medical staff were rushing into and out of a room on the left. He counted the doors. He checked his count. Then he broke into a run.

He looked around for Ty but couldn't see him. A nurse was rushing past. Lock grabbed her arm. 'Melissa Warner? Has she been moved? Is that her room?' he asked, clinging to the hope that he was mistaken.

'Excuse me,' she said, brushing him off with a scowl.

He kept moving. Suddenly Ty was there, although Lock hadn't seen where he had come from. A woman screamed, the sound dissolving into a wail of denial. 'No! No!'

Ty had his arms around her. One look at her told Lock that this was Jan, Melissa's mother. She was trying to fight her way past Ty and into the room. He was struggling to stop her without hurting her. 'Let the doctors do their job. Okay?' he said.

Gradually she began to still until he took his arms away. She slid down the wall, wrenching at her hair with both hands, panic and fear overwhelming her.

'What's going on?' Lock asked him.

'I don't know. One minute she was sitting up, looked fine, the next I'd come out so she could get some rest and all those machines went crazy. Her heart, I'm guessing. I saw them going for a defibrillator and they got a crash team in there.'

Melissa's mother was getting to her feet. Lock and Ty helped her up. 'I need to get some fresh air.'

'You want me to come with you?' Ty offered.

She shook her head, rosary beads falling over her knuckles. 'That's kind of you, but I'll manage.'

Lock stood with Ty and watched her walk unsteadily towards the elevator. They glanced back at the room. The commotion seemed to be ebbing away. Voices were lowered but no one came out. Lock stared at his partner, both men thinking that wasn't a good sign.

They waited. A nurse drifted out, eyes on the floor. A resident in green scrubs was next. He looked at Lock. 'Are you the father?'

The question shook Lock. *What was he to her?* He wasn't any kind of family. He wasn't a friend. He had only met the girl when she had stumbled bleeding into the hotel two nights before. He was a stranger she had turned to for help. 'Her mother just stepped outside. You want me to go get her?'

'If you would,' the doctor said.

'I'll take care of it,' Ty said, striding past them, shoulders down, long legs stalking towards the elevator.

'She's gone?'

The doctor bit at his lower lip. 'I'm very sorry. Sometimes . . .' He trailed off. 'Sometimes when there's been a trauma like she suffered, the body just overloads.'

Lock's gaze drifted towards the room where a dead twenty-year-old girl was lying on a bed, her heart literally broken beyond repair. 'I brought her in after the shooting,' he said to the doctor. 'Would you mind if I saw her?'

The doctor didn't say anything so Lock moved past him and into the room.

She was laid out on the bed. A nurse pulled the gown over her bare breasts as Lock walked in but he could see the raw, livid scar that arced across her abdomen, the stitches still visible from where she had been pieced together after the bullet had been removed. Lock crouched next to the bed, recent history rushing at him. He wasn't at fault for this death, not in any way, but it still weighed on him. Melissa Warner had left him a legacy as sour as any family debt.

He reached up and his hands fell over her forehead. His fingertips drifted down, and he closed her eyes.

Twenty

One Week Later

West Hollywood

Three black Cadillac Escalade SUVs came to a halt outside the restaurant in West Hollywood. Lock emerged from the front passenger seat of the middle vehicle and stepped back to open the rear door. The doors of the other two Escalades also opened curb side. Lock ushered Triple-C's lead rapper, Dwayne Dikes, and his date through a small knot of paparazzi towards the entrance. Ty did likewise with his principal. It was a perfectly choreographed routine, which, in this instance, was effectively there to make the principals look good. The biggest threat Dwayne was under this evening was from some undercooked scallops.

Inside the restaurant, the maître d' escorted the two rappers and their dates to a table in the middle of the room. Lock and Ty took a small table by the window, ordered mineral water and settled in to wait. This was close-protection work as Lock knew it:

watching someone else have a good time while you waited for them to finish.

He paid for the mineral water up front, a habit he had acquired over the years. You got a drink or food and asked for the check at the same time. It meant you could leave in a hurry if you had to.

Out on the sidewalk, three lone paparazzi went back to smoking and talking and sipping their lattes. On the patio, Lock recognized a certain Hollywood actress and her buffed movie-star date, neither of them heterosexual but both with a movie on upcoming general release.

The lead Escalade pulled out into traffic. The other two followed it. Per Lock's instructions, they would circle the block and wait around the corner, ready to pick up their charges as soon as they were finished with dinner.

Across the street there was another vehicle, a red Honda Accord with tinted windows. It was watching Lock and Ty, part of an ongoing surveillance operation. It would have been nothing for them to walk across the street, or get behind it, pull it over, haul out the driver and find out who he was working for and why he was following them. Easy, but redundant. Lock knew who it was. He knew why it was there. He welcomed its presence in the same way that he had welcomed the little black box planted in his Audi. Covert surveillance was a problem when you didn't know it was taking place. When you did, it was a gift from the other side.

He sipped his mineral water. For a change of pace, Ty had ordered a Sprite. When the waiter brought it, Lock gave him some shit to break up the wait: 'That stuff'll rot your teeth.'

That was how their conversations had gone in public for a week now. Sports. Current Affairs. Trivia. No mention of Melissa Warner and what had happened to her. Definitely no mention of

Charlie Mendez. Not in public. Not where there was any chance they could be overheard. Both men were thinking about the girl who had paid with her life in trying to reach Lock, but they didn't talk about it unless they were alone and knew it was safe to do so.

In truth, Melissa was more on their minds today than any other. Lock saw her face when he closed his eyes. She had pushed Carrie to the edge of his unconscious mind and he wasn't sure whether to be resentful or grateful.

Today, more than three thousand miles away, Melissa was being laid to rest at home in Delaware. She was to be buried next to her father. Lock had received an invitation to the funeral. He had placed it in his pocket. Then, outside a clothing store in Burbank, with the red Honda Accord across the street, he had torn it into a few pieces and tossed them into a nearby trash can. That would ensure its retrieval and send a message that, as far as he was concerned, the girl was history, a violent yet random interlude in his life, certainly not worth risking his life over, especially now that she was dead.

The charade had continued, extracting its nightly toll, but he did not waver. His anger burned so hot that when he needed strength he could warm himself by its flame.

Across the restaurant, the rap stars had ordered a three-hundred-dollar bottle of champagne. Their dates giggled. Ty gave them a sour look.

'Could serve those dudes this,' he said, raising his icy glass of Sprite, 'and they wouldn't know the difference.'

'Hey, they're paying you good money to sit in this fancy restaurant sipping Sprite.'

They settled back into their seats and waited out the appetizers, entrées and dessert. As the entrées were cleared, Lock noticed movement across the street. The red Honda Accord nudged its way out into the traffic on Pico Boulevard. It had been rented to a private detective working out of Van Nuys, an ex-cop. He would have been hired by an intermediary who had in turn been instructed by another. A cover story would have been concocted to explain the surveillance. A cheating wife with a penchant for guys like Lock, something of that nature. He would probably never know that he was working for the bad guys and Lock wasn't going to tell him. He was merely a piece on the board. Let him get on and do his job.

Lock checked his watch. The guy had either quit for the night or the week's surveillance that he'd been paid for had expired. He wouldn't know whether it was the former or the latter until to-morrow. He guessed it was the latter. Keeping eyes on someone when nothing was happening would lead to questions and who-ever was ultimately paying him had probably had enough of questions.

Lock ordered another glass of mineral water and reflected that sometimes the best thing you could do was nothing, though for him it was also the hardest. The rappers were arguing over whose Amex Black card, supplied by the record company, would be used to pick up the check. Neither Lock nor Ty had the heart to tell them the company was simply making sure that they would pay for every dollar's worth of their extravagant lifestyle. They would learn the hard way. You never got something for nothing. Everything in life came with a price.

Twenty-one

Lock slotted the plastic key card into the hotel-room door. The light beside the handle flicked to green. He retrieved the card, turned the handle and walked into their temporary operations room. As Ty stood behind him, he pulled a bag from the closet, retrieved a scanner and swept the room for covert listening devices. It was clear. The cleaners had been instructed to leave the room alone, and he had placed a small motion-activated video camera in a far corner. Ty sat down at his desk, opened his laptop and scanned the footage. 'We're good,' he said.

Using a 32-bit encrypted secure Internet connection, Ty logged on to his email account. As he worked through it, Lock laid a map on the bed. Red dots showed locations where Charlie Mendez was thought to have been. Some of the sightings had been confirmed; most had not. The majority were from the period immediately after his flight, before the media had cycled on to the next hot story. Tourists and visitors, eager to help, had called in saying they had seen him in various resorts. One such encounter, confirmed via video footage, had placed him in Cancún, probably the most popular tourist destination for Americans. But that had been months ago. Since Brady's death, he might have been wiped from the face of the planet.

Lock stood behind his partner. 'Anything new?'

'Our boy Charlie's like Brer Rabbit. The mofo, he lay low.'

'You should be a poet, Tyrone.'

Ty smiled. 'Maybe when I retire.'

He returned to the emails, and Lock to the map. Unless Mendez had taken off for another country, the clusters of confirmed sightings had him in the north-east of Mexico, close to the border. It was a puzzle. If Lock had been in his position, he would have driven south, moving deeper into Latin and South America. That he appeared to have stayed within the same three-or-four-hundred-mile radius seemed to back up Lock's suspicion that Mendez was under someone's protection, most likely a cartel or gang.

Five years ago it would have been easy to work out who was shielding him. There had been the Gulf Cartel and the Sinaloa Cartel. Between them they had carved up drug- and people-trafficking in Mexico. Then there had been a US-funded crackdown by the Mexican government, the subsequent emergence of the paramilitary Los Zetas, and a volatile fracturing of the drug-trafficking industry. The cartels were still there, still powerful, but the vertically integrated business structures they had used to operate their business had eroded to the point at which it was very difficult to figure out who was working for whom. Worst of all, with the fragmentation came more violence. Before, it had served a business function; now more and more people were killed, raped and tortured, not to intimidate, clear away competition or for profit, but for almost recreational reasons.

Also, the cartels were outsourcing many aspects of their business, from transport to security to money laundering. As with legitimate business, it saved money, but it also distanced those at the very top from the things that could land you in prison. If a drug lord could claim he had had no idea that a sub-contractor was flouting safety laws, he could wash his hands of the latest criminal outrage. After all, the people committing these atrocities weren't his men. The idea of plausible deniability had found f a v o r with organized crime.

All of these changes had meant that tracking Mendez was proving a lot tougher than Lock had anticipated. To make matters even more difficult, his strategy of convincing whoever was track-ing him that he had no interest in Mendez meant that he couldn't be overt in gathering intelligence. At some point, though, that would have to change. To capture Mendez, they had to find him and, so far, they were getting nowhere fast.

Ty got up and stretched, locking his fingers behind his head and kneading his neck. 'Nothing. No one's seen him. No one's heard of anyone who's seen him.'

Lock kicked at the foot of the bed in frustration. 'He's got to surface at some point.'

'Apart from that detective in Santa Barbara and Brady's wife, did you think about talking to someone at the Department of Justice or in the US Marshals Service?'

Lock walked to the window and looked out over the City of Angels. 'Marshals aren't going to go after him down there and the DOJ have their hands full. Charlie Mendez is old news. Sure, if he gets pinched down there they'll send someone to pick him up, but go looking for him? Nah.'

That was the other difficulty with finding Mendez. Over the

past few months relations between the Mexican and United States governments had become even more frayed. As the narco-wars began to spill over the border and Mexican government corruption became more obvious, cooperation between American state agencies and their counterparts in Mexico had been strained, with distrust on both sides. Simply put, there was no appetite for anyone in Mexico or the US to go looking for a serial rapist. They had bigger fish to fry.

'I'm beat. You mind if I turn in?' Ty said.

'Sure. Go ahead.'

Ty walked to the door. 'We'll find him.'

Lock waved a goodnight and turned back to the map on his bed. He continued to pore over it, hoping it would give up its secrets, willing a pattern into existence, searching for a clue, however small, that would give them a starting point. But none came. Three hours later, he finally fell asleep.

Part Two

Twenty-two

Wrapped in the warmth of the fiery orange sun above the Pacific Ocean, Charlie Mendez stretched his lean, tanned body, and gave a loud yawn. The whole day stretched ahead of him. In a minute or two he would rise from his lounger, grab his surfboard and try to catch some waves. After an hour or so, he would come back into shore, head to the villa to shower, then go out to lunch. Afterwards, he would return to the villa with one of the local girls he rotated on a weekly basis. After a siesta with her, when he often ended up burning more calories than he did surfing, he would rest properly. Around seven, he would go to dinner, then drink in a local bar where he would pick up another girl, almost always a different one from the afternoon's. By midnight he would be alone in bed and asleep.

While most men would tire of such a life, Mendez was used to indolence, to doing a lot of not very much. It had eased his transition to life in Mexico. There was only one problem: the local girls. They were beautiful, some strikingly so, but they were no challenge. He was young, wealthy and American, which meant that getting laid was a lot easier than catching a wave. He missed his old life so badly that he had even drugged one of the girls he had brought back to the villa. But, as she lay there unconscious, the thrill was gone. She would have done what he wanted her to do anyway, no matter how degrading or weird. Where was the fun in that?

That was why, later that evening, he was going to slip away from the villa and drive to nearby Diablo, which had a couple of resort hotels that catered to American tourists, and find some real sport. He had bought a new video camera specially. He had sourced his drugs. He was taking a risk. There was every chance that a bounty hunter might still be looking for him, despite what had happened to the last one. But that made it all the more thrilling. Charlie Mendez would be both hunted and hunter. The thought made his skin tingle with anticipation, and goosebumps rose on his arms.

He got to his feet, flicked off his sandals and picked up his board. Behind him, on the concrete promenade, two of his bodyguards stood next to a red Mercedes saloon, their automatic weapons slung over their shoulders – men openly carrying heavy-duty firearms were no big deal down here. He waved to them. One of them, Hector, waved back. Hector scared him. Although he was the smallest of the men who followed him everywhere, he was the one the others deferred to, the leader of the group. It was in his eyes, which were those of a predator.

Mendez began to run towards the ocean, the promise of a proper evening's entertainment making him feel truly alive for the first time in months. Finally he had something to look forward to. Then he heard Hector calling him from the road.

'Charlie!'

He kept running, but Hector called after him again. He might get away with ignoring the man once, but not a second time. He turned. Hector was beckoning him. He jogged towards the vehicle. 'What's up, Hector?' he asked.

'We have to go back to the house.'

'Why?'

Hector stepped forward. 'I'll take your board. Get in.'

Pissed off, Mendez handed it to him. Hector took the front passenger seat, an assault rifle on his lap.

'What's the problem?' Mendez asked. 'Why do we have to leave?'

Hector swiveled in his seat and smiled at him. 'There's no problem.'

'Is it another bounty hunter?'

'Like I said, there's no problem. It's a precaution.'

'But something's happened, right?'

'The girl who was giving you so much trouble. The Warner girl?'

Mendez hadn't thought about her in ages. For a while he'd had recurring fantasies about killing her in more and more macabre ways, or occasionally he thought back to the night he had raped her. 'Oh, yeah, that bitch – what about her?'

'She's dead,' said Hector.

He greeted the news as if he'd been told that the lunch special had already sold out. 'Oh, yeah? How'd it happen?'

Hector shrugged. 'She was at a rap concert. Someone shot her. It's LA. Bad things happen there sometimes.'

'So how come I have to go back to the house?' *Goddammit Even dead that bitch was cramping his style.* He hated the house where they'd kept him since Brady had arrived. There was no view of the ocean, no mountains, only other buildings, and even those were difficult to glimpse beyond the high walls and razor wire.

Hector's lips thinned to a straight line beneath his fat, bulbous nose. It was a sign that he was growing tired of the questions.

'It doesn't matter, Hector. I'm sure there's a good reason,' he said, with a sigh. He climbed into the back of the vehicle. The air-conditioning was running at full tilt and he shivered as a cold blast hit him. He leaned back in his seat and tried to sleep. His mind drifted back to Melissa but, as he thought of her, images of the night came back to him. Even drugged she had tried to fight him, her hand clawing limply at his face. He had enjoyed that. He thought of it now, and found that he had an erection. What wouldn't he give for another Melissa?

Twenty-three

Five Hours Later

Once a proud *sicario*, Hector resented his demotion to babysitter. Especially when the baby who needed his nappy changing was Charlie Mendez. A spoilt, rich pup of an American who had done terrible things, not for money or survival, as Hector had, but for kicks. A nobody, who had never worked a day in his life. A coward, who didn't even have the balls to take a woman against her will unless he had drugged her first and she couldn't fight back.

Hector did what the boss had asked him to do. He did it well. He made sure that no harm came to Charlie, but that didn't mean he had to like it.

Hector's journey in life had been different. No silver spoon for him. No spoon of any description, in fact. Not even a plastic one.

He had grown up in a family of four boys and one girl, small by the standards of his *colonia*. Hector had been the eldest. His father had died in a farming accident when he was seven. He'd been chewed up and spat out by a threshing machine, then delivered home in a plywood box by a Texas rancher, who probably thought of himself as a good guy for going to the expense.

It was the boss who had saved Hector, and brought him into the plaza, back in the days when there was a plaza and a proper order to business. At first Hector had started out doing some jobs here and there, mostly taking cars across the border. He was never stopped and it was only later he realized that it hadn't been just luck. Actually, that wasn't true. He had been stopped once and the car taken but he had been let go. He had gone straight back to the boss and, because he hadn't waited for him to find out, there had been no repercussions. From that point on, Hector had been trusted and his ascendancy had been swift. Soon afterwards he no longer had a job but a career, with prestige and status and even a pension – if he lived long enough to collect it.

It was a quarter to the hour and darkness had enveloped the streets outside the villa. Dinner would be served soon by the staff. Hector put down his tumbler of Johnnie Walker Blue and walked from the living room, with the french windows that gave on to the swimming pool, into the corridor. At the bedroom he knocked softly. His charge was in the habit of taking a long siesta, but he was usually up, showered and dressed for dinner by now.

There was no answer.

Hector knocked again, a little too loudly, the alcohol kicking in, along with his impatience to lend extra weight to his hand.

When he was ignored again, he reached down and opened the door. Inside the bedroom, the curtains were closed and it was dark.

'Señor,' he whispered. 'Dinner will be served in an hour. You may want to think about . . .'

He crossed to the bed and nudged the lump. He grabbed a corner of the sheet and pulled it off to reveal a bundle of clothes, neatly rolled up and arranged to look like a body.

He checked the bathroom. It was empty. Charlie Mendez was gone and Hector had a problem.

Twenty-four

What kind of twenty-one-year-old still went on vacation with her parents? That had been the question Julia Fisher had been pre-occupied with ever since her dad had come with the brochures for the all-inclusive resort in Mexico. At least it wasn't Disneyland, which had been his suggestion when she was seventeen.

Her mom had wanted to go to Europe but Dad, always one for the cheap option, had ruled that out. He'd f a v o r e d the small resort of Diablo because there was no air travel to deal with and therefore no jet lag, airport security or any of the other annoy- ances you had to deal with when traveling a long distance. If Julia didn't like it, it was only for a week – couldn't she just humor the old man? Remarkably, he had also suggested that perhaps she might bring along the young man she had been seeing, forgetting that they had recently broken up.

So, if for no other reason than to close down the conversation, she had quickly agreed. It was one of those things you said yes to, then immediately regretted, but it was done. And how bad could it be, right? It was only a week, and as a family they liked Mexico. It was strange and foreign without being overly so. And Dad was right: it was a car ride home if they grew tired of it, which Mom did, almost as soon as they had rolled up at the resort.

Perhaps once it had looked like the photographs in the brochure, but it sure didn't any more. Plus, it wasn't even on the coast. In fact, the area they had driven through to get there was almost semi-industrial. But Dad had got a deal – 'Hell, they were practically giving the rooms away,' he'd said, drawing a major eye roll from Mom – and the staff, no doubt eager to make a good impression, had gone out of their way to be welcoming. So much so that Mom had had to agree that the service was pretty much the best they'd had anywhere.

The only real problem for Julia was that she was twenty-one and on vacation alone with her parents. And she was bored.

That evening, Dad being Dad had made a big show of letting her have wine at dinner and joking with the waiter about carding her. Not that she was a big drinker but she didn't have the heart to tell him she'd been drinking at parties since she was eighteen and it wasn't a big deal, like he was making out. Mom, who'd had to clean out Julia's waste basket when she'd thrown up into it after one party, had kept quiet.

In the meanwhile, Julia had spotted the bar down the street on one of their rare forays out of the resort – Dad being a firm believer that all-inclusive meant exactly that, and spending more money was stupid. The staff didn't encourage you to leave the resort either: there had been problems in the area between drug gangs, nothing that had affected any Americans or other tourists but Julia could feel anxiety in the air whenever anyone stepped outside. The hotel had a couple of guards at the entrance, both armed, but you saw armed guards in lots of places, these days, not just in Mexico. If you lived in Arizona, with its gun laws, guns were something you barely registered. Dad had one and he'd made sure that Julia knew how to use one. In any case, it was just three or four hundred yards from the hotel to the bar, where Julia had seen a couple of young American backpackers hanging out when she had passed it.

After dinner she went back to her room, changed and freshened her makeup. Around ten o'clock she left again, slipping out of the resort by a side entrance. Walking down the street, she was glad of the break from her parents. She loved them, and she knew that they were clinging to the last few precious times when they would have her to themselves, but sometimes, like this vacation, it got too much.

The bar was almost empty and all the drinkers were old and local. No Americans. No one under the age of forty. She could feel male eyes on her, which creeped her out. The bartender took pity on her and suggested somewhere else. It wasn't far and it might be more her style. There was live music, although he didn't know on which nights. She shouldn't walk alone under any circumstances. He called her a cab and gave her the firm's number: she should use them to get back to her hotel. They were a local company, reliable and safe.

The cab ride took ten minutes and she was glad she had the phone number because now she had no idea where she was in relation to the hotel. She was just starting to regret her adventure when she noticed him sitting at the bar. American. Bearded, tanned and slim. He was older but not too old – and he was hand-some. Like, really handsome.

*

Sitting next to her at the bar, Charlie Mendez had been wary at first. There had been no Americans in the place when he had arrived and definitely no young American women, never mind one who was on her own. When she had walked in and hopped up on a barstool, looking slightly uncomfortable and out of place, he had taken it as a sign of good fortune, but at the back of his mind he was worried.

Buying her a drink, he had searched her face for a sign that she had recognized him. But since he had fled the United States, he had grown the beard, and his already tanned skin had darkened under the fierce Mexican sun. He had dyed his hair too. He looked different, more like a man coming to terms with his age than the Peter Pan figure he had cut back in Santa Barbara.

'Do you want another beer?' she asked. She had short blonde hair and had on one of those bras that flat-chested chicks wore to make themselves look like they had a rack, but she was pretty.

He dug into his pocket. 'No, I got this. Same again?'

She chewed her bottom lip, then scooted off her stool. 'No, something different.'

'Like what?' he asked, with a smile.

'I gotta go visit the little girls' room. Why don't you surprise me?'

He watched her leave. As she disappeared through the door marked *Señoras*, he leaned over to the bartender and ordered a beer for himself and a margarita for his new friend, Julia. When the drinks came, he slid an extra twenty dollars across the bar and asked the bartender if they had a room upstairs he could rent for a few hours.

The bartender left him, and Mendez went to work on Julia's margarita. A few moments later, she was back, hopping on to the stool and taking a sip of the drink.

'I love margaritas. How did you know?'

Mendez flashed the wide-eyed, puppyish grin that had served him so well back in Santa Barbara. 'Wild guess,' he said, as she took another sip.

Twenty-five

In the car, Hector realized that his anger towards Charlie Mendez had faded. It was the emotion he should have felt rather than the one he did. Inside, he was happy that Charlie had screwed up and gone AWOL without telling anyone. For starters, it gave him something to do. He had a mission – finally. He had to find Charlie and bring him back.

Yes, even if he couldn't find him, or if he was picked up by someone before Hector got to him, that meant the end of the babysitting. It was what his young charge liked to call a win-win situation, a phrase, Hector reflected, that only an American could use with a straight face. In America things might be win-win. In Mexico they were more likely lose-lose.

He pressed down a little harder on the gas pedal as traffic cleared out of his way, the flashing lights on the roof of the car easing his passage. As he drove, he made one more call. Not to the boss, who would only be told about Charlie after Hector knew more, but to the bartender who had called him when word had got out that Hector was looking for the American. There would be good money for the man, a heavier tip than he was used to.

'He's with a girl,' the bartender had told him. 'We have a room upstairs. He's there with her but maybe you should get here soon.'

'Why? What's the matter?' Hector pressed, but he had lost the signal, and in any case it didn't sound like the bartender could do anything about whatever the problem was. Hector flicked the switch on the console that turned on the sirens and picked up his speed.

He left the car down the street and walked to the bar. The parking lot was full. It was a busy place all week round, trade helped by the protection Hector's boss offered. Although neither the boss nor Hector nor anyone they knew drank here often, it was considered safe for locals and tourists so it was often full.

Inside, the bartender nodded for Hector to follow him to a narrow wooden stairway. Hector grabbed his arm and stared at him, his gaze reminding the bartender of who he was before he asked, 'What's the problem?'

'The girl. I've never seen her before.'

He was talking in riddles – and the smell of whisky was tantalizing. 'So what?'

The bartender lowered his voice. 'She came in on her own and sat down next to him.'

The only girls who did that were working girls so Hector didn't see why the man was so anxious, standing there in the narrow hallway, sweating. He shrugged. Then he wondered if maybe Charlie had done something to her. Hurt her. Killed her even. Surely only that would make the bartender so twitchy.

Hector squeezed the man's arm. 'Come on. Spit it out. What's the problem?'

The bartender leaned in towards him and whispered, 'She's American.'

Hector pushed past him, his feet hammering up the stairs, taking them two at a time. He reached the tiny wooden postcard of a landing and threw open the only door.

What confronted him inside told him he had been right. Win-win was for asshole *gringos*, like Charlie Mendez. For a man like Hector there was only ever lose-lose.

Twenty-six

Contrary to its carefully cultivated image as a hotbed of decadence and debauchery, Los Angeles was an early-to-bed, early-to-rise city. There was too much money out there and up for grabs for it not to be. It wasn't even seven in the morning but the diner on the corner of Melrose and Lankershim already had half a dozen people waiting for a table.

In a corner booth, Lock took a sip of coffee and pushed a half-eaten Western omelette around his plate while Ty continued to shovel up a mountain of food. They had walked there from the hotel, Lock wanting to make doubly sure that the surveillance they had been under had ceased. Not that it mattered. A new security team had already moved in to take over the coat-holding and car-door-opening duties demanded by Triple-C, but when it came to Mendez they were still at square one. Despite contacting everyone who might be able to lead them to him, there had been no new sightings, no fresh intelligence of any description.

Ty wiped his mouth with a paper napkin and belched. 'So what's the plan, Señor Lock?

'Apart from you maybe getting some table manners?'

'Sorry about that, just came out.'

'So what do you mean, "What's the plan?"'

'Well, we going to go down there and get this asshole or what?'

Lock eyed him over the table. 'Slight hitch, Señor Johnson.'

Ty smiled and scooped up some more food. Lock swore that his partner had hollow legs. Ty could eat all day every day and not put on a pound. It was irritating in the extreme.

'Like we don't have a goddamn clue where he is?' Ty said.

Lock cleared his throat. 'There's that. But what if he never surfaces? Do we just let it go?'

'Can't do that either, can we?'

'Okay. Let's set ourselves a deadline. If we knew right now where he was, how long do you think we'd need to put everything together for a hostile extraction?' Lock asked.

'Day, maybe two.'

Lock signaled to the waitress for the check. 'Two days' time we head down there. If we don't know where he is, maybe we can flush him out.'

'Or get ourselves killed,' said Ty.

Lock lifted his coffee mug and clinked it against Ty's glass of orange juice. 'That's always an option too.'

The waitress dropped by with the check. Ty gave her his patented never-fails smile. She ignored him but took Lock's credit card and came back with her phone number, which she had written on the back of the receipt.

Ty stared at it as she walked away. 'You gonna call her? I mean the girl's eyesight's clearly not the best, but she is kind of cute.'

'Don't go there.'

'What? You gonna be a monk the rest of your life? You gonna give yourself a bad case of DSB?'

Lock grimaced, knowing he would regret asking the obvious question. 'DSB?'

'Deadly Sperm Back-up, brother. Messes up a dude's mind if he holds on to that dirty water too long.'

Lock pushed away his plate. 'Can't understand why you don't get yourself more dates, Ty. Real old-school charmer such as yourself.'

Ty open-palmed an apology. 'Hey, I'm just sayin'.'

'Well, don't.'

Ty's BlackBerry chimed. He picked it up and took a look at the screen, then clicked the read button to open the email that had just dropped into his inbox.

'Something?' Lock asked him.

'That break we needed?' Ty said. 'American guy I've been talking to down there who's plugged into one or two of the local crews. He thinks he spotted Mendez in a bar.'

'When?'

'Last night,' smiled Ty.

'Where?'

'Little town outside Santa Maria called Diablo.'

Lock tried to think back to his map. He was sure he'd registered that name. 'Wasn't that close to where Brady found him the last time?'

'Think so.' Ty thumbed further down the email. 'Looks like he wasn't alone either.'

'Security?' Lock asked.

Ty's expression clouded. 'Doesn't mention it here but there was an American girl.'

Lock was already at the door. 'Think we'd better move that departure date up.'

'A day?'

'No,' said Lock. 'We leave now.'

'I can be good to go in an hour.'

'Make it thirty minutes,' said Lock, shouldering out on to the sidewalk.

Twenty-seven

The Audi would stay where it was. Lock gave the valet who had seen it in its blood-drenched condition a hefty tip to take it out of the garage and drive it around Los Angeles on a pre-determined schedule that broadly correlated to his previous movements over the past week: a car that didn't move would alert the suspicion of anyone still monitoring the tracking device.

In his hotel room, he gathered some of his belongings. He left some clothes on hangers in the wardrobes in case someone decided to take a closer look. He also left his toothbrush and razor. The toothbrush he would replace; the razor could go unused. He hadn't shaved for the past week, figuring that if Mendez had changed his appearance to deflect attention then so would he.

The hotel was paid for until the end of the following week. That was the time-frame Lock had allowed to locate, kidnap and repatriate Mendez. If it took any longer than ten days they could keep the rest of his stuff or throw it away: the chances were that he wasn't coming back.

He pulled a pre-packed duffel bag on to his shoulders and took one last look at the room, then left. In the corridor, Ty was waiting for him. They walked in silence to the elevator and rode it down to the parking garage. They got out and went to a white Ford Ranger double-cab pick-up truck.

They slung their bags into the back. The Ranger would take them over the border where they would switch vehicles. Ty got behind the wheel and drove out of the garage, both men on the lookout for someone following them.

Lock pulled a picture of Charlie Mendez from his jacket pocket and clipped it to the sun visor as a reminder. Mendez stared back at him with a broad grin. If Lock had his way, he wouldn't be smiling for much longer.

They took Interstate 5 as far south as San Diego, then picked up the Kumeyaay Highway and began to head east through the Cleveland National Forest. Finally, Ty broached the subject that had been preying on their minds. 'He was seen with a girl. You think he was . . .?'

Lock stared out of the window at the dry, scrubby desert, as the road flirted with the Rio Grande only to switch north again. 'A leopard doesn't change its spots.'

Twenty-eight

Towering roadside crosses, painted pink and entwined with dried flowers, greeted Lock and Ty as they crested the hill, the border area of Mexico laid out beneath them. Lock counted six of the twenty-foot-high wooden structures. A hundred yards down the road they came to four more, one after another, high desert stretching off into the distance on either side of the highway. He waved for Ty to pull the white Ranger into the side of the road.

'What's up?' Ty asked.

Lock looked towards the crosses stony-faced but said nothing. 'Just want to take a look.'

Ty pumped the brakes and the car slid to a halt on the gravel.

Lock got out and walked towards the base of the first cross. A photograph, wrapped in clear plastic, was fastened to it. He hunkered down in the dust and studied it.

A young Mexican woman looked back at him. She had long dark hair, soft brown eyes, and the hesitant self-aware smile of someone unused to posing for the camera. She was wearing a black high-school graduation gown over her clothes and clutching a mortarboard in her right hand, her whole life ahead of her. At the bottom of the photograph was a name: Rosa Perez. Beneath that, in the same neat handwriting, were the dates of her birth and death. Rosa had been nineteen when she died.

Lock straightened up and, shielding his eyes from the strengthening mid-morning sun, took in the vista below. Santa Maria lay before him. Official estimates put its population at 1.5 million but that was almost certainly out by at least half a million. Like the other border cities along the Rio Grande, the city had drawn in hundreds of thousands of people from the poorer south of the country to work in its *maquiladoras*. Free trade between the countries had allowed American companies to shift jobs a few miles across the border and save themselves tens of millions of dollars in lower wage costs and taxes.

The workers in the *maquiladoras* were mostly young women. They were considered more dextrous when it came to the assembly line, and the factory owners could pay them less than they would men. They were also the ones who had been turning up dead for more than a decade. Thousands of them, spirited off the streets, raped, murdered and dumped, often mutilated or dis-membered, like trash, all over the city.

The roadside crosses were one part memorial and one part caution. No one in Santa Maria was safe from the ravages of a crime rate that had made it the most dangerous city in the world. But young poor women were the most at risk. It was the same the world over, but here, in Mexico, it had taken on new depths of depravity. Worst of all, no one knew who was behind it. There were theories and whispers, but no answers. Only more killings.

Lock reached out to touch the picture of the girl and his mind forced him back to Melissa. He rose, packing away his feelings. He and Ty had a job to do. A job that wouldn't afford them any distractions. There would be time to mourn the dead when they were done. First they had to find Mendez.

He walked back to the car, opened the trunk and pulled out two large black canvas duffel bags. Staying on the roadside and shielded by the car, he deposited the first bag, marked with a red and white tag, on the back seat. He dropped the second bag, which had no tag, next to it. It was the second that he unzipped. He pulled two hard plastic black gun cases and two side holsters from it.

He opened the first and took out a SIG Sauer 226. He clicked a fresh twelve-round clip into it and checked it over. He repeated the same procedure with the second 226. Then he closed the cases, zipped up the bag, shut the rear door and got back into the front passenger seat.

The guns had been purchased from a contact Ty had in El Paso, a dealer who didn't care whom he sold to as long as the money was good. No paperwork had changed hands, aside from a thick bundle of twenty-dollar bills. If they had to use them, the only way the weapons would be traced back to them was if they left their fingerprints on them. On the other hand, to venture into Mexico looking for Mendez unarmed would have been guaranteed suicide.

The most nerve-racking part had been passing through Customs Control on the US side of the border. Tourists generally didn't use the US/Santa Maria crossing because of what lay on the Mexican side. But gun runners did, although not usually in regular cars. Illegal traffic across the border was a two-way process. Drugs went north, and firearms went south to the cartels.

When they had been questioned, Lock had shown two carry permits and informed the guard that they were private security contractors going south to guard a fictional American executive and his family, who were living in Santa Maria. As cover stories went, it was plenty plausible and they had been waved through.

He handed the second weapon to Ty, who checked it over, put on the holster and slid the gun into it. 'What happens if we get pulled over by the Federales?' Ty asked.

Lock stared hard into the glare of the sun. 'We do what everyone else does. We pay 'em off.'

Ty grimaced. 'And if they won't be bought?'

'What c o l o r do you think we should get our crosses?' Lock asked.

'Well, not pink, that's for damn sure.'

Lock glanced back at the roadside and forced a smile. 'I dunno . . . pink might bring out your eyes.'

Ty waited for a gap in the traffic and pulled back on to the highway as a truck roared past them in the fast lane. As he drove, his eyes flicked back and forth from the road ahead to the rear-view and side mirrors. They were relatively safe on the freeway, but in a moment they would be on surface streets until they reached their first port of call.

Ty nudged his way through the thundering lines of trucks, returning home to pick up fresh loads, towards the off-ramp. He kept the turn signal off. He waited until he was almost at the final stretch of the median, where the ramp ended, then spun the wheel hard right. He gave the rear-view mirror a final check to see if anyone had followed but the ramp behind was clear.

Lock checked the sat-nav app on his cell phone. 'Okay, right at the bottom,' he said to Ty.

Ty didn't signal this time either, and again waited until the last possible moment before making the turn, swinging out wide and almost clipping a green and white taxi cab traveling in the opposite direction. The road opened up into a wide boulevard, with a concrete median running down the middle.

'Over here,' said Lock, and they pulled into a second-hand-car dealership with an auto-repair body shop on one side, presumably operated by the same owner, and a dentist on the other. The body repair and the dealership were two halves of the same business. The place was a *yonque*, or chop shop. They were known as bone-yards, or *huesarios*, in the interior of the country.

Ty pulled the car through a set of gates into a small yard shielded by panels of corrugated iron. A dog sat scratching itself next to a dark blue Dodge Durango with the deep tint on the windows that seemed standard here, rather than a factory option. The dog rose slowly, took a piss against one of the tires and ambled away as Lock went to greet the owner, a portly man wearing a flowery shirt that was two sizes too small, and a fedora.

Lock pointed to the Durango. '*Cuánto cuesta?*' he said to the dealer. How much?

The man took off his fedora and stared at Lock with a bemused smile. The Durango had probably been an insurance write-off, bought at an auction in Texas, repaired in the chop shop, the plates changed to Mexican ones and put up for sale. The car Lock was driving was a white Ford Ranger, worth perhaps ten times what the Durango would fetch. That was the exact reason they couldn't ride around in it. At best they would stand out a mile. At worst they were risking a car jacking, which would be messy. Lock knew that in order to move around they had to do their best to blend in, which, given their coloring, was hardly going to be easy.

The dealer shrugged and walked over to the Durango, no doubt extolling its virtues and leaving behind Lock's scant grasp of Spanish as he did so. Finally, eager to keep the exchange as short as possible, Lock dug into his pocket and pulled out a thousand dollars in cash. 'You give me the keys now, I give you the cash, and we leave,' he said in English, gesturing to the gate.

The man disappeared inside his little wooden shack of an office and reappeared a moment later with a set of car keys. Lock took them and tossed them to Ty. 'Take it for a spin round the block. I'll wait here.'

Less than five minutes later, Ty was back. He climbed out of the driver's seat. 'It's a bucket, but it'll do.'

Lock handed the money to the man, who stuck it quickly inside the lining of his hat, still not quite believing his good luck. Ty took the Durango, and Lock the Ford Ranger, and they drove in convoy out through the gates and on to the road. A half-mile further on, Ty pulled into the multi-storey parking lot of a small shopping mall. They both took a ticket at the barrier, drove past the armed private security guard at the entrance and up on to the roof.

While the lower levels had been crowded, the roof was quiet. Lock scoped the area for cameras but there were none. In a city where violence was explicit and wanton, and where your identity decided whether you would be arrested or face the courts, closed-circuit security systems were hardly a deterrent.

With the Ranger and the Durango next to each other, they moved their gear into the Durango. They pulled two more black canvas bags from the back of the Ranger and placed them in the rear compartment of the Durango. They drove back down a few levels. Lock parked the Ranger, got into the Durango next to Ty and they left the parking lot.

Driving through the middle of Santa Maria, the Durango's down-at-heel exterior, with the blacked-out windows, allowed them to blend in with the rest of the traffic. The stares that the Ranger had drawn from passers-by and fellow motorists fell away. They could watch their surroundings as others did, no longer outsiders, as long as they stayed in the car.

Ahead, on a street corner, a small crowd had gathered. Ty slowed the Durango a little. Outside a convenience store a middle-aged woman was hunched over the body of a young man, blood still fresh on his shirt.

What struck Lock was the expressions of the people who had come to watch. There was no shock or panic, only a dull, tired acceptance. It was the same reaction a minor fender-bender would elicit in LA – just something that happened. Only the woman was crying. It was a scene sadly familiar to him. The only difference between here and the other cities he had seen it played out in was that those had been officially declared war-zones.

He cracked the window just enough to hear her wails as she cried for her dead son. The scene slid past them and the sound of the woman's pain faded.

Twenty-nine

It was the cold that woke her. That, and a sensation of sticky dampness running down her legs. She listened but could hear nothing. Slowly, she became aware of her body and realized she wasn't lying in a bed. Air was moving over her. Her mouth was so dry that her tongue seemed to be glued to the roof. She literally had to will her eyes open and when she did open them it was so dark that she wasn't entirely sure if her eyelids had moved at all.

After a moment, her eyes began to adjust to the gloom. She couldn't see behind her. The floor was bare concrete. The walls were a blank grey. She was lying on the floor. The ceiling was bare, apart from a single light-bulb, which hung from six inches of electrical cord at the far end of the room.

She started to get up but couldn't. She twisted her head to one side. Her neck had a crick in it. She could see her hand. It had a rope around it, which was fastened to a metal ring buried in the concrete floor. She moved her neck to the other side. Her other hand was also tied down. She tried to lift her legs and felt rope around them too.

Panic flooded her. She struggled and thrashed but the ropes held firm. By sheer force of will she forced herself to stop. She had to think.

Her mind felt heavy, as if her brain had been wrapped in cotton wool.

Think.

Think about how you got here.

What do you last remember?

She remembered walking out of the resort hotel and finding the bar.

Charlie.

She had been speaking to him. He was cute. He had bought her a drink. A margarita. She had kissed him.

There had been stairs. She had stumbled. His hands had been all over her as he had helped her up the flight.

Other things were coming back to her now. Things she didn't want to remember, didn't want to think about. Maybe it was better not to think about how she had got here and focus on how she could get out.

What if she had been left here? What if someone had dumped her in this room and something had happened to them? She didn't have water. She would die. The panic rose again and this time she couldn't force it down.

She tried to shout but the noise that came out of her mouth was little more than a croak. She tried again. It was louder. She kept crying out, she didn't know for how long.

After a while a key rattled in a lock. She tried to raise her head.

She hadn't seen a door but she heard one open. It must have been behind her.

A hand settled on the side of her face. She shuddered. It rubbed her cheek. A finger traced a line across her lips.

'Please,' she heard herself say. 'Please don't hurt me.'

She could feel the person crouching behind her. She could hear them breathing. They didn't answer. They withdrew their hand and lifted her head, settling it on their knees.

The hand came back into view, this time holding a water bottle. It tilted the bottle so that she could drink. Some of the water trickled from the side of her mouth on to the floor. She was so thirsty that she chased it with her tongue. When she had finished it, the person lowered her back on to the floor.

'Please, let me go,' she said. 'My parents have money. They'll pay you.'

The person didn't respond. She heard the door close and she was alone again.

Thirty

Arriving in Diablo, they found a hotel in the centre of town. It was part of a large American chain. There were lots of vacant rooms – no surprise, given the wave of violence engulfing some of the border towns and cities.

Ty checked them in using a fake ID, paid in cash, and then they drove straight to the bar to meet his contact. Lock was hoping he would be back for a second evening. He had already decided that if he saw Mendez in public he would take him there and then.

When they arrived, the parking lot behind the bar was already crowded. Ty found them a spot as close to the back door as he could manage and they got out of the Durango. Lock plucked the picture of Mendez from the sun visor as he got out.

They walked around to the front of the bar. Ty glanced up at the sign. 'This is it.'

Lock squared his shoulders and, with Ty a pace behind him, pushed his way through the front door. The first thing he noticed was the smell of cigarette smoke. *Presence of the abnormal if you had just come from California: smoking in public was worse than farting.* He had tucked the picture of Mendez into his back pocket.

At the bar, he ordered two beers and checked out the crowd. It looked to be mostly locals but there were a few Americans.

Lock clinked glasses with Ty.

'What should we drink to?' Ty asked.

Over Ty's shoulder, Lock noticed a white guy sitting alone, nursing a Boilermaker. He seemed to be tuning in to their conversation.

'Let's drink to a great vacation,' Lock said, tipping the neck of his bottle against Ty's. He half turned, so he was square to the bar. The barfly caught his eye. 'You guys American?' the man said.

'How'd you guess?' said Lock.

The guy gave a modest shrug. 'Suppose I'm just good at reading people.'

'You want a drink?' Lock asked.

The guy smiled. 'Sure.'

Ty nodded towards a table of tourists, mostly young and female. 'I'm gonna go circulate, brother.'

Lock slid his beer down towards the guy and grabbed a stool. He'd already spotted something he could use: a battlefield cross tattoo on the guy's right biceps. 'My buddy over there was in the Corps.'

'Good times, man,' the American said, raising his glass. 'Your health.'

'And yours,' Lock said, taking a gulp of beer. 'Where did you serve?'

'Here and there. Did my final tour in Iraq. First time round. Desert Storm.'

That was the phrase Lock had been waiting for, the phrase that told him they had found Ty's contact. He lowered his voice but kept the tone conversational. Just two dumb-ass Americans shooting the bull on vacation. 'So what you got?'

The American dug out a pack of cigarettes. He offered one to Lock, who declined. 'He was in here last night.'

'You're sure it was him?' Lock asked.

The American lit his smoke. 'Yeah. Soon as I saw him I knew who he was. Kind of surprised to see him here, though.'

'How's that?'

'You get tourists in here.'

'He was with a girl?'

The American blew a smoke ring, which settled over the bar. 'There's a resort not too far from here, still gets some trade. She came in on her own. They were talking, he bought her a drink. She must have been pretty blitzed because he had to help her walk out.'

Lock's heart almost stopped. 'She couldn't walk?'

The American shrugged. 'Kids come down here, they can't hold their liquor.'

The bartender was back, asking if they wanted more drinks. Lock waved him away. 'He left with the girl?'

'They went upstairs. I didn't see either of them again for a while until this Mexican dude came to get him.'

'A bodyguard?' said Lock.

'Looked like it. Here,' he said, digging into his pocket and pulling out his cell phone. 'I didn't get a chance to snap your boy but I did get a picture of the muscle.'

The American pulled up a grainy picture on the tiny screen. The bartender was still hovering. 'Great boat, ain't she?'

Lock played along as he took the cell phone and studied the picture. It showed a man in profile as he walked out of the bar. He was dressed in shorts and a wife-beater shirt. Mexican. Heavyset, with hooded eyes and a boxer's squashed nose.

'So why you selling her?' Lock asked.

The American shrugged. 'Low on cash, you know how it is.'

Lock handed the cell phone back. 'Hey, send me that picture so I can show my wife, okay, and we'll work something out.'

'Okay, will do. Listen, good meeting you.'

They shook hands, the American slid off the stool and walked out of the bar. A few seconds later the picture flashed up on Lock's cell. The contact would be paid by wire transfer the next day as per their agreement.

Ty was still talking to the crowd of girls. Lock joined him. 'Hate to break up the party, but we gotta go, brother.'

Ty slid his chair back from the table. 'Catch you later, ladies.' He shot them a backward glance. 'I asked them about an American girl maybe going missing.'

'And?' Lock asked.

'Hadn't heard about anything like that.'

'Well, if it was him and he drugged her, maybe she hasn't remembered it yet.'

They headed back out to the Durango, scanning the parking lot as they made sure no one had followed them. At the rear of the vehicle, Lock shared what the American had told him.

'You believe him?' Ty asked.

Lock nodded. 'Yeah. But I don't think Mendez'll be back anytime soon. Not if he took a girl out of here.'

'So where does that leave us?'

Lock tilted his cell phone so that Ty could see the picture of the bodyguard. 'Leaves us with one more face to pick out of the crowd.'

They sat outside the bar for a while in the Durango, watching as patrons came and went. None was Charlie Mendez or his bodyguard. Exhausted from the long drive, they took it in turns to grab some sleep. After years of practice they were both accomplished at napping when they could. In relative terms, the back seat of a Dodge Durango was luxury compared to some of the places they'd had to sleep in the past.

At around three in the morning, the lot had begun to empty. Their vehicle parked alone with both of them inside it might attract attention. Ty woke Lock.

'He ain't coming.'

Lock sat up, rubbing his face. 'Let's hang on for a while yet.'

Another half-hour passed and the last few drinkers staggered outside, climbed into taxis and headed off into the night. The staff began to leave. The last one out was the bartender who had served Lock. He walked towards his car.

Lock opened the door of the Durango and got out. The man froze as he approached, no doubt figuring he was about to be mugged or forced to let Lock back into the bar to have that evening's takings.

Lock showed him empty palms. 'I just want to ask you a question.' The bartender stepped back, fumbling for his keys, but Lock placed himself between him and his car. 'You speak English?'

The man flicked his head up and down. 'I don't want trouble.'

Lock pulled out the picture of Charlie Mendez as Ty flicked on the headlights of their vehicle. He angled it into the beam so that the man could see. 'This guy was here last night?'

The bartender looked from the picture to Lock and back again. Everything about the way he was holding himself told Lock that he didn't want to say anything. His reluctance was understandable. 'You know him?'

The bartender screwed up his face.

Lock reached out and tapped the man's cheek. 'Look at me. This is important. Was he here?'

The bartender looked at him with pleading eyes. '*Sí*.'

'He was with another man. This man here,' Lock pressed, showing him the picture on his cell phone of the bodyguard. He studied the bartender's face. There was a flicker of recognition, and he swallowed so hard that Lock saw his Adam's apple bob. He didn't answer. He pushed past Lock, trying to get to his car. Lock reached out to grab his arm but he broke away. He started to run. Lock took off after him, his hand falling on the man's shoulder as he fumbled with his car keys, his hands shaking.

'Who is he?' Lock asked. 'What's his name?'

The bartender just stared at him. 'Please, I have a family, children.'

Lock let him get into his car and drive away. He had the answers he needed.

They headed back to their hotel. The elevator was broken. They climbed the three flights of stairs, rigged the door so that anyone coming in unannounced would cause a hellish racket, and fell, exhausted, into a dreamless sleep.

Thirty-one

Lock woke at seven on the button. He got out of bed as Ty slept on, went into the bathroom, took a leak, showered, shaved and worked through some stretches. By the time he came out, Ty was emerging from under the covers, his feet and ankles sticking out at the bottom of the bed. He got up, walked to the window, opened the curtains and looked out over the smoke stacks of a nearby factory.

'Man, there's nothing like being on vacation.'

'I know, and this is *nothing* like being on vacation,' Lock said. 'Go get ready. We got work to do.'

Ty shuffled towards the bathroom, scratching himself as he went. Lock watched him. 'You're going to make some woman very happy one of these days.'

'Thanks, brother.'

'When she divorces you and takes half your money.'

As Ty took his turn in the shower, Lock sat on the edge of the bed. He stared at the number he'd found in Brady's office. Now that he was here, he felt more hesitant about calling it. What if calling it had somehow hastened Brady's death? Could a number summon death? He had no doubt that it could. He had kept the picture of the bodyguard as the screensaver on his cell phone. He stared at the man whose name was too terrifying for someone to utter. Lock clicked on his recent calls list and tried the number.

The cell phone pressed to his ear to block out the hiss of the shower, he listened to the familiar trill. Someone picked up. Lock was so startled that he almost dropped the phone. He stood and walked to the window. 'Hello?'

A woman answered him, in English, but with an accent. 'If you want to fuck me, why don't you just come up to me like a man and ask me?'

Of all the responses, this was one that he hadn't been fully prepared for.

'My name is Francis Brady. I found your number in the personal effects of my brother Joe Brady. He was murdered in Mexico.'

Lock had no idea if Brady had had a brother or not, never mind what his name might be if he had, but he had figured that a family member wishing to ask some questions was about as plausible an explanation as any. Also, he didn't want the person at the other end to know who he was. Her response, though, suggested that perhaps Brady had had a little more going on south of the border than the hunt for Charlie Mendez.

There was silence.

'Hello?' Lock said again.

He could hear the woman clear her throat. 'You are his brother?'

At least she'd heard Joe Brady's name.

'Yes, that's correct,' he said.

Ty had emerged from the bathroom, a towel around his waist. He scratched his chest. 'Think we got bedbugs or something.'

Lock waved at him to shut up. 'I found your number in his office. I'm trying to work out exactly what happened to him when he came down to Mexico. I thought you might be able to help.'

More silence, more hesitancy.

'Can I at least ask your name?'

'Where are you now?' the woman said.

'Santa Maria,' Lock lied, unwilling to give away the precise location to someone he didn't know.

'Are you crazy? You already know what happened to your brother, right? You want to join him?' she asked.

'No, I don't. But I need to know why it happened.'

'Go home, Mr Brady. That's my best advice to you.'

Lock took a breath. Beneath him he watched a crowd of workers clamber on to a bus. He picked out a middle-aged woman who took a seat by the window. She had the worn-out look of someone who didn't so much live as exist. 'I can't do that.' He paused. 'You knew my brother but I don't even know your name.'

More silence. He could hear her, though.

'Meet me in an hour.' She gave him an address in Santa Maria. His lie had caught him out. The drive last night when the roads were quiet had taken an hour and ten minutes. Now it was rush-hour.

'Wait, can we make it a little later?' he said. But she had already hung up.

Thirty-two

An hour wasn't long enough for them to get there. But it was plenty of time to organize their execution. Under normal circumstances, whenever he met with someone he didn't know and was unsure of their motive, Lock liked to check the location ahead of time, find the entry and exit points, have a plan for action on attack. All he could do now was show up. If he was walking into an ambush, he and Ty would have to improvise.

Fifteen minutes after the call, they were only just clearing the outskirts of Diablo. They still had forty plus miles to cover. Then they had to find the place. As Ty drove, Lock navigated.

Ty had his foot pressed hard to the floor but they were still barely touching eighty miles per hour. As they closed in on the outskirts of the city, scrub desert shifted to dense urban jungle. Green and white taxis vied for space on the road with old American school buses ferrying workers to the factories.

Blasting the horn, Ty navigated the crush of traffic as the minutes ticked down. Lock switched to a city map, his attention shifting between it and the vehicles around them. They were on city streets now. Ty swore under his breath.

Lock glanced over the edge of the map to see road works and a road-closed sign. Ty immediately began to turn. It was a firm rule of close-protection work that it was always better to be moving than stationary. It might just be road works. It might be something else. Right now, even though Lock was sure that no one who mattered or wished them ill even knew they were in Santa Maria looking for Mendez, it was safer, and simpler, to assume the opposite was true. 'Prepare for the worst' was a good mantra if you wanted to stay alive.

Cars horns raged as the Durango blocked the intersection. Ty spun the wheel, reversed and roared back in the direction they had come from. They had lost thirty seconds they didn't have.

'Left here – we'll loop back around,' said Lock.

They were parallel to a railway line when he realized he was taking them in the wrong direction, a rare mis-step. 'Sorry, brother, we need to be over there.'

Not missing a beat, Ty pulled the wheel down hard, the Dodge bumping straight across the tracks. Lock felt the blood drain from his face. His partner looked at him and laughed. 'What? You said over there.'

'I'm driving next time.'

Ty shrugged. 'The way you're navigating, that might not be a bad idea.'

They reached the address five minutes after the deadline. It was a shopping mall. As an RV, Lock liked it. Lots of traffic. Lots of entry and exit points. Lots of innocent bystanders, not that narco-traffickers worried too much about that, but an empty parking lot with nothing nearby would have had him more on edge than he might normally have been.

The only question remaining was whether the woman had waited for him. His cell rang. It was the number.

'Where are you?'

'We got lost.'

'I gave you an hour,' the woman said.

'I'm sorry.'

'I'm on the third level. In the café opposite the elevators. You have one more minute before I leave. I don't have time for this bullshit.'

She hung up. Ty had his arm out, waiting to get a ticket from the machine and then for the barrier to rise.

'Catch me up.' Lock grabbed the door handle and jumped out.

Ty called after him but Lock kept going, running hard towards the entrance, almost catching himself on the automatic doors as they glided open. Dodging around a woman pushing a baby in a stroller, he looked about. People were waiting for the elevator but the display s i g n a l e d that it had only just begun its descent.

He headed for the stairwell, exploding through the doors and launching himself upwards, heart pounding and gasping for breath.

Head throbbing, out of breath, he made it to the third floor, pushed through another set of doors on to a walkway and out into an open courtyard of stores. Frantically, sweat running down his back, he looked for a café.

Nothing. No restaurant. No cafés. Only stores. So many of the names were American that you might think you were still on the other side of the border.

He began to walk past the stores, people shooting glances at the sweaty *gringo*. He called the number.

'There's no café on the third level,' he said, when she answered.

'And Joe Brady didn't have a brother. So why don't you tell me who you are and what you want?'

Decision time. He took a breath. Whoever she was, she was smart. If she was linked to a cartel or someone protecting Mendez she knew that he'd lied, and would probably be able to guess that his intentions towards Mendez were unlikely to be favorable.

'My name is Ryan Lock. I'm here to find Charlie Mendez and bring him back with me to the States.'

'Who are you with?' she asked.

She was close by. She was watching him right now. He could feel her eyes on him.

'You mean, like an agency?'

'Yes.'

'I'm not with anyone. I'm a private citizen,' he said.

'A bounty hunter?'

'No.'

'What do you want with Mendez?'

'I told you already. Listen, I was contacted by one of his victims, a young woman he had raped. She asked me to return him to serve his sentence.'

There was silence. He thought of how his words must have sounded to someone who didn't know him. Absurd. A madman on a suicide mission on behalf of someone he hadn't even met a week before. He scanned the crowd, trying to guess what she looked like from the sound of her voice. 'Hello? Are you there?'

'If you're not a bounty hunter, then who are you?'

'I work as a close-protection operative, a bodyguard. Will you tell me who you are? Hello?'

'Be quiet. I'm thinking.'

Lock was searching with his eyes for a woman on a cell phone. If she had a clear line of vision to him, which he was sure she did, he had to have the same.

The mall had a semi-circular walkway with an atrium that extended the full height of all five floors. He looked up and saw movement as someone who had been leaning over a glass barrier looking down suddenly retreated. He had a flash of a tailored black suit, bright red lipstick, long brown hair, and then she was gone.

'That was you,' he said, into the cell phone.

'I'll call you back,' she said, and hung up on him.

He walked across to the escalator and rode it up to where he had seen her, all the while scanning the crowds. Looking down he saw Ty doing the same, searching for him. He found the spot where she had been standing. She was long gone. All he could do now was wait and hope that she was as good as her word.

Thirty-three

While they waited for the woman to call back, Lock and Ty drove around Santa Maria, using the time to get a sense of the city. Outwardly, as far as Lock could see, it didn't look like the most dangerous city in the world but, then, on a good day neither did Kabul nor Baghdad. Violence came in spasms, and then it was gone, leaving wounds that were mostly invisible to the naked eye: broken hearts and minds. In between times, people worked and ate and made love and went to school and raised their kids, all the while hoping they wouldn't be sucked into the swamp.

They drove round a rectangle of main roads, first heading north, then east, then south and then back west. They were on Hermanos Escobar Street, passing a Pemex gas station, when Lock noticed a black and white Policía Federal Dodge Charger moving up to overtake them. Ty eased off the gas to let it pass but it stayed directly in front of them.

Immediately Lock had a bad feeling. In the labyrinthine world of Mexican law enforcement, where most cops were lucky to clear five hundred dollars a month, the cartels had infiltrated certain sections of the police to the extent that the government tended to rely on the army when it needed to get things done. There were clean cops but there were a lot of dirty ones too. Once you added into the mix the fact that this part of the world had a history of suspects disappearing before they even made court, his bad feeling had some foundation in fact.

'What d'you want me to do?' Ty asked.

The Policía Federal vehicle had slowed slightly, almost willing Ty to try to go round it. 'Sit tight where we are.'

They weren't going to outrun them and even if that was a possibility it would have been a bad idea. The city was saturated with police and army units. They could turn off and hope that they weren't followed but this was a busy main artery with lots of people around and that was good, as far as Lock was concerned. If they were going to be stopped, he wanted witnesses.

He reached down, unfastened his holster, and threw it into the back of the vehicle. Ty did the same. Glancing into the side mirror, Lock saw two more Policía Federal vehicles bearing down on them. One was an SUV, the other a pick-up truck. Both had their lights on. The pick-up tucked in behind them as the SUV moved out and pulled up alongside.

It was a textbook stop, leaving them nowhere to go. The Dodge in front slowed and Ty braked, easing their vehicle to a halt. Ty, with his upbringing in Long Beach, was well versed in being stopped by the law. He switched off the engine and kept his hands on the wheel.

The door of the Federal pick-up snapped open and the barrel of a Heckler & Koch UMP popped through the gap between sill and door to cover the rear of their vehicle. More doors opened.

More cops emerged, all of them kitted out in black body armor. They began to move in, slowly at first, then more rapidly.

A cop faced Lock, who had his hands at shoulder level, palms open, fingers wiggling in the air to make it clear as crystal that he wasn't carrying. The passenger door was wrenched open, and before he had a chance to step out, a gloved hand gripped his shoulder and hauled him out, forcing him face down on to the blacktop. Boots kicked at his feet, forcing his legs apart. His hands were grabbed and pulled painfully behind his back, then cinched with cuffs so tight that the metal was crushing his wrists. Hands delved into pockets, fingers jabbing against thighs and chest, before his wallet was taken, along with his cell phone and the picture he had been carrying of Charlie Mendez.

He lifted his head long enough to glimpse Ty getting the same treatment. His friend followed his lead, not saying anything and offering zero resistance. The sole of a boot squashed the back of his neck, forcing his back down on to the road. He heard their vehicle being opened, and shouts of excitement from the Federales as they went through their bags.

Pain screaming from his wrists and up into his shoulders, he was hauled to his feet and marched across to a black and white meat wagon. Two bench seats ran either side. He slumped down into one, his back to the metal panel. At least now he could get a better view of what was happening. Above, he heard chopper blades thrashing the air. The metal cage door of the wagon swung open and Ty was pushed in. He sat opposite him and flashed a smile.

'We're screwed, ain't we?' he said.

Lock took a moment to think it over. 'Pretty much.'

The cage door was shut and two bolts slid across to secure it.

The rear door slammed. The engine chugged into life and the wagon trundled forward, slowly picking up speed.

They had to brace their feet against the opposite bench to avoid being thrown on to the floor. Bouncing along in the back, Lock wondered if Brady had enjoyed a ride like this on the day he had died.

Thirty-four

Fifteen minutes later, the police wagon began to slow. Then it came to a halt. The engine died. Car doors opened and closed and excited voices were speaking in Spanish. The next few moments would give Lock some clue as to their fate. If the rear doors opened to fields or a disused warehouse, it was all over.

In the next moments that passed, he felt strangely calm. Normally he would have been going back over what he might have done differently, how he might have avoided the situation. But he found himself feeling supremely indifferent to everything. No one had forced him to come here looking for Mendez. He had done it because it was the right thing to do and because someone had to. If it ended in his death, he could accept that.

What did he have to live for anyway?

The words appeared from the ether. They felt simultaneously juvenile and right. He looked at Ty, who had closed his eyes. The man sitting across from him was his only cause for regret.

'Hey, Ty.'

'Whassup?'

'I'm sorry, man.'

'Nobody put a gun to my head. Not yet anyway. I knew what I was getting into. Felt bad for that girl too. Fuck it. If this is how I go out then so be it. I've lasted longer than most of my homeboys. I ain't gonna go out crying about how life ain't fair and shit. Hell, even if it's over now, it's turned out better than I thought it would. Kinda have one regret, though.'

'What's that?'

'Eighth grade. Tynisha Brown offered to blow me at her grandma's house when we were walking back from church. I turned her down because she was supposed to be dating one of my boys. Kind of wish I'd let her now. Man, she had some pair of lips. I tell you, she didn't get 'em sucking oranges either, boy. Tynisha. Goddamn. Fine like cherry wine.'

'Ty?' said Lock.

'Yeah?'

'Do me a favor?'

'Name it.'

'Shut the hell up.'

'What can I say? I talk too much when I'm nervous.'

Outside, the voices fell away to be replaced by silence. The temperature in the back of the wagon began to rise. Sweat prickled on Lock's forehead until he could taste the salt on his lips. They sat in silence, baking in the heat and waited. If they were to be interrogated, this was probably part of it. Let them marinate for a little while and become dehydrated. Keep them quiet. Give them time to think the worst. An hour or two would be nothing to a bunch of cops sitting in an air-conditioned station house playing cards and watching TV. To two men sitting in the back of a wagon in a foreign country, uncertain of their fate, it would be an eternity. Unless, of course, they were men to whom waiting for something bad to happen was part of the fabric of their working lives.

Lock got as comfortable as he could, closed his eyes and went to sleep. Take it where you can, he figured – even if the big sleep might be just around the corner. Plus, Lock knew from experience that there was nothing more guaranteed to tee off a cop than finding a prisoner so nonchalant and unconcerned about his fate that he didn't have the nervous energy required to keep his eyes open.

No sooner had he drifted off than the faces were appearing, floating somewhere between him and Ty. The first few he recognized. Carrie. Melissa. His mother, who had been dead a long time. Then others came, and these were the ones he found most unsettling. He could see them completely clearly, yet he had no idea who they were and why they were staring at him, silently pleading for his help. One was white but the others were Hispanic. All women. All young. All scared. Their fear and despair rolled from their eyes like vapor.

'Ryan! Ryan!'

His name was being called. His eyes flew open. Ty had stretched out a boot to kick him in the shin. 'Wake up, man.'

He took a moment to find his bearings. 'What is it?'

'You were twitching like a hound dog chasing rabbits in his sleep.'

Lock tilted his head back. 'I was dreaming.'

A voice could be heard outside. A woman's.

Ty called, 'Can we get some water in here?'

There was no reply. A second later a hatch at the front of the cage opened and a bottle of water was thrown through. It bounced on to the floor.

'We still got cuffs on,' Ty called out, but the hatch closed with a snap of metal.

The cab door opened, and the bench under Lock shifted fractionally as someone got in and sat down. The door slammed. The engine roared back into life. There was a grinding of gears, as if the person at the wheel hadn't driven it before. Lock looked at Ty as the wagon began to reverse, jolted to a stop and lurched forward, slowly picking up speed. Whatever was happening, wherever they were going, it wasn't good.

The only up-side so far was that there seemed to be just one person besides themselves in the vehicle, and even though they were cuffed, that gave them a chance.

Sounds of traffic and the steady thrum of the wheels over smooth blacktop told Lock that they were still in the city. They picked up speed. After five more minutes they seemed to hit traffic because the driver stood on the brakes so hard that both he and Ty slid down the bench seats towards the cab. The bottle of water was at his feet but there was no way of getting to it.

They set off again. Occasionally a truck would pass them or another car but the traffic seemed to thin. The wagon kept moving at a steady speed. The air changed and grew fresher. The stench of the city fell away and so did the heat.

The minutes passed. Looking at Ty, he sensed that his partner was starting to suffer the effects of dehydration. His chin had fallen on to his chest, his eyes were sunken and his shoulders were slumped.

'Ty, stay with me, okay?'

His head snapped up. 'I'm good.'

'Listen, they're gonna have to stop at some point, and if either of us gets a chance we're going to have to take it.'

'Gonna be tough with these cuffs on but I hear you.'

They had been cuffed behind their backs, their feet and heads were all they had at their disposal. Sometimes cuffs could be popped open by banging them hard against a solid surface but Lock had already tried slamming them into the side of the wagon with no result.

The vehicle must have hit a rut in the road because it bumped violently and he almost fell off the bench. Another rut, and this time he had to stick out a foot to brace himself in place.

They were on a dirt track or off road entirely. The wagon bounced and juddered along for what he estimated was five or six hundred yards. Then it stopped and the engine was switched off. The driver's door opened and someone got out, then slammed it shut.

Silence.

Lock began to shift towards the rear door, shuffling along the bench on his ass. Ty did the same. When the door opened, they wanted to be as close to it as possible. Even with their hands cuffed behind their backs, two on one gave them a shot.

The rear door was unlocked and thrown open. Sunlight flooded in, blinding them both. Having been in the dark for so long, and now unable to shield his eyes, the best Lock could do was squint. He could make out the outline of the driver, who was around five foot eight inches tall and of average build, but that was about it. He couldn't see their face.

Whoever it was removed the padlock from the second door, threw back the bolts and flung it open. Then, perhaps anticipating the prisoners' plan, they took half a dozen steps back, their right hand resting on the butt of their service weapon, which rode high in its holster.

'Get out!'

It was a woman's voice.

Ty went first, toeing the cage door open, shuffling forward and jumping out of the wagon on to bare desert. Lock followed him. The woman backed up a little further, making sure to keep a proper distance.

Gradually Lock's eyes adjusted to the low blazing sunset. There were juniper trees, desert and tumbleweed and that was pretty much it. No buildings in sight. No vehicles. No other people. It was the perfect spot to kill someone.

'Turn around,' said the woman, unholstering her service weapon.

There was too much distance for either of them to rush her. She would shoot them before they got within striking distance, and even if she didn't, all she had to do was move back. Maybe this was it, he thought, doing as she had asked.

Executed in the desert. Two more bodies for the coyotes.

'Kneel down.'

Lock glanced across at Ty.

'You got a plan? I'd sure like to hear it,' he said.

'No talking. Now get on your knees.'

As being killed went, you wouldn't know too much about a single shot to the back of the head. There was only one problem, as far as Lock was concerned. He'd come here for a reason.

He turned and faced the woman. His eyes had adjusted to the glare and this time he could pick out her features. She was the woman he had seen in the shopping mall.

'Turn back around,' she said.

'You're a cop?' he asked her.

She didn't answer.

'Was this how they got Brady?' Lock went on.

She took a step back. Her body language didn't suggest she was hesitant as much as irritated. 'I'm not going to shoot you, I'm going to take the cuffs off, and I'm not going to do that unless you're kneeling. And, for the record, I had nothing to do with what happened to Joe Brady. If he'd listened to me he'd still be alive.'

'Is that so?' Lock said.

Still clutching her weapon in her right hand, her left hand fell to her hip. 'Okay, then, don't turn around. I'll just leave you two out here in the desert.'

'Maybe we should do what she's asked,' said Ty.

Lock stood beside Ty and rubbed at his wrists as the woman threw them each a bottle of water. When they had finished slaking their thirst, Lock said, 'Now what?'

She nodded to a dip in the terrain. 'You walk. It's about two miles to the border. Border Patrol will pick you up near the fence. Two miles should give you time to come up with a story about why you're breaking back into your own country.'

'And if we don't want to leave?'

'Then it's about fifty miles back into town and the next cop who picks you up might just turn you over to the cartel. Or throw you into jail for bringing firearms into the country. Your choice.'

'I'm liking the first option,' offered Ty.

'You should listen to your friend,' the female cop said. She bent down and picked up two plastic bags. She threw one to each man. 'Your cell phones and wallets. Your weapons are illegal.'

They stooped and gathered their belongings.

Lock scraped at the ground with the toe of his boot. He looked up at her. She had big brown eyes and long, unruly black hair tied into a ponytail. She was carrying a little extra weight around the hips, but so was he. There was an intensity about her that he admired. But something didn't square.

'I came here for Charlie Mendez. Why are you protecting him?' Lock asked.

She holstered her weapon. Judging by her expression, Lock's question demonstrated such a degree of naïvety that she no longer considered him a credible threat to her safety. But her hand stayed on the butt just in case.

'You Americans. You're so arrogant.'

'You've done it now,' Ty said, under his breath.

'You know how many young women's funerals I've been to this year?'

Lock shrugged.

'Dozens. All of them young women taken off the streets on the way back from the *maquiladoras*. Raped. Tortured. Mutilated. Their breasts cut off. Left out in the open. On display. And for what? For pleasure. And yet you stand there, Mr Tough Guy Bounty Hunter, and you tell me I'm protecting a rapist?'

'Then let me go get him.'

'Go home, Mr Lock. Take your friend and go home before you end up like Brady. Which was what was going to happen to you if I hadn't offered to bring you out here. Sooner or later Mendez will be caught, but right now, someone like you only makes my job more difficult. We have enough crazy men out for revenge around here. We don't need any more.'

Lock considered his options. It didn't take long. He wasn't

going to try to overpower her. They couldn't walk back into town. The only real option was to do as she said, then come back and try again.

'Okay,' he said eventually. 'We'll go. But will you do me one favor?'

'What?'

Lock switched on his cell phone and pulled up the picture he had of Mendez's bodyguard. 'Mendez is supposed to have picked up an American girl in a bar. I'm concerned for her safety. Could you at least look into it? I can tell you where he was last seen.'

He stepped forward and angled the cell-phone screen towards her. 'He was with this man,' he said, showing her the picture of the bodyguard.

She took the phone from him, looked at the picture and back at Lock. 'Where?'

Lock didn't follow her. 'What do you mean?'

'Where was this taken?' she asked.

'A bar out near . . .' He stopped himself. Now he had something she wanted.

She had her gun out again. It was a Browning. 'Where? Where was that taken?'

'We'll show you.'

'Tell me.'

Finally he had some traction. 'You help us and we'll help you. No games. No tricks. I give you my word.'

She started for the wagon. She opened the driver's door. 'You'll have to ride in back.'

With the cage door at the back of the wagon wedged open, Lock sat with Ty as the woman, who had finally introduced herself as

Detective Rafaela Carcharon of the Policía Federal, drove them back towards the highway. A hatch opened from the mobile holding area into the cab. A grille covered it but Rafaela kept the windows open so that they got some breeze. Lock didn't blame her for having them ride in the back. She had taken a risk helping them in the first place. It was clear from what she'd said that, as soon as they'd been arrested, they had been marked for death.

It had been the picture of the bodyguard and the mention of the girl. He had asked her who the man was but she had said she didn't know. She was lying to him. She knew exactly who he was and, tough cop or not, she was frightened of him. It had shown in her eyes and her fear told him that for someone like her, who lived every day in a war-zone filled with atrocity and horror, he must be a very bad man indeed. And he was the man who stood between Lock and Charlie Mendez. At least now he was beginning to understand why Mendez had stayed untouched for so long. But it still didn't explain why these people were protecting him.

That was the real mystery that lay at the heart of this business. *What was in it for them?*

Thirty-five

Turning away from the windows that looked over the swimming pool, Hector walked out of the room and down the corridor to the kitchen where he fixed the girl something to eat. He put it all on a tray and walked it down to the room.

At the door, he set the tray on the floor, unlocked the door and stepped inside. She was where he had left her. She eyed him with a mixture of fear and relief. Fear of what he would do. Relief at not having been abandoned. He didn't speak to her. It was better that way. He might still have to kill her and he felt badly enough for her without getting to know her more than he had.

People on the outside might laugh at that, but it was true. He was a killer many times over. On more than one occasion his hands and arms, all the way up to his elbows, had been immersed in blood. He was an executioner. A *sicario*. But he still felt pain, and grief, and sympathy, and fear, and every emotion that others did.

He propped the door open with a case of beer, one of many stacked in the narrow corridor outside the room, brought the tray in and set it down next to her. There was bread and eggs, juice and coffee. An American breakfast. Bland but filling. 'The coffee is hot,' he said to her. 'But don't get any ideas about throwing it at me. I am used to pain.'

She didn't react but she seemed to take in what he was saying. He took the keys from his pocket and released her from the restraints. He retreated to the door as she ate. She had an appetite, which was good.

As she finished her coffee, she looked up at him. 'Why are you keeping me here? If it's money, my parents do okay but they don't have millions or anything.'

So young, he thought. So naïve.

He motioned for her to sit back so he could put the manacles on again. She did as she was told. As he knelt next to her, he sensed that someone else was in the room with them. Not a person. Something much bigger than they were. Bigger than the boss.

Later, he would reflect that he didn't think it was God, or the Virgin, or Santa Muerte, because what washed over him was beyond a thought: it was something far more powerful. His face was close to hers and for a split second he thought he might throw himself on the floor and weep for what he was doing. But the core of him, which allowed him to function, reared up again, pulling him back from what was surely an abyss. The feeling didn't abate entirely but it retreated, like the tide.

'Don't tell anyone your family is poor, okay?' he whispered. 'If you have no money, they won't keep you alive.'

He was so close that he could see flecks of green in her blue eyes.

She nodded.

He stood up, took the tray, walked out and locked the door behind him. His hands were shaking so hard that the coffee cup rattled in its saucer. He needed a drink. Needed it bad.

Thirty-six

Rafaela left them at a fast-food restaurant while she went to return the police wagon. They took a table near the back and ate in silence, the only Americans in the place. It was Ty, the only African American they had seen since they had crossed the border, who drew the stares. It had been the same everywhere they'd been. Not that Ty seemed to mind. Maybe he didn't notice it, or maybe, thought Lock, he just figured that with his height, build and rugged good looks, he was a pretty tough guy to ignore.

Thirty-five minutes later, Lock received a text: 'Meet me out back.'

He tapped Ty's arm. They got up, went outside and strolled round to the back. Rafaela pulled up next to them in a Chevy Camaro. They got into the back seat. She had changed into sneakers, jeans and a white blouse. 'Okay,' she said. 'Show me this bar.'

'It's in Diablo. I'll tell you the name when we get there.'

She eyed him in the rear-view mirror. 'You don't trust me?'

'You were ready to kick us out of the country a couple of hours ago.'

'I was saving your skin.'

'Anybody ask what happened to your prisoners?' Ty said.

Ty's question seemed to leave her on the verge of laughter. 'Here, when you don't come back with prisoners, no one asks questions. Not if they're smart. Some things are better not to know about.'

Rafaela's cell phone rang. She reached over on to the passenger seat and plucked it from her handbag, answering in Spanish. A few seconds later she ended the call. She glanced at her passengers. 'We have to go somewhere else first. When we get there, stay in the car, and don't move. If anyone asks who you are don't say anything.'

'I think we can manage that,' said Ty.

She eyed Lock. 'I'm not so sure about your friend.'

Ty shrugged. 'Don't worry. Nobody is.'

She tugged down hard on the steering-wheel and spun the car round. Lock was thrown back in his seat as she buried the gas pedal, weaving through the late-night traffic. As they drove through the city one thing stood out to him: an absence of the normal. There were no young women out alone, and the people who were on the streets scuttled purposefully towards their destination, like beetles, heads down, focused solely on getting to where they had to go.

A truck full of soldiers was parked at an intersection. They eyed each passing car, weapons tucked between their knees, cigarettes dangling from their lips. Rafaela didn't appear to register their presence as she zipped past. They were so much background scenery, so commonplace that they warranted no comment.

The lights of the city fell away as they hit the freeway. Lock opened the window for some air. He leaned forward in his seat. 'Can I ask you something?'

Rafaela turned her head slightly to look at him. 'What is it?'

'Who's the bodyguard?'

'I don't know.'

'I thought we were going to be straight with each other. I told you exactly why we're here. You only got interested when you saw that picture so you have to know who it is.'

'I don't know his name. But, yes, I recognized him.'

'From where?'

Her hands tightened on the wheel and she stared out of the windshield as the car swallowed the surface of the road. 'He's one of them. Very dangerous.'

'Who's them? Part of a cartel?'

He saw her eyes shift towards him and her jaw tighten. She looked down and away before her eyes settled back on the road. 'Yes.'

He grabbed the back of the front passenger seat, and pulled himself forward. 'That's not what you meant, though, is it? When you said "them", you weren't talking about a cartel.'

'No, I wasn't.'

'So what did you mean? Who are *they*?'

Another army truck sped past them. One of the soldiers leered at Rafaela from the back.

'He's one of the men who are killing the women here.'

'If you know he's killing women, why don't you go arrest him?' he asked.

He caught sight of Rafaela's lips parting in a sad smile in

the rear-view mirror. 'How long have you been in this part of the country?'

'People don't get arrested here?'

'That depends on the evidence – and who they are.'

'So, who is he? There's something you're not telling me.'

She turned, facing him briefly. 'He's a police officer.'

Thirty-seven

Rafaela turned off towards the centre of Diablo. They were moving down a main avenue, busy with bars, stores and restaurants. The traffic began to slow. Through the front windshield, Lock could see people crowding a small section of sidewalk and spilling out on to the road. At first he thought it must be another killing, with the inevitable ghoulish assembly that death attracted. Rafaela braked.

'Someone been shot?' Ty asked.

'No,' said Rafaela. 'It's a shrine.'

As they drew level it didn't look much like a shrine, and the people gathered around it didn't look much like worshippers. It was a plain storefront with a couple of tables stacked out front, and the crowd was low rent – lots of overweight girls sporting tattoos, and men clutching beer bottles or smoking spliffs.

'A shrine to Santa Muerte,' Rafaela said. 'Saint Death.'

That was when Lock, who was still digesting the notion of a police officer moonlighting for a major drugs cartel, saw it. Right at the front, bathed in candlelight, a human skeleton was wearing a blonde wig covered with a black shawl.

'They believe she can offer protection. They come here every night and bring her offerings.'

Next to him, Ty sucked his teeth. 'Maybe someone should bring her something to eat – she looks like she could use a good meal. I mean, I like my chicks skinny an' all, but there's such a thing as taking it too far.'

'We shouldn't stick around here. A lot of the people who work for the traffickers come to worship,' Rafaela said, nudging the car past the edge of the crowd.

Lock looked through the rear window as a hulking Mexican guy, with full sleeves of tattoos running up his arms, made the sign of the cross before the skeleton, then retreated back into the gathering. 'This why they call it Diablo?' he asked Rafaela.

'No. They worship Santa Muerte all over the country.'

'What's with the name?' said Ty.

Rafaela shrugged. 'It's an old name, but the joke now is that Santa Maria is so bad that the devil himself is afraid to come within forty miles of it. This is the closest he'll get to the city, hence Diablo.'

Lock chewed it over. 'You believe in the devil, Rafaela?'

'I'm Catholic. It comes with the territory. God. Jesus. The Holy Mother. Can't have God without the devil, right?'

Before they turned the corner and saw the bar, they smelt smoke. Two fire crews were still at work, dousing it with water, even though all that was left was the charred outline of the frame. Forgetting himself, Lock opened the door and got out as Rafaela pulled up opposite.

The crowd here was sparser than the one that had stood around the skeleton with the bad haircut but the smell of death was more real. There were four bodies laid out on the sidewalk. A fireman was covering each with a white cotton sheet, but Lock could see that they were badly burned. As he drifted through the crowd towards them, he felt a hand on his shoulder. He turned.

'Go and wait in the car,' Rafaela said.

He shrugged her off and kept walking. Perhaps not wanting to make a scene, she let him go. As Lock reached the bodies, the fireman had covered two. The others lay on their backs, clothes burned from them, faces blackened by smoke.

He knelt down beside them, recognizing the American who had given him the picture of the bodyguard. There was a gaping hole in the man's chest. Before he'd been asphyxiated by the smoke, he had been shot.

'*Señor!*' A fireman waved at him to move back. A couple of local cops were eyeballing him. Lock filtered into the small crowd of bystanders.

Ten minutes later, Rafaela got into the driver's seat and slammed the door. She had spent several minutes talking to one of the fire crew as the bodies were loaded on to a truck for the short journey to the local morgue. 'They were all men. One American, your friend, the bartender and two locals. They're saying it was an electrical fire.'

'What about the gunshot wounds?' Lock asked.

She gave him the same sad smile as when he'd asked about arresting the bodyguard. 'You must have a fertile imagination. They are saying no one was shot, even though I saw the same thing you did.'

'Any sign of the girl?' Ty asked.

Rafaela shook her head. 'Did your friend tell you what she looked like?'

Lock detailed the thumbnail sketch he'd been given.

'If she was American, we can check the hotels, see if anyone has been reported missing,' Rafaela said, turning the key in the ignition and pulling away from the sickly sweet smell of charred flesh, which hung in the air. 'If she's missing, they may have taken her with them.'

'And if they have?' Lock asked. 'What then?'

Rafaela stared straight ahead. 'It might be better for her if she had died in the fire back there.'

They stayed in the car while Rafaela went inside each of the hotels that catered to American tourists. When she emerged from the third, they knew before she reached the car that it was bad news.

She got in, massaging her temple. 'I spoke to the manager. They are trying to keep it quiet but an American girl went missing at the same time as your friend saw the girl in the bar with Mendez. Her parents are going crazy. They've contacted the American consulate.'

'What about the local cops?' Ty asked. 'I mean, they have to make it look like they're doing something, right?'

'When they first went in to make the report, they told them that a person has to be missing for forty-eight hours before they can do anything,' Rafaela said.

'I take it that's not procedure,' Lock said.

'No, it's not. They have to start investigating as soon as a report is taken, but if they say they can't take a report and the person doesn't insist, they have forty-eight hours. They use it all the time to put off the families of the girls who go missing.'

'I'm guessing these folks didn't buy it,' Ty asked.

'No. They went straight to the American consulate so the cops are out looking for her,' Rafaela said somberly.

Lock leaned forward. 'And after that?'

'They'll get to her,' said Rafaela, her shoulders slumping. 'But she won't be alive when they do. Then they'll find someone to take the blame. They'll arrest them, plant evidence, torture a confession out of them, send them to prison, wait until things settle down, and then it will start all over again.'

Lock met her eye. 'You know who's doing this, don't you?'

'Knowing isn't enough, Mr Lock.'

'Listen, your hands are tied down here. But ours aren't. Let us help you. If we can find the girl, find Mendez, then maybe we can get you the evidence you need.'

Thirty-eight

Rafaela's home was a one-bedroom apartment on the third floor of a four-story walk-up where the communal areas smelt of fetid garbage and even staler urine. Lock knew that he could be sure of one thing about her now: she wasn't on the take.

Inside, the place was clean, tidy and ordered in the way you'd expect of someone who lived alone and spent most of their time at work. It was a look he recognized. As Rafaela made tea and coffee for her guests, he and Ty settled themselves on a couch in the tiny open-plan living and kitchen area.

'You can take a shower if you want,' she said, dunking a teabag in a mug of hot water.

They thanked her. As the tea steeped, she disappeared into the bedroom. They heard her rummaging in a closet and then she reappeared with a large blue binder. She handed it to Lock.

'These are my girls,' she said.

Lock had a feeling he wasn't about to flip through a family album full of cotton candy on sticks and visits to whatever passed for Disneyland down here. As he opened the binder, he wasn't disappointed. Photographs of every murdered girl had been slipped into a clear plastic sleeve. Two for each victim, sometimes three or four where there had been some level of dismemberment. The first showed a girl alive – as an awkward teenager in a school uniform or a younger girl in a confirmation dress, all gangly limbs and big brown eyes and gappy teeth – and the second was of the dead body, either laid out on a stainless-steel mortuary platform, on waste-ground, or simply dumped at a roadside.

Rafaela plucked the teabag out of the mug and put it into the garbage pail. 'That's this year.'

Flicking through, Lock reckoned there had to be at least thirty victims. One year, he thought. *Sweet Jesus.* He reached the back, where the sleeves were empty, awaiting the next communion photograph, the next dead girl, and passed it to Ty. 'When did the killings start?' he asked.

Rafaela brought over two mugs of coffee, handing one to Lock and one to Ty. 'Twelve years ago.'

Ty glanced up from a teenage girl with her hair in braids and a small silver cross at her throat. 'And no one's been caught?'

Rafaela blew on the hot tea in her mug. 'Sure. Lots of people have been caught. Caught, convicted, sent to prison. One or two might even have had something to do with one or two of the killings.' She caught Lock's expression of surprise. 'I'm sure there have been copycat murders as well.'

'But you think you know who's really behind it?'

She put her tea on the counter that separated the kitchen from the living area and went back into the bedroom. This time there was no binder, just a thin brown folder with half a dozen or so newspaper clippings. She handed them to Lock, who flicked through them. He had expected crime stories but instead found puff pieces about local dignitaries.

The first article concerned a local politician called Manuel Managua. He was in his early forties, and good-looking in a bland sort of way, with the horn-rimmed glasses and studious look of an accountant. The article talked about him as a rising star, who was almost certain to serve as city mayor, a stepping stone to bigger and better things. Managua was pictured with his wife and two cherubic little boys, every inch the family man. 'What's this guy's story? You're really saying he's caught up in this?'

'I know. A politician. Hard to believe,' Rafaela said, her sarcastic tone not lost on him.

'Feeling up a Congressional page or photocopying your wing-wang and sending it to your secretary, that I'd believe. But Lock's got a point here. This is heavy stuff for a guy who wants people to vote for him,' said Ty.

'Getting elected in Mexico is about money. His friends,' she said, gesturing at the clippings, 'have all the money.'

That was certainly the case with the second person featured in the file. Lock already knew the name. Federico Tibialis was the alleged leader of one of the largest drug cartels in Mexico. This piece was an interview with him in which he volubly denied any involvement with drugs and complained about the endless rumors. He was, he said, merely a businessman. Lock guessed that indeed he was. It was just that his business was death and despair. Rafaela leaned over to jab at the clipping. 'He is the one they all look to. The real leader. The boss of bosses. He funds Managua's campaigns. He has money in most of the local businesses around here.'

'Laundering?' said Ty.

'Of course,' Rafaela agreed.

Lock passed the cutting to Ty and flipped to the last one. This one did shock him, although he wasn't sure why. The man was also middle-aged and puffed up with his own importance. He had the same big-shark-in-a-small-pond look as his buddies. The only difference was that, rather than a suit, he was wearing a uniform or, to be more precise, a police uniform complete with stripes, epaulettes and service medals.

'Gabriel Zapatero,' said Rafaela. 'The city's chief of police. The boss of the man who's looking after Mendez. My boss too.' She looked evenly at Lock. 'Now do you see why it might be difficult to just go arrest them?'

Thirty-nine

'I don't get it.'

Lock rose from the couch, walked five steps into the tiny kitchen and rinsed his coffee mug in the sink. 'They take girls off the streets, then rape and kill them. Why?'

'I'll give you my answer, but you won't like it,' said Rafaela.

Lock dried the mug and placed it carefully on the counter. 'Try me.'

'They do it . . .' she sighed '. . . because they can and because they believe that no one's going to touch them. When the public outcry gets too much, they have one of Zapatero's men in the department pick someone up. They threaten his family or torture a confession out of him, he's convicted and everyone quietens down. In terms of why you'd want to rape and murder, I don't think the attraction's hard to grasp, if you think about a certain type of man.'

'So where does Mendez fit in?' Ty said, his long legs stretched out, fingers steepled under his chin. 'He ain't one of them.'

'I don't know,' Rafaela confessed. 'That part is strange. They can manipulate the courts here, but by protecting him, they're inviting the Americans to look at them more closely.'

'Well, there has to be a reason,' said Lock. 'And it's got to be more than that they've found a kindred spirit.'

'You think?' said Ty. 'Why couldn't it be that? He's as sick as they are. He comes down here, they work out who he is and offer him an invite into the club.'

Rafaela shook her head. 'No, Ryan is correct,' she said to Ty. 'There's more to this.'

Lock and Ty took turns to shower in her tiny bathroom and then Rafaela suggested they get some rest. Lock took the couch, Ty the living-room floor and they grabbed a meagre few hours' sleep. Rafaela slept in her bedroom, or at least she tried to, but her mind was over-occupied. Part of her wanted to drive the Americans back over the border, but another part told her that finally she had people she could trust, whose interests were broadly aligned with hers and that this opportunity might never arise again. She could probe the killings but eventually the group of men, or those around her, would tire of her interference, or she might gather too much evidence and she, too, would be gone. If she was killed that would be one person fewer to protect the young women who were asleep in their beds tonight – with a bloody future awaiting them.

All the horror and despair of recent years had cemented rather than eroded her belief in God. She believed in Him and in the grace of the Holy Mother. Perhaps He had sent these two men to help her. Their arrival might be a sign that the Almighty had grown tired of the wickedness, that He wished Rafaela to call the killers to account.

She got out of bed, clicked on the lamp and began to make a list of places to check. Yesterday she had been one but now she was three. And Lock was right: if they had the American girl, she wouldn't be kept alive for ever. Eventually, thought Rafaela, standing next to the window and looking out over the rooftops of the city she still loved, they would tire of her, as they had tired of the others.

Rafaela wasn't the only one having difficulty getting to sleep. Despite his exhaustion, Lock's mind wouldn't rest. He lay in darkness in the tiny apartment and worried over one aspect of the American girl's disappearance.

In the normal run of things, he could go to the American consul with what he knew. Or, if he wanted to remain in the shadows, he could share what Rafaela had told him with the parents and they could relay the information. He was in no doubt that if they were believed, which was by no means certain, the consulate would call in other authorities and apply pressure on the Mexicans to do everything they could to find the girl. It would be more than an abduction: it would be a full-blown diplomatic incident. It would also, he was pretty certain, guarantee that, if she was still alive, whoever had her would get rid of her as quickly as they could and start covering their tracks.

If Rafaela's belief in the previous pattern was true, Julia would turn up next to some rail tracks and some dumb unfortunate would take the rap. Justice would be seen to be done. The parents might not buy it, but the American government would want to move on. After all, there was money to be made along the border and business deals to be completed. It was a cynical view but, in Lock's experience, when the stakes were so high, and particularly when there was money in the mix, it was safer to err on the side of cynicism. Idealism was best saved for happier times.

They reconvened over more coffee and tea in the tiny apartment. Together they decided that the key to finding the girl was tracking down Charlie Mendez. If he was found first, though, Lock and Ty would be in a quandary. Mendez was still the reason they were there, and Lock didn't want Melissa's death to be lost in the midst of this. But Melissa would not have wanted another young life sacrificed in order to secure justice or revenge.

Rafaela was aware of three residences where Mendez might be found. One was an apartment in the centre of the city. The second was a house owned by Managua, the third a vast narco-mansion owned by Tibialis in an area that was as close to leafy suburb as any area got here. The house, according to Rafaela, was often used as a party location by the four men.

She would take the apartment and the boss's house. She had been keeping an eye on the narco-mansion, when she could, and had an observation post nearby in the shape of a small apartment across the street. She would drop Lock and Ty there to keep watch.

Forty

As the sun crept over the horizon, Lock scanned the narco-mansion with a pair of binoculars, careful to angle them in such a way that he avoided the sharp sunlight striking the lens. From his vantage-point in the front room of the small, dusty apartment, he had a clear view of the house's back yard with its shimmering swimming pool. To the right of the pool, french windows led into the main house; to the left there was a small single-story guest- house, perhaps eighty feet long and forty deep.

No one was around, save a gardener, who was clearing leaves from the water. Lock counted two fixed-position closed-circuit cameras, one mounted on either corner of the house, their lenses triangulating over the pool and the yard towards the guesthouse. The first hour of watching had already started to weigh on him. Ty, pacing the floor behind him, didn't help. By definition, surveillance was a waiting game that required patience and, with the American girl missing, he was all out of it.

Their plan was needle-in-a-haystack stuff. Between them, the men connected to Mendez would have dozens of possible safe-houses at their disposal. With all the drugs that flowed through the city, hiding places would be legion and of good quality. Lock imagined that if you had something, or someone, you wanted to hide, there would be plenty of options available to you.

The only plus for them was that Rafaela had managed to retrieve not only their vehicle but also the gear they had brought down and their weapons, checking everything out from the police station on the pretext that, with them gone, it was better destroyed. The vehicle was no good to them now so they had emptied it of its contents and hidden it close to her apartment.

On the hour, Lock handed the binoculars to Ty. This was no good. For all they knew the house might be completely empty and, in any event, they had only a partial view of it. If he was there, Charlie Mendez could walk out of the front door with the girl, and they would be oblivious to the whole thing.

'This sucks,' he said to Ty.

'Yup. You have other ideas?'

Lock unscrewed the top from a bottle of water and took a sip. The building was hot: there was no air-conditioning, and because the apartment was supposedly unoccupied, the windows had to stay closed, the drapes, too, apart from a narrow gap. 'They're protecting Mendez, they have the girl, and we have no clue where either of them is, so, no, I'm all out of ideas. You?'

Ty lowered the binoculars. 'I was counting on you coming up with something. Man, this country is messed up. How'd you figure a place gets like this?'

'Corrupt?'

'Yeah.'

Lock hadn't given it much thought until Ty had asked the question. 'Slowly, I guess. You do someone a favor, look to make some easy money, and once you're in, there's no going back. I don't know.'

'And how do you figure these people get their country back?' Ty said. 'That's gonna be even slower, right? Easy to get into the dirt, harder to get clean again.'

'There are good people, like Rafaela.'

'Not many of them,' said Ty. 'I mean, most people aren't going to stand up to these guys. They don't want to take the risk. They got families, kids.'

Lock stood behind Tyrone and stared down at the shimmering surface of the swimming pool as the gardener dumped the last of the leaves into a wheelbarrow. An idea was forming. It was a bad idea, bordering on reckless, but right now it was the only one he had.

Forty-one

Rafaela walked into her office at Police Headquarters and closed the door behind her. It was after lunch, and the building was close to empty, not that it was ever full. The city of Santa Maria had eight hundred officers but at least three hundred of them never showed up or did anything that people would recognize as police work. They were on the payroll of the cartels, recruited even before they had entered the academy to train. They wore the uniform, they were paid by the city or the government (as well as the cartels), they carried a badge and a gun and drove around in police cars, but they spent their days and nights working for the bad guys. They escorted shipments of money and drugs. They kidnapped low-level dealers, people who owed the cartel money or who had crossed them in some way, however significant or slight. Often, after a phone call from their superior, they killed those people and buried them in the dozens of hidden mass graves around the city. Rafaela believed that some had taken the girls, killed them and buried them too. It was said that, as a cop in the borderlands, you had only two choices. *Plata o plomo?* Silver or lead? You took a pay-off or you took a bullet.

Now that she was alone, and had time to think, she was regretting her change of heart with the Americans. More than regretting it. She had done many stupid things in her life, but this had to be the dumbest of them all. She should have insisted that they go home. But Lock had swayed her. How could he change things here? She wasn't even sure that he could help her find the American girl. Before she arrived at the office, she had checked the two locations but seen nothing out of the ordinary. If the girl was there she would have sighted extra security but everything had been as always.

There was a tap at her office door. A young police officer poked his head in. He was always earnest. He took the job seriously. Rafaela wondered how long his idealism would last. Probably until the first time he was shown five thousand dollars to look the other way or the first time his mother received a phone call asking if she had reserved a cemetery plot for him.

'The boss wants to see you.'

'Thank you. Tell him I'll be there in a moment.'

'He said it's urgent.'

'Very well.'

She got up and followed him out into the corridor. He headed back to his cubicle and she kept going. She was more curious than nervous when the boss's secretary made her wait for a few moments before she ushered her in.

Zapatero was at his desk. He was wearing a white dress shirt, slacks and loafers. This was his new uniform since his return from a management seminar in America about leadership. She wondered if the DEA, who had paid for his attendance, knew that he took money from the cartel. That was the thing about the people who had been bought: unless you had been close to them for a long time it was difficult to tell. The only obvious clue was how they could afford to send their kids to private school and drive the cars they did. Other than that, they spoke and behaved in exactly the same manner as the others. Some probably believed that by aligning themselves with one cartel they were somehow bringing order to a bad situation, that they were doing the right thing.

'Detective Carcharon, please, sit down,' he said, with a wave of his hand. When he opened his mouth all she could think of were the disgusting words he hissed down the phone at her late at night when he was drunk.

She sat opposite him. There were family pictures on his desk. A wife and two girls. She wondered what the children would think if they knew about their father. Presumably he loved them and wouldn't want any harm to come to them. She found it strange that someone could feel so deeply about their own, yet have no regard for the children of others. That was the heart of the sickness that had enveloped these people. As long as their own needs were fulfilled, their own children safe, they didn't care about anything else.

'The two American bounty hunters we apprehended,' he began. 'I understand they have left the country.'

She cleared her throat. 'Yes, I made sure of it myself.'

He smiled across his desk at her. 'Good, that's very good. We have enough problems of our own without these . . .' he paused theatrically '. . . mavericks causing trouble. We will find the man they are looking for. This Charles Mendez.'

'Yes, sir. I'm sure of it,' she said.

He picked up a file from his desk. 'And speaking of Americans, it seems we have another to cause us concern.'

He passed a file to Rafaela, his eyes scouring her blouse for a loose button as she leaned over to take it from him. He truly made her skin crawl.

She opened the file. There was a missing person's report and a photograph.

'This girl is missing. Her parents are very concerned,' he said. 'It's probably nothing. No doubt she is with some boy she has met. I'm sure we all know how young women can behave at that age. Anyway, the consulate are very concerned, too, so I told them that even though a missing person is hardly a priority, with everything that is happening now, I would assign one of my top people to investigate.' He smiled again. She felt sick. 'Someone whose integrity could never be questioned. Someone of the highest moral standards.'

'You think something has happened to her?' she asked, wanting, needing to hear the lies pour from his mouth.

'I don't think so. But who knows? There are so many criminals out there, bad people. We know that better than most. We have to deal with them every day.'

She smiled back at him. 'Yes, we do. Very bad people.'

He gave a little nod, his sign that the meeting was over. She got up and walked out. She could feel his eyes all over her every step of the way.

In the corridor, she opened the file again. It was as much as she could do not to laugh. This was perfect. This was how they operated. They gave the case to someone whom everyone, the Americans included, knew was beyond reproach, not because they wanted the girl found – hell, they could do that with a phone call – but to give the appearance that they did. Smoke and mirrors. Deception. Double talk. But perhaps this time they had been too clever for their own good. She was looking for the girl in any case, but now she had their approval. They were counting on her not being crazy enough to find her. Maybe they were right. Or maybe they were wrong. By doing her job and finding a girl whom important people did care about then perhaps she could secure justice for all those whom no one cared about.

And if she was wrong about that she could be wrong about the Americans. As her boss had told them when he had returned from his management training across the border, 'There is no such thing as a problem. There is only an opportunity in disguise.'

Forty-two

Every time the door opened, Julia flinched. She couldn't help it. It was the sound. The groan it made as it shifted on its hinges. She knew it would stay with her for a very long time – if she lived.

The older man was standing over her, legs apart, chest stuck out.

'Julia,' he said. He was Mexican and his words held the accent but his English was good.

She opened her eyes and looked up at him. 'Yes?'

'I am going to take off these handcuffs now, okay? You can go to the bathroom, take a shower, clean yourself up. But I want you to know that if you try to run there is nowhere for you to go. There is no way you can escape until I decide to let you go. Do you understand me, Julia?'

As he said that, she felt like she might cry. Her throat tightened and tears gathered in her eyes. It was the thought of home, of being free from this nightmare. She fought it. She didn't want him to see her break down. She hadn't broken down when it was happening. She had taken her mind somewhere else and it had worked. She had been aware of what they were doing but she hadn't felt present. 'I understand,' she said.

'That's good, Julia. Because if you behave and do what we say then maybe you'll be able to go home. But first we have to get you cleaned up.'

He knelt down and freed her arms and legs. She noticed that he was very deliberate about where he placed himself when he clicked each shackle. He stayed out of range of a kick or a punch. Her ankles and wrists were bruised and swollen. She had lost all feeling in her feet hours before. She wiggled her fingers and rubbed the sensation back into her feet and calves.

'That's okay, take your time. There's no rush,' he said.

Eventually, she felt she could stand. Putting her palms on the floor, she started to lever herself to her feet.

'Here,' he said. 'Let me help you.'

He put his hands under her armpits and lifted her. She recoiled a little at his touch, but as soon as she was standing, he let her go.

'Will you be okay on the stairs?' he asked her. So polite. So solicitous. The situation was so surreal that part of her expected to wake in her room in the resort.

As she took the stairs he stayed behind her. His presence seemed reassuring rather than threatening. At the top, the door was wedged open. She began to walk along a corridor. Halfway down, he tapped her elbow. She half turned. He held out a pair of sunglasses. 'If you have been in the dark too long, the sun can hurt your eyes,' he said.

She took them from him and put them on. The corridor darkened but not by much. He directed her through a door into another corridor. They passed a large room, the door open, sunlight blazing through a window. He was right: she would have been blinded without the sunglasses. She felt a breeze, then heard something that brought a lump to her throat. Outside a bird was chirping, running up and down a warbling set of scales. She realized that while she had been in that room she had heard nothing from outside. No birds. No footsteps. Nothing. It must have been soundproofed.

Past a bedroom there was another door. He darted ahead of her and opened it into a large, tiled bathroom. 'There is a lock on the inside,' he said, 'so you can have some privacy. But please remember what I said. There is no escape unless you follow my orders.'

She walked past him and into the bathroom. There was a tub and a separate shower, a washbasin and toilet, even a bidet. The tiles were green, yellow and red. The door closed behind her. Without thinking she walked back to it and turned the key. She had gone from one locked room to another, but this time she had secured the door herself.

As she ran a bath, she sat on the toilet and thought about what the man had said. If she did as they said and didn't try to escape, she might be released. He had sounded so sincere when he had said it. She hadn't thought to question him.

Forty-three

Walking into the small resort hotel, Rafaela had to steel herself for what lay ahead. For those who never knew the fate of a loved one, hope obstructed healing. As the days passed, hope itself became twisted and cancerous, an emotion that turned in on itself. Rafaela had seen it more times than she cared to remember. It was a cliché, but not knowing what had happened to someone you loved was the worst part of an abduction. With human remains came certainty. And certainty gave grief a starting point. That wasn't to say that someone who lost a child was ever free of the pain, they weren't, but knowledge of what had happened during a loved one's final hours was almost always preferable to what the imagination conjured.

Of course, Julia's family were only at the beginning of the road. Hope was there, and hope was real. They still had that glimmer of light in the darkness. It was Rafaela's job to convince them that the best way of keeping it burning was to do as she asked. And she was about to ask them to do the one thing that went against every single parental instinct. For now the best thing they could do was nothing. No press. No public plea. No drawing attention to their plight. All it would do was make Julia's survival less likely – assuming she was still alive.

Julia's parents and a young man from the US consulate were sitting outside in the sun as the hotel staff scuttled around their table, trading anxious glances. It wasn't just that a guest at the resort had gone missing – presumed abducted: it was akin to having wealthy relatives visit, when their worst suspicions about how you lived were confirmed and your dirtiest secrets were laid bare before them.

Julia's father was a tall, lean man in his fifties with a shock of white hair and frameless glasses. The girl's mother was, Rafaela guessed, a few years younger, with long, strawberry-blonde hair pulled back into a ponytail. She was clutching a picture of her daughter, taken only a few days before, the backdrop of the hotel's pool visible from where they sat. Julia was standing next to her father, one hand raised to shield her eyes. She looked tanned, happy and relaxed. Her smile, a little forced, a little over-sincere, suggested a young woman who was mature enough to understand her parents' need to cling to her as she began to carve out a life apart from them.

Rafaela began by asking the father to take her through the period before his daughter had gone missing. She didn't interrupt him. He was already frustrated at having to tread again over old ground. He wanted his daughter back.

She made notes as he talked. The young man from the consulate tapped his fingers on the table. A glance from the mother stopped him as the father concluded his story, his voice cracking as he told of the last time he had seen Julia.

Rafaela cleared her throat and thanked him for his patience. Her next job was to offer some reassurance. 'I already have at least a dozen officers making enquiries. I want you and the US government to know how seriously we're taking this. That's the first thing.'

The mother leaned forward. 'So you think something's happened to her?'

This was where things got difficult. Rafaela didn't think, she knew, but sharing that information wasn't going to help them.

Straightening in her seat, Rafaela made sure she met the woman's gaze. 'I don't know anything for certain other than that your daughter is missing.'

The father stiffened. 'I don't believe you.'

The young consular official intervened: 'I think for now we have to—'

The father cut him off: 'I'm believing shit from these people.' He stared straight at Rafaela, whose heart was racing now. 'You know something, and don't tell me you don't because I can see it in your eyes.' His hand shot out across the table and grabbed her wrist.

'John, please!'

Rafaela made a quick calculation. 'I don't know anything for definite,' she said, 'but I have my suspicions based upon recent events here.'

His grip loosened a little. He must have felt he was getting somewhere. 'What events?'

'Kidnap for ransom is a growing problem. I'm not saying that's what this is but it's a possibility.'

He let go of her and slumped in his chair. 'I'll pay whatever it takes. You hear me? I'll sell the house, take out a loan if I have to.'

'It may not be that. But, as I said, it does happen now. And if someone has Julia, you can help me.'

The father looked at her, his eyes wet. He swiped at them with his sleeve. 'How?'

'By staying away from the press for a start. Often these cases can be resolved quietly. A lot of publicity can spook the kidnapper,' she said.

The official raised his hand, palm open. 'She's right. This is something that needs to be handled carefully.'

'So if we do what you tell us we'll get Julia back?'

'I can't promise you that. It wouldn't be fair if I did. But there will be a better chance, yes.'

The father's chin was resting on his chest. He took his wife's hand. 'We understand.'

Outside the hotel, Rafaela sat alone in her car for a few moments. She could have told them that she knew where their daughter had last been seen and whom she had been with. She could have told them those things and more. Would she have wanted the truth if she'd been them? It went without saying.

What right had she to deny them the truth? Who was she to decide?

Questions. Those were her problem. Did the men behind these things calibrate their choices like this? No. They took action. They made decisions. They stuck to them.

She was about to turn the key in the ignition when she stopped. She'd been so preoccupied that she had forgotten the routine that had become like a reflex. She opened the driver's door and, using a mirror she kept on the back seat, checked beneath the car.

Her husband had died four years ago when the cartels had

ramped up the violence. A bomb had been planted under his car. He had been a newspaper reporter whose crime had been to report the news. At first he had reported on the cartels with no problems. But as the violence had escalated the public had become more indignant at the failure of government and politicians to stop it. In turn, the cartels had grown more sensitive to how they were covered in the newspapers and on television. Like pushy celebrities, they wanted to use the media but on their terms. Her husband had received two threats. The third time they had made good on their promise and blown him up. She even knew who had planted the bomb but, as she had told Lock, knowing wasn't enough. Not if the person was powerful or connected to those who were.

Satisfied that there was no bomb, she got back behind the steering-wheel, started the engine and pulled away from the hotel, leaving the girl's parents to their tear-stained vigil. No more questions, she told herself. That time was gone.

Forty-four

They met in a private dining room at the back of the restaurant. The first there was the chief of police, Gabriel Zapatero. He slid into a chair and immediately ordered a whisky, which evaporated almost as soon as it was placed in front of him. He ordered another, then a third.

Manuel Managua arrived five minutes later, greeting the hostess with a kiss on both cheeks and shaking their hands with the v i g o r of a career politician, then settling in to stare at the menu over the top of his horn-rimmed glasses. Zapatero often imagined him shaking his family's hands at breakfast, pledging cookies for all if he could count upon their support. It had made his continued presence at these festivities all the more surprising. Even a whisper of his involvement could end his career.

Zapatero had often wondered about Managua until Federico, Zapatero's childhood friend, had pointed out that many politicians seemed to seek out, or at least flirt with, the seeds of their own destruction. Managua's flirting was overt, but that,

Federico said, was merely a reflection of where they lived and at what point in history. In comparison to the Roman Empire under Caligula, or the Holy Church under the Borgias, things were not so extreme. The rich had always craved decadent pleasures. It was entirely natural.

As the politician fussed over the menu Federico, the boss of bosses, arrived with his two bodyguards. Of course, they all carried security, but Federico's was of a different magnitude. The joke was that if he woke in the middle of the night and rolled over, he would find a bodyguard beside him, rather than his wife or mistress. He took his seat at the head of the table and dismissed the guards – one headed for the door that led back into the restaurant and the other took up a position just outside in the courtyard. He accepted a menu and a waiter took their orders while another poured the wine. Then they were left alone.

Managua took off his glasses and cleaned the lenses. Zapatero checked emails on his BlackBerry, until a look from Federico prompted him to power it down. The rule was that all cell phones had to be turned off. Finally, Federico spoke.

'I see from the newspapers that a young American woman is missing,' he said, his gaze bypassing all of them and settling on the far wall of whitewashed stone.

Zapatero cleared his throat, his eyes shuttling back and forth to his powered-down BlackBerry. 'I have assigned one of my best people to find her. A woman. The family and the American government have been reassured,' Zapatero said.

'Really, I don't know what the world's coming to,' Federico said, with a sigh.

Managua put his glasses back on. 'We wouldn't have a picture of her, would we?'

Zapatero glanced towards his BlackBerry. 'With your permission, Federico?'

Federico couldn't contain his smile as he nodded. They all knew what Managua was like when it came to women. A regular Bill Clinton.

The police chief turned his BlackBerry on, opened an email attachment, full-screening a picture of the girl, and handed it to Managua, who studied it. 'She's pretty,' he said. 'I hope she's still alive.'

'Still alive?' Zapatero mused. 'Of course I hope she is, but nothing has been confirmed one way or the other.' He turned his gaze to Federico, who was staring fixedly at the silverware laid out on the table in front of him.

Managua put down the BlackBerry. Zapatero could see the girl's face staring up at him but he, too, turned to see what Federico would do. Would he pick up his knife or his fork? Pick up one, and the girl would be allowed to live, at least for the time being – and, no doubt, to satisfy Managua. Pick up the other, and she would be disposed of.

Federico drummed the fingers of his right hand on the table, his thumb nearest the fork, his pinkie nearest the knife. He took a sip of red wine, enjoying the attention and his role as final arbiter between life and death. That was what it was all about, thought Zapatero. For Managua it was an appetite. But Federico was the one who had sanctioned it. He had brought along the first girl, and had let things get out of hand when she had tried to escape from the bedroom. He could have called a halt to it at any time. But he hadn't. He enjoyed the power too much.

'I think it is mostly likely,' Federico began, his hand shifting slightly, 'that she will be returned to her family.'

'Alive or dead?' Zapatero asked, unable to endure any more tension. After all, he would have to call Hector and alert him to the decision.

Forty-five

Twilight. Apart from the gardener and a few flitting shapes at the rear of the house, they had seen no one all day. Rafaela had called to say that she had scoped out the two other likely locations and come up with as much as they had: nothing. There was no sign of Charlie Mendez, and no sign of the girl. She had also told Lock how her boss had put her in charge of the hunt for Julia.

Lock walked to the back of the room, picked up his light canvas jacket and put it on. Ty reached into one of the black canvas bags, pulled out a radio and threw it to him. Lock caught it one-handed.

'You sure this is a good idea?' Ty asked.

'Nope. But it beats sitting here watching leaves float to the bottom of a swimming pool.'

'Want some company?' Ty said, shifting in his seat.

'On my signal,' said Lock. He tucked a baseball cap on to his head, the brim low, checked his weapon and dialed down the volume on the radio. He walked out of the apartment.

He took the steps two at a time, eager to get as much distance between himself and the apartment door before someone saw him. He had no need to worry. The communal stairs and ground-floor hallway were empty, apart from a couple of bags of rotting garbage placed outside one of the doors. He picked the bags up as he passed, a good n e i g h b o r on a mission, and headed out into the street.

It was quiet there too. A dog skulked uncertainly near a tree while simultaneously eyeing a nearby fire hydrant. *Decisions. Decisions.* Lock knew how he felt.

The high wall of the narco-mansion was to Lock's left. He stayed on the opposite side of the street but walked parallel to it, still carrying the bags. At the end of the street there was a narrow alleyway with a dumpster. He dropped the bags into it. As he wiped his hands on his jeans he looked across at the front of the house. The wall here was broken by high metal railings that ran for about eighty feet before the wall began again, took a ninety-degree turn and continued to circle the house.

A solitary armed guard, wearing black trousers and a black T-shirt emblazoned with the logo of a local security company, stood at the gated entrance looking bored. He was completely dis-engaged. He didn't even register Lock's presence. In terms of actual bodies, that seemed to be it. Lock walked back in the direction he'd come. Dusk was giving way to night, and as the light died, so did his patience.

The recon had provided him with one interesting piece of information. Just as there was no way to glimpse the house from street level so there was no view of the street, or the street side of the wall, from the house. The cameras, apart from the ones at the front to monitor arrivals and departures, didn't record what happened outside the footprint of the grounds.

He keyed the radio. Two minutes later Ty emerged from the apartment block and joined him beside the wall. Lock vaulted up, Ty giving him a boost. Then Ty returned to the observation point from which he could warn Lock of any approach.

Lock sat astride the wall for a moment and looked down into the grassy yard with the swimming pool. The rear of the house was closer than he had anticipated. The rooms were dark. He scanned for cameras and lights. There was a single fixed-mount camera looking out over the pool and two motion-sensor lights, both attached to the house. A set of french windows was the sole entry point to the rear of the house that he could see.

Slowly he lowered himself into a row of shrubs. He tried not to make his movements too sudden or abrupt, while at the same time trying to limit the amount of time his back was exposed.

With a dull thud, which seemed thunderous to his ears but was probably no louder than a cat's landing, his boots were on the ground. He stood still for a moment, his legs partially camouflaged by a bush, and listened.

Twenty feet away he heard scuffing. He hunkered down into a squatting position, his hand moving to the butt of his SIG Sauer 226. A Mexican male in his early forties sauntered around the corner, an AK47 hanging as casually from a leather strap at his side as if it was a man-bag. Lock could track his progress by the glowing red tip of his cigarillo. He was carrying about fifty extra pounds and was clearly relying on his weapon to get him out of any trouble.

He wandered over to the edge of the pool, unzipped his trousers and proceeded to urinate into the shallow end. He sighed with satisfaction, zipped up, wiped his hands on his shirt and continued his patrol.

There was more good news. Neither of what Lock had suspected were motion-activated lights had switched on.

He waited a few more minutes, then broke cover, moving slowly towards the rear of the house, careful to skirt the area covered by the fixed security camera. From its height, the lens and the angle it was sitting at, he had estimated its coverage – and peeing in the pool was an off-camera activity.

The up-lighters at the bottom of the pool were bright enough for Lock to take a closer look at the frames surrounding the windows. The depth and composition of the glass told him it was blast-proof. He kept moving, staying close to the building out of the camera's range. At the doors, he cupped his hands over his eyes and peered inside. There was a large living area, with a drop-down viewing screen. The remnants of a party – empty glasses, bottles and drug paraphernalia – covered a low wooden coffee-table.

From nowhere, a light snapped on. He hugged the wall beside the windows, pulled out his gun, and held it by his side. Seconds passed before he realized that what he had thought was a motion-activated external light was in fact the main light in the living room. If whoever had switched it on hadn't seen him, it was by pure dumb luck. Or they had seen him and were raising the alarm. He risked taking a peek, craning his neck to the window and look-ing inside.

Separated by a few inches of bomb-proof glass and less than fifteen feet of carpet, he found himself staring straight at the missing girl. She was wearing a long floral dress and looked drained but in reasonable shape. Better yet, standing behind her, weatherbeaten but still clearly recognizable, stood Charlie Mendez. Between them was the bodyguard.

Lock ducked out of sight, a shiver of excitement running through him, like an electric current. He got it now. He understood why Brady had risked everything. There was no feeling like this.

He keyed his radio and spoke to Ty. 'I got them both inside.'

Forty-six

Back in the apartment, Lock weighed the options. A hostile extraction, where you take someone who is either unwilling to leave or being prevented from doing so, is hard to pull off and it sure as hell required more than two bodies. But that was all they had – three, if they counted Rafaela – and Lock was a firm believer in working with the tools at your disposal rather than cursing your ill-fortune. Under normal circumstances, a task of this nature would require ten times the resources if it was to be carefully and safely executed. The surveillance and intelligence team would be one component, the extraction team another. There would be a quartermaster, a transport coordinator and all manner of other personnel.

Complicating matters even further, they had two targets. One would, Lock hoped, go willingly, although that couldn't be guaranteed when you were dealing with someone already traumatized by an abduction and who might have begun to identify with her captors. Mendez, on the other hand, would go kicking and screaming.

As they gathered together their gear, Rafaela on her way to them, Lock looked at his partner. 'We're going to have to forget Mendez. We take the girl, get her out of there, and deal with him later.'

He could tell that Ty didn't like the idea of giving up on the fugitive they had come to collect. 'We can't take 'em both?' Ty asked.

Lock tucked a spare clip into his jacket. 'We could try, but it halves our chances and right now they're pretty slim as it goes.'

'So he gets off again?'

'Maybe we can come back for him,' said Lock.

'That ain't gonna happen. You and me both know it.'

'If he's implicated in kidnapping the girl the State Department will have to get off their fat ass and put pressure on the Mexicans to get him back.'

'Or he floats on down to Venezuela or catches a slow boat to Cuba,' said Ty.

Lock zipped up a bag. 'What do you want me to tell you here, Ty? It sucks, but taking them both is too risky.'

'What about Melissa and what she wanted?'

There was a long silence. Lock flushed and his jaw tightened. He advanced on Ty, fists clenched. 'Melissa's dead. Carrie's dead. When they're gone, they're gone. The girl's alive. We can get her home. There's no debate.'

They froze as the apartment door opened and Rafaela walked in. 'Am I interrupting something?'

'No, we're good,' said Ty, breaking eye contact with Lock. 'Just talking things over.'

'Now what?' Rafaela asked.

Lock looked at Ty.

'We go get the girl,' Ty said.

Lock gave Rafaela a grim smile. 'You're the cop in charge of finding her. Should be straightforward, right?'

She smiled back, all three knowing that for Rafaela to knock at the door and demand they hand over the girl was about as likely as building a snowman in Palm Springs in June. Of course, they might hand her over, and that would be it, until a bomb turned up under Rafaela's car or someone arrived at her apartment to kill her. But, Lock thought, there might be a way for them to extract the girl while everyone saved face. In him and Ty, Rafaela might not have two accomplices so much as two scapegoats.

'Sure,' Rafaela said. 'Piece of cake.'

Forty-seven

Lock had already run through the choices in his head, dismissing most of them out of hand. They could try a covert entry, breaking in without anyone noticing and taking the girl out. That was Fantasy Land, the domain of movies. Even if they could sneak in, which in itself was unlikely, getting out unnoticed with the girl was pushing the boundaries of possibility.

The second approach was a dynamic, and therefore overt, entry. In other words, forcing their way in. From the cursory glance he'd had of the location that, too, was unlikely. They would almost certainly have something akin to a panic room. The girl, Mendez or both would be put there and then it was a siege, with plenty of reinforcements to hand.

Their only real shot at this was if the girl left the house, and there was no way of knowing if that would happen. And even if it did she might not necessarily leave alive. If she had been retained for Mendez's amusement, then history suggested he would tire of her – there had been no sequels in his date-rape movie collection – and she was far too risky to keep. She would be killed, dumped, and Rafaela would be handed a prime suspect. The case would be closed, and Lock would find himself a lone voice trying to persuade people that Mendez had been involved in her disappearance.

No, the only real shot they had was if she was moved – and that would have to be prompted. They would have to find a way of dictating the kidnapper's next play.

He wrote out what he needed and handed it to Ty. Ty looked at the list and his eyes widened a little. 'You sure about this?' he asked.

'That's Plan B.'

'And Plan A?' Rafaela asked.

'Once Ty's got what we need and it's all in place I want you to call your boss and tell him you have a lead. Give him this address. They'll have to move her and that'll give us a shot.'

Rafaela looked unconvinced. 'And what if they decide to kill her, then move her? You might be better going with your second plan first. That way they won't have time to think, just to react.'

Lock walked to the window and stared over the wall. The light was still on in the living room but there was no sign of anyone. Rafaela had a point and he wasn't one for letting his ego get in the way. 'None of this is without risk, but okay. Can you take Ty and gather the materials?'

She gave a curt nod. 'Sure.'

As Ty followed her to the door, Lock called him back. 'And we're going to need a new vehicle as well.'

Ty raised an eyebrow. 'Oh, yeah? Ask the black guy to jack the car. Y'know, just because I grew up in Long Beach doesn't mean that—'

Lock put up his hand. 'Tyrone. How many cars have I seen you steal? Not how many cars have you actually stolen. Just how many have I seen you steal?'

'"Steal" is kind of a judgmental term to apply under the circumstances.'

'Okay – borrowed without asking first,' said Lock.

Ty glanced at the ceiling as he did the math. 'I dunno. Maybe a dozen?'

Lock nodded outside toward the villa. 'Okay, so can we have the racial stereotyping discussion after we've taken care of business?'

'Fine,' said Ty. He turned to Rafaela. 'See what I have to deal with here?'

As they headed out, Lock stayed at the window, torn, not sure if he wasn't deluding himself, that maybe he shouldn't just pick up the phone to the State Department. He packed that idea away. Who would they call? Rafaela's boss? That was one sure way of getting the girl killed.

Ty sat out of direct sight in the back seat as Rafaela navigated the empty streets. Her eyes flicked to him in the rear-view mirror. 'You want Mendez, don't you?'

Ty shrugged. 'Can't always get what you want. Ryan's right, the girl's more important.'

They got to the gas station. A couple of kids were hanging around out front, kicking a soccer ball back and forth. Ty helped Rafaela fill the two gas containers and load them into the back of her vehicle. She went in to pay and he put the small tank of propane next to the gas.

*

Lock had already worked out that the guard he'd seen walking round the grounds stuck to a regular routine, leaving on the hour every hour and taking less than seven minutes, even with a stop to pee in the pool, to complete his patrol. So, barring someone coming out of the house, that left the grounds empty and un-patrolled for fifty-three minutes. The rest of the time, Lock figured, they were relying on someone inside watching the security monitors, but the cameras were mostly at the front of the property, leaving a couple of large blind areas at the side and rear. One of those areas covered the wood pile.

With Ty and Rafaela back safely with supplies and a new model, recently 'borrowed', white, Toyota RAV 4, with heavily tinted windows. Lock checked his watch. It showed a quarter past the hour. He set to work, climbing on top of the wall, then haul-ing up the two gas containers and the cylinder full of propane. He lowered them to the ground on the other side, then followed them.

Having been over the wall once already, this time he felt more sure of himself. He doused the wood pile with one container of petrol, set the second a few feet away, but closer to the house, and the propane cylinder closer still. He was counting on no one find-ing the initial fire until the other items had exploded. It was an imprecise science.

Satisfied, he used a rag soaked with gas to start the bonfire, then headed back to the wall. Ty's hand reached down and pulled him back over. They had already abandoned the apartment so they retreated to their vehicle, retrieved from the back of the apartment block, and climbed in.

Now all they had to do was wait.

Forty-eight

Hector anxiously checked his watch. They were running late. They should have left the mansion five minutes ago. They would have to make up the lost time on the road.

At the front door, he pulled Julia to one side. 'Remember what I told you, and you'll be fine. You understand me?'

'I understand,' she said softly, eyes focused on the hallway's red terracotta-tiled floor. Charlie was standing a few feet away, looking awkward. Hector assumed this was a new experience for him – having to be around one of the girls after he was finished with her.

Eager to get moving, Hector opened the front door and ushered them out. A red Escalade SUV was waiting to take them to the party. Hector opened the rear passenger door. Charlie walked past Julia and climbed in. Julia didn't move. The look she gave Hector told him that, while she wouldn't try to escape, there was no way she was sitting in the back with Charlie.

'What's the problem?' asked Hector.

'I don't want to sit next to him,' she said, shooting a glance at Charlie.

'Fuck it,' Charlie said, scooting across the seats and getting out again. 'I'll ride up front.'

He squeezed past her as he got in, his crotch deliberately brushing her backside, even though there was plenty of room. She shuddered and got into the back. Hector climbed in and started the engine. He put the Escalade into drive and released the parking brake.

A second later she caught sight of one of the guards from the back window. He was shouting and waving his arms. Hector stopped, put the Escalade in park and got out, leaving the door open.

The guard was still animated, waving his arms and pointing to the back of the house.

Julia's Spanish was rusty but she picked out the word *fuego*. Fire. She couldn't smell smoke but the breeze was blowing towards the house and they were at the front.

Hector snapped at the guard, telling him to deal with it. Then he slammed the door, put the Escalade into drive and gunned it, roaring down the driveway, the gates gliding open just in time for them to scrape through and out on to the road.

Behind them there was a loud bang. Louder than a gunshot. Louder than a car backfiring. She looked at Hector. If he had heard it, it didn't seem to register. His eyes were fixed on the road and that was where they stayed.

In the front seat. Charlie was staring out of the window at a vague orange glow behind them.

'What was that?' he asked, unclipping his seatbelt so that he could turn around for a better view. 'It sounded like an explosion.'

Hector shrugged. 'Don't worry about it.'

Lock's hand slammed down hard on the steering-wheel of the Toyota RAV 4. They had still been moving into position when the gates had opened and the red Escalade had come barreling out on to the road. The guards couldn't have anticipated the fire so it was down to bad luck, plain and simple. But it left in shreds his plan to grab the girl as the occupants fled the house.

Given the Escalade's tinted windows and that they were parked behind it, they'd had no clear view through the windshield so no idea about who was inside it. For all Lock knew, it might be a decoy.

Glancing to his left, he saw a column of dense black smoke rising from behind the wall as an alarm screamed a warning. The Escalade was almost a full block clear of them now.

'Call Rafaela – ask her to hang back here,' he said to Ty, pulling out from the curb and falling in behind the fleeing Escalade.

Ty pulled out a pre-paid throwaway cell phone and made the call. A few moments later, he tucked it back into his pocket. 'She ain't happy about staying back there but she said she'll check the house when the fire crew arrives.'

Lock's hands tightened on the steering-wheel. 'All right, then.'

Up ahead, the Escalade was stopped at a red light. Lock eased up and the Ranger dropped back. If it hadn't been for the possibility that the girl was in the vehicle, and on the way to who knew where, he would have dropped out of the pursuit.

The lights flipped to green and the Escalade drove on. Lock followed at a respectful distance, keeping his eyes on the car but also looking out for other vehicles around and behind them. If the driver of the Escalade had spotted them, which was possible, there was every chance he or she would call in reinforcements.

Presumably sensing Lock's tension, Ty straightened up in the passenger seat, his head on a swivel, his gun in his hand. They passed a side road. A car pulled out in front of them. Lock swerved around it, careful to keep his hand off the horn. He checked it out in the rear-view. The driver, a middle-aged woman, was the sole occupant. It had been bad driving, nothing more. When he looked up again, the Escalade was out of sight.

Ty pointed at a crossroads. 'He took a left up there.'

Lock accelerated a little, trying not to get over-anxious, but aware that if they lost the Escalade they might also lose the girl. Ty's cell phone rang.

Lock spotted the car again as Ty took a call from Rafaela.

'You're sure?' he heard Ty ask. 'Okay.'

He gave Rafaela their current location and killed the call. 'Looks like the girl and Charlie Mendez were there but they're not now.'

'Did she see any other vehicles exit the property after this one?'

Ty shook his head. 'Better than evens they're both inside, so what you want to do, Ryan?'

Lock took a moment. The Escalade's movements were deliberate. It wasn't as if the driver was idly circling the town. He had a destination in mind where, it was safe to assume, there would be reinforcements. The Escalade could hold maybe seven individuals. Not great odds, but better than they would be at another narco-mansion where they would have the same problems of entry.

'I think we roll the dice,' Lock said, burying the gas pedal and going hard after the fleeing Escalade.

Forty-nine

Hector had spotted the Toyota RAV 4 dropping in behind them a few blocks from the house. When you lived your entire life with one eye open at all times, it became second nature to pick out a car that was following you.

The white splash of headlights in his rear-view prevented him seeing exactly who was inside, but it hardly mattered. No doubt it was connected to whoever had set the fire at the side of the house as they were leaving – to which he'd been alerted by one of the guards as he'd pulled out of the driveway.

As he drove he had made a phone call, bringing his boss up to speed on what was going on. Zapatero had been freaked that he hadn't travelled with additional security but Hector had assured him that he was fine: he had precautions in place. But if they were being followed it left a question mark over the girl. What did his boss want him to do now?

The original plan had been to bring her out to the ranch for a special party before she was disposed of. But with all four men set to be there, delivering her might mean delivering trouble too. It wasn't Hector's job to offer opinions so he simply asked whether or not he should continue as ordered, or whether the plan should change. Zapatero had told him he would call him back.

At the end of the call, Charlie asked, 'Everything okay?'

Hector smiled. 'Sure. Everything's fine.'

He glanced into the rear-view mirror to see the girl sitting awkwardly in the back. His cell phone rang.

'Her attendance is no longer needed,' Zapatero said, and hung up.

Over the years Hector had received many such calls. The language was always oblique. Not once had anyone ever told him to kill or maim someone. Instead they had told him to 'deal with the situation' or that a particular person was 'no longer required'. The words were corporate, and unemotional. It left no doubt about what was expected and Hector had never been troubled by the task, but as the horrors had stacked up, his ability to block them out with alcohol or drugs had diminished.

He snuck another glance at Charlie and an idea took hold in his head. What was that phrase about two birds and one stone? Perhaps it was time Charlie Mendez was forced to confront the consequences of his actions and clean up his own mess for once.

Fifty

In the back seat, Julia knew she had to escape before they reached their destination or she was dead. Since her kidnapping, when anyone had spoken Spanish to or around her, she had played dumb and pretended not to understand what was being said. The truth was different. Though she was far from fluent, she could broadly follow a conversation. And she could certainly pick out enough words to work out that Hector had just discussed whether she should live or die.

Sitting alone in the back seat, she had already tried the door. It was centrally locked, with no way of overriding it from where she was. Her only chance, she figured, was to cause some kind of distraction, and find a way to make them pull over. But it couldn't be obvious, like pretending she had to pee. It had to be something from left field that would throw them off balance. Her mind flashed back to her childhood and road trips with her parents.

Leaning slightly forward in her seat, so that neither Charlie nor

Hector could see her, she jammed the index and middle fingers of her right hand into her mouth, forcing them down her throat until she began to gag.

Fifty-one

Startled by the sound of retching, Hector twisted in the driver's seat, just in time to catch the vomit as it arced from back seat to front. It splashed on the side of his face. His foot tapped at the brake as he piloted the Escalade to the side of the road. Next to him, Charlie must have caught some too because he exclaimed, 'Jesus Christ,' as Julia retched again.

'I'm sorry,' she mumbled.

Hector brought the Escalade to a complete stop and turned to assess the damage. The Escalade would have to be cleaned. He could do it when they got to the ranch.

Charlie swiped at the vomit on his jacket. 'Jesus, that's disgusting,' he said, opening the passenger door before Hector could stop him.

'Where are you going?' Hector asked.

Charlie shot him a you're-only-the-help look and kept going. 'To get some air. It freakin' reeks in here.'

'Can I get some air too?' Julia asked, eyes pleading.

'No,' said Hector, firmly. In the seconds of confusion he had forgotten about the vehicle that had been following them. Now, as he checked the mirrors, he couldn't see it anywhere. Something told him it had kept going, driving past when he had stopped, but he couldn't be sure. Maybe it hadn't been following them after all. If it was someone who intended doing them harm surely they would have taken this opportunity.

'Stay where you are,' he said, and clambered out to retrieve Charlie. He slammed the door behind him and clicked the key fob to lock it. Let Julia suffer the stench.

A chill desert breeze caught him off guard. Charlie was standing a few feet at the back of the Escalade, hands cupped protectively around the red tip of a cigarette as the wind bit at the tobacco. Hector took a moment to study their surroundings. There was traffic, but not much. Maybe one car passing in either direction every forty seconds or so. He could see the city lights in the far distance. There was a metal crash barrier, and beyond that scrub desert. He glanced up into the night sky. A full moon hung high overhead.

He peered down the road for the RAV 4 or any other vehicle that might have stopped but there was nothing and no one. He walked to the back of the Escalade and repeated the procedure as a bus whizzed by on its way home from a *maquiladora*.

No one would stop. Hector knew that much. If someone broke down here it was their hard luck. It wasn't only men such as him who were paranoid. It was the defining feeling on this side of the border. Good Samaritans had long since been snuffed out. A car at the side of the road would only be approached by someone looking for trouble.

This was his opportunity. The girl's sickness had been a signal. He turned to Charlie. 'Finish your cigarette.'

Charlie took a long final drag and crushed the butt under his heel. He started back towards the front passenger seat but Hector blocked his path with a meaty arm. Beyond the crash barrier the ground sloped down for about seven feet before leveling off and extending into the distance.

'Wait down there,' Hector said, with a nod towards the open ground.

Charlie stared at him. 'What the hell are you doing?'

'It's not what I'm going to do, Señor Mendez. It's what *you* are going to do.'

Fifty-two

Julia watched as Hector walked back towards the car. He stopped at the rear passenger door. She tried to read his expression but it was impossible. He had one of those faces.

He started to open the door and her heart began to thump a little harder. This would be her chance. He was letting her out so he could clean the inside of the vehicle. All she needed was his back to be turned for a few seconds and she would run. If she could get over the barrier and down the slope before he had a chance to draw his weapon she had a chance to get away. If Charlie was still outside the vehicle she would have to make sure she was a good ten feet from him when she made her break. That would be enough. She ran every morning – at least two miles. She wasn't the fastest but she had enough pace to put some distance between them, and she had stamina, which she doubted either man possessed. Hector was strong but out of shape, and Charlie was only good for catching girls he'd drugged.

It was only when the door was open and she caught the look on

Hector's face as they made eye contact that she knew he wasn't planning to clean the interior. He was letting her out so he could kill her. His face betrayed him: it spoke of shame and regret in equal measure.

Her mind racing, she shuffled along the seat, swung her legs out and emerged from the Escalade. She needed distance, a few feet between herself and Hector, but he stayed close. Glancing over, she saw Charlie, hands at his sides, his fingers drumming against his legs in agitation. He must know as well.

She would have to play along. If Hector suspected she knew, her fate was sealed. He would put a bullet in her then and there. A car was approaching. She thought for a moment about dashing towards it but Hector was so close she could feel him, and the chance of the car stopping in time, if it stopped at all, was slim.

'I'm sorry about being sick,' she said, half turning her head.

Hector shrugged, head down, eyes looking everywhere but at her. 'Don't worry.'

Testing his reaction, she took a half-step to the side. He didn't appear to notice.

How far? she asked herself. How much distance would there have to be before she could make a run for it? Too much of a gap between them and he would notice; too little and she would stand no chance of getting away.

She looked again at the crash barrier, the slope beyond. That was when she noticed the gap in the barrier – a gap big enough for the Escalade to squeeze through. Even if she ran, Hector could take the Escalade down there. She could outrun him, and Charlie if she had to, but she wouldn't be able to outrun the vehicle. Her shoulders slumped. She felt like crying. Her stomach lurched. She started towards the front of the vehicle. Hector began to follow her. But as she doubled over to heave, she put out her arm to push him away. He backed off a little and she retched. A pathetic string of bile dribbled from her mouth. Something shifted in her mind. It was as if the fear she had felt all this time had been switched off.

As she groaned in apparent pain, s i g n a l i n g with her hand for them to give her space, she looked back at the road. On the other side of the road she spotted two sets of headlights in the distance approaching from the opposite direction. Between the side of the road they were on and the other there was another barrier with a gap, but it was close to a hundred feet away. On the other side, a matching barrier offered no such breach.

She straightened up for a second, hands falling to her hips. She tried to gauge the speed of the approaching vehicles by the ever-expanding orbit of their headlights. Hector was growing impatient. He was shouting to Charlie to join them. Then he turned to her.

'Come on, we take a little walk. The air will be good for you,' he said, his voice like an echo as she focused on what she had to do.

'Give me a second,' she said, losing the last of the sentence as she doubled over one more time, her right leg falling back a little to give her more of an explosive start.

Now, she thought, pushing off on her right foot, twisting round the front of the Escalade and hurtling across the blacktop, everything around her a blur. Pressing her hands down on the crash barrier, she vaulted over it, stumbling as her feet touched down on the other side but quickly recovering her balance.

She could hear the approaching vehicles, the roar of their engines, but she didn't dare stop to check how close they were. Hector had reacted faster than she had anticipated. For a big man he moved fast. She couldn't be certain but as she had run across the road she thought she had felt the toe of his sneaker brush the heel of her trailing foot. He could be only feet behind her, close enough that if she hesitated, even for a second, he would take her down.

She dashed straight across the road, white light enveloping her along with the nail-on-a-blackboard grating of brakes – more sensation than sound – and the chemical cloy of burning rubber. A gust of warm air dipped around her, so sudden and violent that her dress billowed. She felt dirt under her feet and the crash barrier on the other side loomed almost from nowhere. She started to vault it but her balance, thrown off by having been a split second from going under the wheels of what she knew now was a trucker's rig, was off, and she half fell, half stumbled over it, landing painfully on her left leg, her ankle folding under the weight.

The slope on this side of the road matched that on the other. If anything it was a little steeper. Knees folding, she allowed gravity to take her, and rolled down, a good fifteen feet, bits of dirt and shale flying up into her face as she went.

She pushed herself back on to her feet as the whipcrack of a gunshot rang out close by. *A warning shot to stop her?*

Back up on the road, she could just about glimpse the truck jack-knifed across two lanes, the cab slicing across them, the trailer lying on its side. Rubber smeared the surface in two curved trails behind it.

She struggled to her feet. A jolt of pain surged up her leg as she tried to put weight on the twisted ankle. She hobbled forward. She had to keep moving. If she didn't, she was dead. She broke into a jog. After half a dozen steps the pain l e v e l e d off.

Another gunshot. Then voices. She could hear Hector shouting, telling her to stop. She kept moving, and threw a glance over her shoulder. He had one leg over the barrier. He was heading towards her. He was moving faster than she was. Without the twisted ankle she could have outpaced him, but not now.

She bit down hard on her lower lip and propelled herself on into the moonlit desert. She had to be within range of his gun. She looked around for cover. A lone juniper tree stood about twenty feet to her left, its trunk barely thick enough to hide her, even if she could get to it before he pulled the trigger.

There was noise from the road now too. Men's voices. She thought she heard Charlie shouting but she couldn't be sure: the words were drowned by the blood pounding in her ears.

She kept moving. The pain was receding. Either that or she was simply becoming used to it. Whatever the reason, her strides were getting longer. The juniper tree was close now. When she got there she would find something beyond it to fix on. She would keep moving, keep running, until her back took a bullet and she went down. The thought gave her comfort and spurred her on.

She brushed past the outer branches of the tree, and moved left so that its trunk was behind her. It was only then that she noticed the man. Her breath caught in her throat as a huge hand shot out, grabbed her by the shoulder and spun her round a hundred and eighty degrees. She caught the merest glimpse of him. He had appeared from nowhere as his hand bunched the dress fabric at the back of her neck and held her in place, her back to his. It was like being taken by a riptide. A second later there was the ear-shredding sound of a gun being fired less than two feet from her and a bright yellow muzzle flash.

Time seemed to fracture as she was spun back round so that she was alongside the man, the fingers of his giant left hand grasping her elbow as he moved her back towards the road, circling wide where Hector had been only moments ago. She didn't struggle against him but she was hobbling as he covered the ground in long, loping strides. He stopped for a second. 'Are you okay to keep going?' he asked, his tone, like his movements, strikingly relaxed, as if he had saved her from being pushed over in the playground, rather than from a midnight execution in the middle of the desert.

She nodded. 'I twisted my ankle.'

'Here,' he said, picking her up as if she weighed nothing, and tucking her over his back with one hand while he held the gun in his other and broke into a run. 'We gotta get you out of here.'

Fifty-three

Charlie Mendez opened the glove box of the Escalade and rifled through the contents, hoping to find a spare set of keys or, better yet, a gun. There were wads of receipts, and an owner's manual for the vehicle, but no gun. There was no Hector either: he had disappeared. He slammed the glove compartment shut, panic threatening to overwhelm him.

He had to get the hell out of there before the cops showed up. If he was picked up it would complicate an already difficult situation. To take him from custody would involve a lot of explaining and there were limits – he had been told so when he'd got here. There was only so much the cartel could do to protect him, and there would surely come a point where he was more trouble than he was worth – even though he was worth a lot.

He climbed back out of the vehicle and looked around with pinprick pupils. On the other side of the highway, the trailer was lying on its side. Behind it a white SUV was inching its way through the debris. Hector still hadn't appeared. There had been two gunshots a minute or so ago but then nothing. For all he knew Hector could be dead and he could be stuck in the middle of this mayhem, a sitting duck, with no idea where he was, never mind how to get away.

He was still debating with himself whether to sit tight or get out of the Escalade when he saw the girl being hustled towards the SUV by a tall man, who opened the vehicle's back door for her. She got inside.

Charlie felt a breath of relief. The girl was gone. Alive. Whoever the guy was, he was obviously there for her, not for him. Charlie would wait for one more minute to see if Hector came back. If he didn't, he would leave the vehicle and get out of there. There were plenty of hours until sunrise. If he stayed off the road there would be little chance of anyone spotting him. At daybreak he could flag someone down and offer them money to take him back into town. There, he could make a phone call and arrange for someone to pick him up.

Making his plan calmed him. Everything was going to be okay. He opened the driver's door and that was when he saw him. A guy standing next to the man who had just put the girl into his vehicle. They were talking: the conversation was animated – a disagreement. From the look of him, the second guy was almost certainly an American. He was tall, over six foot, and more than wiry but a long way short of muscle-bound. And there was an intensity to him that crackled, like the air before a flash of lightning.

A sedan had pulled up next to the Escalade and an elderly man had got out to take a look at the accident. Charlie didn't recognize him, but by the time he looked back across the highway, the vehicle the girl was inside was pulling away. The second guy was still there, standing at the edge of the highway, staring straight at

Charlie, even though the tinted windows and interior cabin of the Escalade must have blocked his line of sight. It was as if the Escalade didn't even exist. Charlie felt himself meet the man's gaze, and shuddered. He had seen that look before, in the eyes of the lead prosecutor at his trial. It was the look of someone who had already weighed and measured him, delivered his own judgement and was now set to carry it through.

From the chaos of grinding metal and gunfire, fear rose in him. He turned and ran. Across the barrier, down the slope and into the barren desert.

He didn't look back. He didn't have to. He already knew that the man was coming after him.

Fifty-four

The smell of sweat and vomit came at Lock like heat from a blast furnace as he opened the door of the Escalade. He took a deep breath, drawing the fetid air into his nose and down his throat, searching for the coppery tang of blood. There was none.

A five-second check of the interior revealed no one balled up in a footwell, only empty space. He got back out, opened the rear tailgate, made sure it was clear and ran to the barrier.

About a hundred yards out there was movement. *Mendez.* Or maybe the bodyguard. He vaulted the barrier and watched the person make a final break from the cover of a juniper tree. From the figure's outline, he was sure it was Mendez.

He skidded down the slope, letting the gradient and gravity do the work as Mendez took flight, heels kicking up in a steady pulse. He was moving at a good pace, while Lock was going about as fast as he could manage. Mendez was a surfer, young and fit. It would be no easy foot chase but maybe he'd have an edge when it came to stamina. He settled into his stride, hoping that his quarry would overreach himself and tire quickly.

The decision to go after Mendez, rather than stay with Ty and the girl, had been a snap one. Something that defied his own logic. Ty's gambling instinct had suggested they rescue the girl and take Mendez. Lock had argued that to split the mission reduced the chance of attaining either goal. Cold calculation said the same, even by the roadside. Getting Julia back to her parents, or better yet straight across the border and to sanctuary, was hardly straightforward. An extra body would always be useful – not fundamental, but useful. Throw an entirely separate and ongoing hostile extraction of Mendez into the mix and things got very complicated. In short, it was a bad idea.

That was still Lock's thinking as they had watched the Escalade pull over. Assuming they might have been spotted by the bodyguard, they had kept moving. They were on a highway. Unless the bodyguard was going to drive back down it the wrong way, he had nowhere to go and no way of losing them. They had coasted along until they were out of sight.

Ty had got out and moved back down the road on foot. He had watched as the occupants had popped out of the vehicle, happy that they hadn't been following a decoy. He had jogged back and relayed the news to Lock, who had decided that this was the best opportunity they would get. But by the time they had found a gap to cross to the other side of the highway, the girl had already made a run for it.

Lock had been there to see her dash for freedom. The echo of Carrie's death had brought his heart into his mouth and a fresh rage to his heart. Julia had made it, but all of a sudden, standing at the edge of that dark desert highway, ghosts had been all around him, popping up like so many plants after a summer storm. He looked back to the desert and they were everywhere, completely real. The men who had pursued his fiancée to her death stood like gunslingers, staring at him. At their feet, Carrie lay dying. Melissa Warner was there too. The girl whose rape and subsequent death he had come to avenge.

As Ty had put Julia into the RAV 4, the pull of the dead, and the rage he felt towards Mendez, had sucked his heart into his boots. His decision was made. There was no time to do anything other than tell Ty to get the girl out of there and that he was going to find what they had come down here for: justice for Melissa Warner.

Now, without the vantage-point afforded by high ground, Lock stopped for a moment, scanning the dinner-plate flat landscape for Mendez. The desert breeze rustled through his shirt. He was five hundred yards out from the highway. Flashing lights near the jack-knifed truck announced the arrival of the authorities. Lock doubted Mendez would double back and risk running into cops who might not be aligned to the cartel. Lock couldn't go back in case they were. That left no turning back for either of them.

He plunged forwards into the darkness.

Fifty-five

Police Chief Gabriel Zapatero listened quietly, put the phone down and walked outside to find the others. The atmosphere was light and festive. A mariachi band played on a raised dais overlooking the swimming pool. Waiters circulated with trays of food and drinks. There were no wives but lots of girls, beautiful but hard-faced professionals. The men were businessmen, lawyers, cops, one or two doctors.

The first person Zapatero saw was Manuel Managua, who was working the assembled guests like a true politician, seemingly oblivious to the fact that he already had the votes of everyone here, and that hookers rarely made it to the polls on election day. The problem with telling Managua was that in a crisis he panicked. He was the one who had most wanted the American girl, yet now that she was a problem he would no doubt deny he had ever said any such thing. A classic politician.

Zapatero smiled broadly at the crowd of people surrounding Managua as he lectured them about how the unions would destroy the prosperity of the area if they weren't reined in. 'Excuse me. I need to borrow our country's future president. We will only be a moment.'

He led Managua off to one side.

'Is she here? The American girl?' he asked, as eager as a child on Christmas Eve.

Zapatero wondered what it was with politicians and situations they shouldn't be within miles of. 'No, she's not here yet,' he said, choosing his words with care. 'But let's go inside.'

'Why? What's going on?' Managua asked, picking up on the tension.

'Let's wait for Federico,' Zapatero said.

It wasn't a long wait. Federico Tibialis, the boss of bosses, strode in, buttoning his shirt. He poured himself a drink. He seemed the calmest and most collected of them all. That was why he always made the final call. A man in his line of work who was unable to cope in a crisis usually lasted all of five minutes. The narcotics trade was one of perpetual crisis management, and his job as pressured as that of any Fortune 500 company CEO. He took big decisions every week. Decisions that involved life and death.

Managua shifted from foot to foot, apparently beside himself that he seemed to be the only one out of the loop. Zapatero felt like slapping him but instead he poured him a drink and told him to sit down. 'There's been an accident,' was how he phrased it. 'The girl and the other American. They're gone.'

Managua's brow furrowed. 'Dead?' And then he was off, spinning the whole thing in his mind before anyone had the chance to correct him 'That's not so bad in a way. I mean, if it was an accident, a real accident, it may solve many of our problems with—'

Federico cut in: 'No, the chief means they're missing. We don't know where they are.'

Managua lapsed into silence. He took off his glasses and began to rub at the lenses with a silk handkerchief plucked from his top pocket.

Zapatero watched Federico as he walked towards the window. The villa was on a flat plateau with a single road that snaked up to the entrance. You could see everyone coming and everyone leaving. From this room you could take in the entire panorama of *maquiladoras* clustered along the border, busy twenty-four hours a day churning out products for the *gringos*.

Finally Federico Tibialis, the drug lord of all drug lords, seemed to have assembled his thoughts. He turned to Zapatero. 'I heard there was a man with them. Hector somebody or other, one of our corrupt police officers, who are such a problem. I heard he was protecting the American.'

Even in private Federico always spoke as if there was a Federal prosecutor in the next room, listening to his every word. It was a good assumption to make. He never spoke directly, always left room for interpretation, and Zapatero knew all too well that in a courtroom that was all that was required.

'This Hector, I have heard rumors that he is dangerous. A killer,' Federico continued. 'If I was a betting man I would wager that somehow he has got himself mixed up in all this. But I'm sure you and your men will be able to stop him, won't you, Chief?'

'What about the American man, the rapist?' Managua asked, of Mendez.

Federico shrugged. 'There was a crash of some kind. Perhaps if he was hurt in it and he has stumbled out into the desert, the coyotes will finish him off. There is only so much we can do to look after our visitors in this town. Sometimes nature must simply take its course.'

'And the other matter? Surely we can't ignore that,' said Managua.

Federico sipped at his whisky. He whirled the ice cubes around in the bottom of the crystal tumbler. 'The papers were signed yesterday. There's no backing out for either party now.'

Police Chief Zapatero felt satisfied with what Federico was proposing. They had done everything they could to protect Charlie Mendez but he had brought this upon himself by seeking out the girl. His family would have to understand that. The time had come to draw a line under the whole affair. The girl had forced their hand. Of course, for their story to stick they would all have to die. Mendez. The girl. Hector could take the fall and, once he was safely in prison, he could be taken care of too. They had reporters who would be helpful in tying it all together in a neat enough bundle for the Americans to be satisfied. Of course, first they had to be tracked down and that meant finding Charlie Mendez, and the two men Rafaela Carcharon was supposed to have kicked out of the country.

It made for a lot of loose ends. By the end of this, they were going to have to dig one hell of a big hole in the desert. The police chief straightened and looked at the other three men. 'Gentlemen, leave it to me. My men will find them, although you understand that I can't guarantee their safe return. The border is a dangerous place. Especially at night.'

Fifty-six

Two Hours Later

Local and Policía Federal vehicles were massed along the highway, the wash from their lights turning the blacktop a deep crimson. Paramilitary black-clad cops swaggered back and forth. Two separate forensic units swarmed over the abandoned Escalade. Traffic had been halted in both directions, and roadblocks set up, not only on the highway but at all the off- and on-ramps in both directions for five miles. Federal and local police officers moved in pairs along the lines of vehicles, flashlights probing the interiors. A tarpaulin was ripped from the back of a truck carrying produce, the driver held at gunpoint as the tailgate was lowered, his wares spilling out on to the road.

Further down the line a bus disgorged its human cargo of exhausted women from a *maquiladora*. They stepped sleepy-eyed down on to the road while a search dog, which had already sniffed the Escalade, was led on to the vehicle by its handler.

Thick black hair tied back in a ponytail, Rafaela stood in the middle of the throng, her silver police ID clipped to her belt, an AR-15 semi-automatic rifle slung over her shoulders, the barrel pointing to the ground. She watched the search unfold, her feelings a blend of anger, anxiety and awe. If a local woman had been found dead, never mind merely missing, Rafaela would have been there with, perhaps, one or two bored officers and a hard-pressed forensic team, who would have had fifteen minutes to gather what they could before they were called away. Her pleas for more resources and the time to conduct a thorough investigation would have been met with a resigned shrug. No one cared about dead factory girls by the side of the road. The contrast couldn't have been sharper. The size and scale of the operation told her that the cartel wanted Mendez and the missing American girl bad.

At a fresh wail of sirens she looked round and saw a motorcade muscling its way through the jam of black and white Dodge Chargers and Ford F-150s. A sleek black town car stopped less than twenty feet from her, the rear door opened and Zapatero stepped out, sporting full dress uniform and ready to take personal command of the search. He moved among his men, slapping backs and shaking hands. When he spotted Rafaela, his expression tightened.

As he got closer to her, he nodded towards the cell phone she had clasped in her right hand. She had been waiting for a call from one of the Americans. She had risked a call to both of them but Lock's cell phone was switched off and Ty's had defaulted to voicemail.

'I've been trying to reach you,' Zapatero said, business-like. 'You're on duty but you don't answer the phone?'

She thought back to his late-night calls. The heavy breathing. The obscenities. And the following day he would talk to her as if everything was completely normal, even though they both knew what kind of a man he was. Carry on as usual, she thought. The whole country was like that: the crazier things were, the greater the denial. It was the land of the looking glass where an empty SUV drew more police officers than a ton of cocaine or a pile of dead bodies.

Zapatero was waiting for an answer. She feigned surprise. 'I'm sorry, I didn't hear it.'

Clearly he didn't believe her but he didn't press the point. 'Someone saw the American girl,' he said. 'She was here.'

It was as much as Rafaela could do not to laugh in his face. The truck driver, whom she had already spoken to, had mentioned a girl fleeing the scene in another vehicle but he'd had no idea who she was. It had been dark and everything had happened quickly, he'd told her. Even if he had seen more, he would not have mentioned it: in this part of the borderlands, you gave enough information to satisfy the police but not so much that you were seen as too helpful.

'We have a witness who said they saw a young woman. Who told you it was the American girl?'

Zapatero puffed out his cheeks. 'It's disappointing that I should be more aware of the situation than the officer I placed in charge, wouldn't you say?'

Rafaela could think of many words to describe it but disappointing wasn't one of them. She kept her mouth shut, deciding that she had already pushed too hard. Retribution wouldn't come in the shape of a reprimand or a lack of promotion: it would come in the shape of a bullet to the back of the head.

'No matter,' Zapatero continued. 'But we must find her. And the men she was with. They were all American.'

She tried to keep her face set. *How did he know about Lock?*

'Two of them had been arrested previously,' he continued. 'I believe you dealt with them, Detective Carcharon,'

She flushed, and was glad of the darkness as he stared at her.

Fifty-seven

Ty pulled into an alleyway behind a row of shacks, killed the headlights and switched off the engine. The girl was curled up against the passenger door. She had his jacket wrapped around her and her eyes were closed. He pushed the button to crack the window for some fresh air. The stench of rotting food and bad sanitation, the smell of poverty, wafted in on a cold breeze. He closed it again.

After leaving Lock to go after Mendez, he had got off the highway as quickly as he could and pulled into a residential neighborhood. Driving at night, with so many police cars tearing around and no way of knowing who they were really working for, he'd decided that their best chance lay in waiting for sunrise before he contacted the American consulate or made a dash for the border. Anywhere in the world, a strange car in a poor neighborhood was less likely to go reported than one parked in a rich area. A phone call to Rafaela had only confirmed his worst fears. Half the police department had been pulled from their beds with instructions to find him, Lock and Julia.

Conversation with the girl had been minimal. Ty had told her that he was here to return her to her parents but that it was too dangerous to do it directly. She seemed to understand. He didn't ask much about her ordeal. It wasn't his place and, in a way, he didn't want to know the details. Knowledge might cloud his judgement, just as it seemed to have tipped his partner over the edge when he had darted off after Mendez.

It seemed cruel to wake her, but he leaned over and tapped her on the shoulder. She started and opened her eyes.

'Sorry,' he said. 'We're going to park here until sunrise.' He gave a nod towards the back seat. 'I thought you might be more comfortable there. You can stretch out.'

She eyed it with suspicion. He didn't blame her. It would be a long time before she trusted another man.

'Don't worry, I'm going to be right here and staying awake. Don't want anyone sneaking up on us,' he said.

The thought of him standing watch over her while she slept seemed to reassure her. 'Okay, thanks,' she said, clambering into the back. 'I'm so tired.'

'You've been through a lot. Don't worry, I'll wake you when we need to get moving.'

She lay down, knees tucked into her chest. Melissa had slept in a similar position at the hospital in Los Angeles. Ty wondered how many of Mendez's other victims slept like that now, or still had nightmares about their ordeal.

'Tyrone?' the girl asked, as outside a rat scuttled across the alleyway, stopping briefly to size up one of the SUV's tires.

'Yeah?'

'Thank you.'

In the dark, Ty shrugged. He was wondering if this went some way towards atoning for past mistakes, past misdeeds.

'Can I ask you something?' she said.

'Sure, go ahead.'

'The man you were with.'

'Ryan? What about him?'

'Did he go after Charlie?'

Ty didn't say anything at first. He was still unsettled and angry at Lock's change of heart. He had been right in the first place. They should have forgotten Mendez. It was too risky to try to take him and rescue the girl at the same time. But something had changed in Lock when he had seen Mendez across the highway. A dark flame had burned inside him since Carrie's death. He kept it hidden but Ty knew it was there. It had blazed up momentarily when they had been watching the house. It was like a pilot light, burning low but with the capacity to explode into an inferno at any moment – as it had when he had seen Mendez.

'Yes, he did,' Ty said finally.

'Why?'

Ty sighed. 'How long have you got?'

'You said we can't move anywhere until sunrise.'

'You know you're not the first person Charlie Mendez has hurt, right? I mean, you know who he is.'

She nodded. 'I didn't at first. But after, yes . . . I felt so stupid. I'd read about him and heard about what he'd done on the news. I just didn't connect him with the man I met in the bar until it was too late.'

Again, she spared him the details, and he was thankful. He settled into his seat and told her about Melissa, and how he and Lock had come to bring Mendez back to the United States to face justice. At the end of the telling, she raised her head and stared at him. 'That still doesn't explain why he agreed.'

He didn't have it in him to tell her about Carrie's death and Lock's guilt over it – his own guilt about what had happened. Instead, he said, 'You should get some sleep.'

She closed her eyes, and within a minute she was asleep, leaving Ty alone in the driver's seat with his gun, enveloped in the darkness of a place where people too poor to afford dreams made their lives.

Fifty-eight

With the desert landscape still cloaked in darkness, Lock continued his search. A four-armed saguaro cactus loomed over him, spines ready to spear him. He skirted it as the land dipped, then leveled out. For the most part the terrain had been flat and even: ground he could cover at a rapid clip. It was cold but not freezing, and dry.

He could see the outline of a man ahead on a ridge. He was standing perfectly still. Lock held his position. There was no way of knowing whether Mendez knew he was there and was watching him or whether he was simply catching his breath.

The outline moved over the ridge and out of sight. Lock took a bearing from the point he had last seen him and broke into a jog, splitting his attention between the ground beneath his boots and the far horizon. His chest felt tight as his heart protested at the continued exertion. The sweat on his back had cooled and now ran uncomfortably into the crack of his butt. In contrast, his feet were hot and swollen. His boots chafed at the back of his heels and he could almost feel the blisters as they formed. He switched his mind to Melissa, staggering into the hotel lobby, bleeding and so close to death that he had felt its presence as he had rushed her, cradled in his arms, to his car. The image pushed away his fatigue. He doubled his pace, taking measured breaths, every stride drawing him closer to Mendez.

At first he took the distant wash of noise he could hear to be the pounding of the blood in his ears but then it grew louder and more persistent. He stopped for a moment, and turned a full three hundred and sixty degrees, searching out the sound. It was coming from behind him – the distinctive *thwump* of rotor blades slicing through the air. A helicopter was buzzing low overhead, searching them out. A near-celestial arc of light from a front-mounted searchlight swept the landscape.

Lock was closing in on Mendez, but someone up there was closing in on both of them. He'd thought he had hours to hunt down his quarry, but now he realized he had minutes. He broke into a run. The ridge where Mendez had stood moments before was empty. Behind him, he watched the helicopter sweep sharply to his left, then double back.

He scoured the terrain for movement. Nothing. Not that it was barren. Far from it. They had come further than he had imagined. The edge of the city was within striking distance, and with it the urban camouflage that would shield him from the aircraft. But it was also a place for Mendez to find refuge if Lock didn't reach him first.

Fifty-nine

A lone cloud swept silently across the moon, plunging the land into darkness for the briefest of moments. Charlie Mendez watched it pass as the helicopter faded into the distance. The man following him was gone, swallowed by the vast landscape. He had kept moving, putting one foot in front of the other, until his pursuer had been lost in the shadows, and with him Charlie's fear.

He had made it and now straight ahead he could see a row of low buildings. He dug into his front pocket and pulled out a roll of dollars. It was more than enough to buy him sanctuary, a place to hide out until he could be picked up. No one would ask too many questions. No one around here did. People like him, crazy *gringos* in trouble, simply materialized, and then they were gone.

Tired after the long trek, and on the down slope of an adrenalin rush, he started forward. Less than two hundred yards away there was a tiny one-room shack, one wall made from cinder blocks, the others cobbled together from pieces of wood with a corrugated-iron roof. A child's bicycle lay on its side. Next to it were two large cooking pots, left out for the rats and mice to clear. Charlie picked up the bicycle and stood it up. It was too small for him even to attempt to ride it. He let it fall back to the ground.

He kept moving. There were more shacks and, beyond them, he could see lone pairs of headlights signaling a road. Sooner or later he had to find someone who could give him a ride, and if the money didn't cut it he had a back-up plan, something he had rifled from the Escalade.

Sixty

A thousand yards. That was all that stood between Lock and the retreating figure of Mendez as the *colonia* folded around them. Mendez was pushing open a three-bar gate, which guarded the entrance to the row of shacks. Beyond was a road.

The beam of the helicopter patterned the ridge above them, the edge of the cone of light seeping over to touch the shack. As Lock ran, his foot caught on something. He stumbled and fell. The back wheel of a child's bike spun where his trailing leg had caught it. He got back to his feet and set off again, breaking into a full-on sprint.

A car was heading down the road. Mendez had stopped in the middle and was waving his arms, trying to flag it down. Lock still had four hundred yards to go as the car slowed and halted.

As he reached the gate, he saw Mendez lean towards the driver's window, speaking to the driver, and waving something at him or her. The next word he heard was '*Gracias*', and then Mendez was skirting around the car. Drawing his weapon, Lock screamed at the driver to stop as the helicopter roared above him and he was engulfed in a blinding light.

The car – clearly the driver had thought better of their offer – sped away, leaving Mendez stranded in the middle of the road. The helicopter dropped lower, Lock still in the circle of light, as people emerged from the nearby shacks, roused by the commotion, curiosity getting the snap on fear.

Lock ran towards Mendez, aware that he could be taken down at any minute by a hail of gunfire from the helicopter. For a second, Mendez seemed paralyzed by Lock's sudden appearance or, perhaps, by how close he'd been to getting away. He stared after the departing car. When he looked back, Lock was a hundred yards from him, and the circle of light was covering both men as the helicopter rose into the air on an updraught of desert wind.

Lock gun-faced him. 'Don't move!'

But Mendez wasn't about to start doing as he was told. He pivoted round and made a break for a patch of ground next to the road, beyond which was another set of shacks, the fringe of a bigger, more densely packed *colonia*.

The blacktop behind Mendez splintered as a couple of rounds dug into the tarmac. They had come from the helicopter because Lock had yet to fire. It banked to one side, the pilot moving into position so that whoever was firing had a better angle from which to take out Mendez.

Mendez zigzagged across the ground as the helicopter moved alongside him, the pilot struggling to keep it steady, the searchlight punching its cone of light into the *colonia*. Lock saw the barrel of a semi-automatic pop out from the side door as another gust of desert wind caught the helicopter, lifting it fractionally and taking out the gunman's angle.

He took the shot anyway, the mark of an amateur, and a three-round burst fractured the air, threatening everyone but Mendez. The downside of the maneuver was that the searchlight lost Mendez as he sprinted towards the *colonia*.

Lock went after him, temporarily holstering his weapon, and charging over ground littered with broken glass. Mendez slipped through a gap between two houses as the downdraught from the aircraft blew up a thick cloud of dust.

In the narrow alley, as the helicopter climbed, Lock looked around. There was no sign of Mendez. He walked slowly now, trying to block out the noise of the thrashing rotor blades and pick out his target, but it was an impossible task.

The alley, if it qualified for alley status, was about three feet wide and ran for about eighteen. It seemed devoid of life. Lock slowed before he stepped out into the street – and from nowhere a fist slammed into the side of his face just below the right eye, throwing him off balance.

Lock stumbled, taking two steps back, then found his balance and moved on to his toes, like a boxer. He shook his head, centered himself and looked to his left. Charlie Mendez was right there, but he had frozen again. Lock rushed him, driving his shoulder hard up into Mendez's chest, catching him slap-bang in the solar plexus. He followed with two quick but full-force elbows to the man's face. By the time the second landed, Mendez had his hands up but Lock hadn't finished. Stepping in close, he butted his opponent full in the face, hearing the satisfying dull crunch of the cartilage in his nose cracking with the force of the blow. Mendez let out a whimper as Lock stepped back, fished in a pocket for some plastic ties and went to work securing his wrists. When they were cinched tight enough to be painful, Lock gave him the fastest of pat-downs.

With the helicopter directing reinforcements straight towards them, Lock propelled his prisoner forwards, down the street, as a sea of small brown faces peered from the houses, only to be dragged away from the windows by mothers and grandmothers.

He felt no sense of accomplishment. If at all, it would come later. He had Mendez but the chances of being able to keep him long enough to get him back across the border were slim. And if the action of the gunman who had fired from the helicopter was anything to go by, Mendez's protectors had experienced a change of heart. If they both stayed alive long enough, Lock might even discover why.

In the meantime, he pushed the whining Mendez down the narrow street, praying for a miracle with every step he took.

Sixty-one

The American consulate was housed on the third floor of a down-
town office building. Once they had stepped inside no one outside
could do anything to either Ty or Julia. Consulates and embassies
counted as American soil so, to all intents and purposes, they
would be on home turf. But there was a snag.

The consulate didn't open for another hour and, right now,
reaching it in one piece was looking about as likely as fashioning
a rocket out of baking trays and flying to the moon. Hunched
over the steering-wheel, Ty watched as the traffic snaked along the
road towards a police checkpoint. Twenty vehicles ahead, a squad
of local cops were interrogating a smartly dressed man, who was
leaning out of his car, no doubt protesting at the lengthy delay.

Julia shuffled forward from the back seat. 'Can't we just ask
those cops there to give us an escort?'

'We could,' Ty growled. 'The only problem is they might just
escort us somewhere else instead. Like right back to the people
who were looking after Charlie Mendez.'

'The police?'

Ty thought back to when he'd been that naïve about the world. Nope, his memory didn't go back that far. Not that he blamed Julia: we were all products of our experience and her experience, growing up as a white, middle-class American in a loving family, had left her lacking the necessary insight into just how messed up large parts of the planet actually were. In her world, cops were on your side. Down here some of them were, and some of them were with the bad guys. The problem was that they both wore the same uniform, so there was no knowing for sure which type an individual was.

A few feet ahead there was a side street. Ty waited until he was sure the cops running the checkpoint were busy, then spun the wheel and turned down it. Cars parked on either side meant that he had to squeeze past yet another Policia Federal Dodge Charger, driving in the opposite direction. The driver was in a hurry and didn't check them out.

'What are you doing? Why are you turning off?' Julia asked, her voice panicked and rising in pitch and volume as he tried to stay aware of everything around them and get round the checkpoint.

'What does it look like I'm doing? I'm trying to get us there safely,' Ty barked. The road was widening but any extra room was taken up by food stalls and street vendors. Even at this early hour, crowds of people milled around. Something about the area was beginning to look familiar to him, but his mind might have been playing tricks.

He glanced in the rear-view mirror and saw that Julia's face was pressed against the window. 'Sit back. Someone might see you.'

It was already too late. The SUV, even with the tinted glass, was drawing gawkers on either side. This was hardly a tourist area.

Two small boys, brothers by the look of them, raced over to Ty's window, jumping up to tap on the glass, smiling excitedly and motioning for him to lower the window. He kept it closed. Give them a few pesos and it would only draw more kids and more attention. An old man wearing a straw hat and drawing hard on an unfiltered cigarette eyed them warily from the corner.

Ty nudged the RAV 4 forward, but the car ahead of him had stopped to allow an old lady to cross the road. Dressed in black, perhaps fresh from morning mass, she took her time as Ty's long fingers drummed on the steering-wheel and he searched for an escape route. Barring mowing down the old lady or squelching the kids, who were still running alongside and tapping at the glass, there was nothing to do but wait.

As the old lady cleared the road, Ty pressed down on the horn. The vehicle in front stayed put. He pulled out, trying to get an angle to see if he could get round it. It looked too tight a squeeze. It inched forward again and he dropped back in behind it, eyes flicking from rear-view to side mirrors as he watched for any sudden movement from the crowd.

In the back seat, Julia was growing agitated. Ty had seen it before in Iraq: some people made it through the most traumatic situations by surfing on a tide of grit and adrenalin, only for the wheels to come off as they neared safety. The mind simply wasn't built to contain what Julia must have endured at the hands of Mendez.

'Why don't we just get out and walk?' she asked suddenly.

'Hey, be cool for me, 'kay? The traffic will clear in a minute.'

She was rocking back and forth. He saw her arm move. 'I can't breathe in here. I need to get some air.'

As she reached for the handle to open the door, his hand

shot out and the central-locking clicked into place with a *thunk*.

'What are you doing?' she screamed. 'You're not taking me to my parents, are you? Who are you?'

Inching forward, Ty hit the brakes then the button to unlock the doors. 'You want to get out? Be my guest. But you're on your own. Now, I know you've been through hell. I get that. But if they catch us, you might be safe, you might not, but I am definitely going to be dead. So, if you don't trust me, go. You're not the only one who's scared here. You hear me?'

He eyed her in the mirror. His words seemed to be having an effect. Her chin slumped to her chest and she lapsed into silence

Ahead the traffic was moving, not in fits and starts but at a steady clip. They were getting past the last of the street vendors. Ty glanced at the GPS. They had less than a mile to go before they reached the consulate building. Less than a mile to safety.

He settled back into his seat, and checked the sat-nav screen in front of him, plotting a route through the side-streets that would take him close to the consulate. His plan was to leave the vehicle somewhere close by, make the phone call, and then, before word could leak from anyone at the consulate to the local authorities, walk her in. If he was stopped, he would inform whoever was doing the stopping that the consulate officials already knew they were there. He doubted any regular cop, no matter how corrupt or plugged into the cartel, would have the balls to block their safe passage at that point.

His eyes flicked back to Julia just as she glanced to her right. Her pupils snapped from pinpricks to full dilation faster than he had ever seen. She opened her mouth and began to scream.

Sixty-two

The hollowed-out eye sockets of Santa Muerte stared back at Julia through tangles of damp white hair. A part of her rational mind knew it was just a shrine, just a skeleton dressed as a woman, but that part was a lost, lonely voice drowned by a cacophony of others screaming at her, telling her that she had to get the hell out of there – now.

She opened the door and stepped out into the road. The people clustered around the shrine turned to look. A heroin-thin man shuffled towards her, eyes as vacant as those of the saint he had come to worship. A fat girl with a baby wedged against her hip whispered something to an older woman. All the while, Santa Muerte shot that demonic smile in Julia's direction.

She jumped as she felt a hand in the small of her back. Someone giggled at her reaction, the laughter rippling through the crowd. She spun round to see Ty.

'We have to get out of here, Julia. You understand me?'

Her eyes flicked to the row of gifts laid at the skeleton's feet.

Cigarettes and bottles of beer and tequila jostled with baby bootees and tourist-tat jewelery.

'Who is she?' she asked Ty.

He hesitated. 'It's some messed up bullshit is all. Now, let's go.'

She didn't move. 'I asked who she is.'

'Santa Muerte,' he said.

Muerte. She knew that word. *Muerte* was Spanish for 'death'. *Santa Muerte*. Saint Death.

The junkie had stepped from the semi-circle of the crowd towards her. He had his hand out, asking her for money. Ty took a step towards him, 'Back off, asshole,' his hand resting on the butt of his handgun. The junkie lurched back into the crowd, spitting at Ty's feet as he went.

'Okay,' he said to her quietly. 'You have until the count of three. When I hit three you are on your own, Julia. You got me?'

She said nothing. She knew she had to leave, that she had no choice if she wanted to stay alive, but the shrine was drawing her towards it.

'One.' His voice betrayed the weakness of a parent who has threatened a sanction they're not sure they'll be able to deliver.

'Two.'

She turned back towards the SUV, ready to get back in but his hand grasped her elbow. 'No,' he said. 'Too many people have seen us now. Seen the vehicle we're in. We're going to have to walk.'

Tears bulged at the corners of her eyes. Her lack of control had made the hole they were in even deeper than it had been. 'I'm sorry.'

'Save it,' said Ty. A huge arm folded over her back and he led her meekly away from the shrine. She glanced back at the vehicle, abandoned in the middle of the road, the rear passenger door still open.

Ty set a brisk pace but eventually he had to slow down. The only way she would have been able to match his long, loping strides would have been if she had jogged and she was too tired for that. Beyond the shrine, he shepherded her down a side-street, away from the prying eyes of the crowd, who, no doubt, were still discussing the behavior of the two crazy Americans who had offered up an SUV to Saint Death.

The GPS clasped in his hand, Ty was busy recalculating their route. He turned down the volume and zoomed out, trying to commit the new route to memory, aware that he would need his eyes on the girl and the surrounding streets rather than the screen.

They had under a mile to cover. Given the traffic, walking wouldn't take much longer than driving. They might be more mobile too, and it would be easier to adjust their route, to duck into a doorway if he saw the cops. The drawback was that they were both exposed. You could hide in a car. Now everyone they passed could see them.

As they walked, he scanned the buildings. He and Julia drew interest but it lasted no more than half a block.

He wondered how long it would take the cops to find the abandoned RAV 4 and work out who the occupants had been. Less time than it would take him and the girl to cover the mile, that was for sure. And if they knew he had her so close to the consulate they would be able to figure where they were headed.

At the end of the block, he spotted a store with racks of clothes left out on the sidewalk. As they reached it, he guided Julia in as a Federal Policía car sped down the next street. 'What are we doing?' she asked.

Three minutes later and fifty dollars lighter (twenty for the clothes and thirty for the owner's silence), they emerged from the store, the girl's long hair tucked up under a baseball cap, both of them wearing long sleeves, the tall man with a wind-breaker zipped up to his chin. Hand in hand, they strolled across the street, without a care in the world.

Looking ahead, Ty swore that if he pulled this off he would head back to that old witch Santa Muerte and leave her the biggest goddamn spliff he could find, with a whole goddamn case of tequila.

Sixty-three

Lock hunkered down next to the thin plywood door of the one-room shack where he was holed up with Charlie Mendez. Outside, a group of children were busy kicking a soccer ball. Behind him, Mendez was sprawled on a threadbare floral couch, his chest rising and falling as he slept. Sunlight splashed lazily through a Perspex window, etching a yellow square on the bare floorboards. The facilities were meagre – a chemical toilet out back, but no electricity.

After a nerve-shredding night spent one step ahead of the police search party, they had chanced upon the owner, a heavy-set middle-aged woman, as she was leaving for work at around four in the morning. As soon as she had turned the corner at the end of the street, Lock had snuck them inside, figuring they would probably have the place to themselves until early evening when she would return from one of the factories or a day spent cleaning rich people's houses.

Mendez had fallen asleep quickly, the exhaustion of the pursuit and the consequent huge dump of adrenalin taking its toll. Lock had kept guard by the door. A cursory check of the GPS on his cell phone, before he had powered it down, had given him their position.

They were approximately five miles north of the city centre, and south of the Rio Grande by less than a mile. To the west lay the highway they had fled. To the east lay the desert. But to the north lay another highway where headlights twinkled in the distance, and that highway lay in the United States. They were closer than he would have dared believe possible, but it was an agonizing proximity.

Though the distance may have been less than a mile, more and more cops were pouring into the *colonia* with every minute that passed, and even if they could make good their escape, they still had to cross the border. Ten, even five years ago, it would have been a matter of wading the river. But now they faced not only the river but a whole host of defenses aimed at keeping people out of the United States. The irony of an American trying to break back into his own country wasn't lost on him but that was what he faced, and the plain fact of the matter was that they wouldn't be able to achieve it during daylight. They would have to sit out a long day and wait until night fell again.

On the up-side, he had Mendez, and the shots aimed at him from the helicopter had made him broadly compliant. Mendez knew that, on his own, he was most probably dead. The knowledge had served – it often did – as a calming influence. Lock wasn't sure how long it would last but Mendez was aware that, at this very second, the only person who appeared even vaguely interested in him staying alive was Lock. If it hadn't been for him, he'd already be dead.

Sixty-four

Ty stood at the edge of the crossing, directly opposite the office building that held the consulate, and gave Julia's hand a reassuring squeeze. He had talked to her the whole way there, as they played the part of a happy couple, trying to keep her calm. He had asked her about her family, about her memories of growing up. Safe stuff designed to reassure.

The walk had gone quickly. There had been a moment when, darting through traffic, a motorcycle cop had stopped to stare at them. Ty had bluffed with a friendly wave, and that single nonchalant act had been enough to satisfy the cop's curiosity as he took off with a macho twist of his handlebars.

It was as they started to cross that Ty noticed the two men. Both Hispanic, both wearing wrap-around sunglasses, each man posted within twenty yards of the two entrances to the consulate building. They might have been working for the Americans – US consulates were often staffed by locals and now, with military resources stretched, regularly used private security. As they hit the opposite sidewalk and Julia made towards the nearest entrance, a set of glass double doors, Ty pulled her in the opposite direction towards a row of stores on the ground floor of the building.

He cursed his own stupidity. If the cartel and their buddies had guessed that he wasn't going to risk the border crossing, where they could easily be detained in Mexico on a pretext, and instead head straight for the the consulate, they wouldn't have cops on show to scare them off. They would be watching from the shadows. A spider didn't sit in the middle of a web waiting for the fly: he clung to the edges.

Ty studied the storefronts. 'Here,' he said, guiding her towards a nail salon as one of the men swiveled around to watch them.

Inside, the salon was quiet. The owner bustled over and, without asking, got Julia to sit down. Ty pulled out his cell phone and motioned towards the back of the salon. 'Okay if I make a call back there?'

'What's wrong?' Julia asked, as the owner shrugged in agreement.

'Just be cool.'

Ty stepped away and pulled up the number Lock had given him. A few seconds later a woman answered, speaking in English but with an accent: 'American Citizen Services Unit.'

Without explaining who he was or why he was calling, Ty asked to be put through to a member of the consular staff. He was put on hold. The phone pressed to his ear, he walked to the front of the store and peered out. The two men he had spotted were standing next to each other now. One was nodding towards Ty, who was only partially obscured by the gaudy stenciled advertising plastered across the window.

Finally there was a click, and for a second he thought he had been cut off or placed in some kind of automated queue. A second later there was a voice, a real live human being. 'How may I help you?'

He stepped away from the window, and started to speak. He gave the man at the end of the line Julia's name and explained that they were across the street but that two men were positioned outside the consulate who, he believed, had been placed there by people who wished to prevent Julia's safe return to her family.

'Mr Johnson, please stay on the line, and I'll be right back to you.'

Before he had a chance to protest he was put on hold. He walked back to the window and took a peek. The two men were still in heated discussion. One was on a radio. Not a cell phone but a walkie-talkie. From the corner of his eye, Ty caught a flash of red light as a patrol car sped down the avenue. The two men watched it pull up not far from them. Walkie-talkie Man keyed his radio again. At the same time the consular official came back on the line.

'Mr Johnson, I want you and Julia to stay exactly where you are. If you have a weapon please do not draw it. Do you understand me?'

'Yeah, got it.'

The patrol car was joined by another. One of the two men, the one without the radio, broke off to go and speak to the cops as the one with the radio started towards the salon. The owner, completely oblivious to the scene unfolding outside, remonstrated with Julia, who was fidgeting in her seat.

Walkie-talkie Man was walking at a clip now, his right hand dropping into his jacket and under his left shoulder. Not wishing to be overheard, Ty killed the call. He didn't know what kind of bullshit was going down and he wasn't about to stick around to find out. *Sit tight, my ass.*

He crossed to Julia. 'We gotta go,' he said, tossing twenty bucks in the direction of the protesting salon owner, for whom a half-finished manicure was clearly some severe breach of beauty-shop etiquette.

Walkie-talkie Man was no more than ten seconds from the door. His partner's discussion with a cop who had got out of the patrol car was proving animated.

Ty turned to the salon owner as he pulled Julia to the back of the store. 'You have a way out back here?'

She stared at him, uncomprehending. Julia tried to translate her few words of stitched-together Spanish, earning a shake of the head and a finger pointed at the front door, which was now open-ing as Walkie-talkie Man shouldered his way through. Beyond him the Federales were making their move too, running not walk-ing towards the salon.

Ty's right hand came up, with the gun, finger on the trigger.

Walkie-talkie Man froze. 'Dude, chill out,' he said, his accent pure California surfer. 'I'm from the consulate. We've been wait-ing for you. If you hadn't stopped to get your goddamn nails filed we would have had you inside by now.'

Ty lowered the gun. The guy flashed his State Department identification to prove his point and apologized in fluent Spanish to the salon lady. He motioned Julia towards him. 'Stay close. They're going to give us some static but they touch you and I have four men across the street ready to turn this place into the goddamn Alamo.'

Julia managed a smile, which soon dissolved into tears of relief. The State Department official, whose ID had him down as

Armando Hernandez, turned to Ty. 'You too. Stay close to me. You're not exactly flavor of the month with some of these assholes.'

He walked them to the door, shielding Julia with his stocky frame as Ty brought up the rear. Halfway across the street, he glanced back at Ty. 'Kind of disappointed in you, Mr Johnson. All us Hispanics look alike to you or something?'

Sixty-five

Rafaela walked back into her apartment, threw her bag and keys on to the kitchen counter and took off her jacket, but kept on her holster with her loaded service weapon. She had been relieved of her duties pending an official inquiry into the 'unauthorized release of the two Americans': her boss wanted her out of the way while he assured the consul general that everything was being done to find Charlie Mendez. That part was true enough. For once they weren't just putting on a show. They did want Mendez – and Lock – just not alive and talking.

She filled a plastic jug from the kitchen tap and watered the plants out on her little terrace balcony. After the death of her husband and everything that had followed, she had clung to work, though in her darker moments she told herself that she was more social worker than cop. Cops found the bad guys, gathered evidence and made sure they were put behind bars. Rafaela picked up the rag-doll bodies of young women from the streets and comforted their heartbroken parents as best she could. *What good was that? What good was she?* The bodies piled up anyway and she made no difference. The streets weren't any safer. Worst of all, the dead girls weren't even the main event: they were a sideshow. Sure, the media got excited as they speculated on the serial killer or killers but really they were nothing. There was a war on drugs. There would never be a war on the rape and torture of young women.

She put the jug away in a kitchen cupboard, walked into the bathroom, took off her clothes, dumping them in a small wicker laundry basket, and turned on the shower. She hung the holster with her service weapon on a hook at the back of the door, stepped into the shower and closed her eyes as the hot water pounded her face.

Sixty-six

Hector parked around the corner and made a final check of the address. He should have been happy. For one, he was alive, not chopped into pieces in the bathtub of a rent-by-the-hour motel at the edge of town. For another he was back to his regular job, working as a *sicario*. He had been granted something rarely afforded by his boss: a chance to redeem himself. Two weeks ago, he would have welcomed it, and in some way he still did. A man doing a job he felt ill-suited to couldn't be happy and Hector was a man who had defined himself, like so many men, by his work. He enjoyed the fact that he was useful and that his work was valued. But ever since the American girl's kidnap something in him had changed.

Walking up to the entrance of the apartment building, he tried to put this shift in his thinking to one side. Second chances in his world were a rarity.

He pressed the buzzer above the one he needed. I have a chance to redeem myself, he thought. A woman answered, and he muttered something about delivering a parcel to one of the other apartments. He waited. A few seconds later a window opened above him. He kept looking straight ahead so that all she caught was the top of his navy blue baseball cap. She called down and buzzed him inside.

There were four apartments on each floor, two at the front and two at the back. The one he was looking for was on the front right-hand side if you faced the building from the street. He knew his target was there because he had seen her a few minutes before, watering the plants on the tiny balcony.

He rested his hand on the balustrade at the bottom of the staircase and started to make his way up. After only one flight, he was sweating. It wasn't hot but the stairwell was stuffy and he'd had to wear a jacket, plus he was carrying the big brown leather bag that usually accompanied him on a job like this. It held his special knives. For the most part there were two broad types of job. In the first they wanted the person dead quickly with the minimum of fuss. This one was of the second type, in which they wished to send a message. Message killings were messy.

On the landing, he stopped to catch his breath. That had been the other problem with babysitting Charlie Mendez. All the sitting around had left him out of shape. Once this job was done, he would change that with a few workouts. He had a friend with a boxing gym in the south of the city. He would go there. He made it a promise to himself. It took more than strength to kill someone, it took stamina as well. People fought, and the ones you least expected to be a problem were often the most difficult to kill.

He took the second flight at a steadier pace. This time he didn't stop on the landing but kept going. He stayed out of sight of the door and took a moment to compose himself. It was only when he looked over that he saw it was already ajar. Immediately, he was on guard.

He glanced around and saw that the apartment door diagonally opposite was also open. He could hear women's voices. He tuned into the conversation. One woman was saying how she had to go out of town and would the other take a key.

Hector looked at the two chains dangling by the door and the two deadbolts. He knew better than to hesitate. He walked into the apartment, and pulled the door back to the position it had been in when he had arrived.

Inside, the apartment was neat. A damp towel lay over a stool next to the kitchen counter. He didn't want the woman screaming if she saw him as soon as she walked in so he decided to wait in the bathroom. Locks and chains worked in two ways: when he heard the apartment door close and the chains go in he would emerge. He crossed to an iPod docking station. The woman's iPod was already in it. He cued up a track, hit pause and lifted the volume by five or six notches. He found the small white remote control for it on a table next to the couch and picked it up. The music would cover him long enough to place the tape around her mouth. She would fight, he knew that for sure. A woman like her knew where this would end.

The remote in one hand, he retreated to the bathroom. The floor was still wet around a white mat laid on the floor and condensation fogged the mirror. He was glad. He didn't enjoy looking at himself. He sat down on the toilet and waited for the woman to return.

Sixty-seven

Armando Hernandez took a slug of water from an Evian bottle, and offered some to Ty, who declined with a wave of his hand. They were in a conference room with long windows that looked out on to the avenue. Posters on the wall advised tourists to be cautious when they were out at night. Hernandez cleared his throat. 'You and your buddy Lock think you just stumbled into the middle of this fucking mess and worked it all out while we were sitting round here like a bunch of hicks? Mendez was being left where he was for a reason.'

Ty didn't like getting lectures, not from some college kid like Armando Hernandez, not from anyone. 'And the girl was what exactly?' he asked.

Hernandez rolled his neck. 'No one saw that coming. Not the traffickers, not us, not anyone. In that regard, Mendez had been behaving himself. Anyway, she's safe now.'

Fists clenched, Ty bit down on his lower lip. 'And that's it? She was *raped*. By a guy you knew was here. But, hey, you're trying to bust these dudes so what's a little collateral damage, right? I *served*, motherfucker, so I know how shit like this goes – people get thrown under the bus so that someone else can make a name for themselves. But don't try and piss on my leg and tell me it's raining. You assholes turned to look the other way. If it wasn't for Ryan and me, she'd be hanging out at that ranch like a frickin' piñata. Now, what you gonna do about finding my boy?'

'You don't even know where he is.'

Ty said nothing.

Hernandez walked over to the window and tapped the glass with the knuckle of his right index finger. 'In case you haven't noticed, Mr Johnson, we're not in Kansas any more. Mexico is a sovereign state so we have to work with the local authorities.'

'That's a joke, right? The authorities here? They're in on it.'

'And what do you suggest? We call them up and tell them that? This entire situation is a mess and it's way bigger than me or you or your buddy or some scumbag like Charlie Mendez.' He gestured for Ty to sit back down.

'I'll stand,' said Ty, irritated.

'When you first spoke to me, you said that your buddy had Mendez and he'd be heading for the border. If they're on foot there's probably only a twenty-mile stretch either way where they'd be looking to cross. If we can find them and if they can make it even an inch on to American soil we can help, but the way things are right now, that's the best we can do.'

'If anyone can get across, Lock can,' said Ty.

'Then that's good. Believe me, we want Mendez alive too. He's the key to a lot of stuff. Now, what's your plan, Mr Johnson?'

Ty looked out on to the avenue where cops were still massing. Right now the city was a symphony of sirens. The military were out too, along with the local police, the Federal Policia and numerous special units. Moments before there had been a stand-off between a small group of soldiers and some cops. Hernandez had explained that, after it had given up on certain sections of the civilian police as too corrupt even to attempt reform, the government had been using the military instead. But even that hadn't been without its problems: members of Mexican special forces had been offered lavish amounts of money to work for the cartels. It was one massive pissing contest in which no one had any real way of knowing precisely where a lot of loyalties lay.

'I go out there, I don't stand much chance, do I?' said Ty.

Hernandez folded his arms. 'You stand no chance and we can't protect you.'

'Who are you going to have looking for them?'

'Border Patrol for Lock. US Marshals for Mendez. We're pulling some strings.'

'What about Rafaela Carcharon?' Ty asked.

'We have people trying to contact her. From what you've said she could be an important intelligence resource. She comes in, we can help her out.'

'You haven't heard from her?' Ty asked, with another glance at the window.

Hernandez seemed to read his mind. 'One white knight out there is about our limit right now. You step outside the consulate, you're on your own.'

Ty started towards the door. 'Way I see it, we've been on our own from the jump.'

Hernandez got up, blocking his passage. 'I already said, there's a lot more to this.'

'But you won't share?' Ty asked.

'It's not a question of won't. I can't.'

Sixty-eight

Her service weapon raised, Rafaela nudged the apartment door open with her toe and stepped inside. She waited, listening for the sound of movement, but none came.

Across the border, she would have walked downstairs and called the cops. Here, she was the cops and, in all likelihood, so was the delivery man who had come to take her life. Alerted by the sound of the bell and of another neighbor shouting down to the street, she had watched him walk up the stairs and into her apartment. The only thing that surprised her was how quickly they had moved to kill her. Usually when something big was going down, the cartels waited in the long grass for a while. It was clear from the *sicario*'s arrival that they wanted her dead quickly for a reason.

She moved into the living room, anticipating the rush of a body only to be met by stillness. Gun arm out, she moved towards the tiny balcony, approaching it side on so that she never exposed her back to the interior. The balcony was empty. She moved back into the body of the apartment, finding nothing.

Then she noticed the closed bathroom door.

She lowered her weapon. She could shoot through the door and hope to get lucky but even if she caught him it would create one hell of a mess. And she didn't want the man dead, not yet anyway.

She moved back, gathering her bag and car keys, making sure that it would be audible to the man waiting in her bathroom. She went to the door and slammed it shut then threw the locks but left the chains where they were. As quietly as she could, she took up a position facing the bathroom door and stood there.

Less than three minutes later, she heard a deep sigh followed by the splash of water. A minute after that the door opened. She already had the gun raised and level, the hammer thrown back, her finger on the trigger.

The man she knew as Hector, bodyguard to Charlie Mendez, and one of the most prolific *sicarios* operating in the borderlands, as well as a serving police officer, stepped out of the bathroom and looked at her. There was no wry smile on his face, no sign of irritation either, but neither was there any fear. If anything, she was looking at what she thought she would never see. Someone who was as world-weary and exhausted by life as she was.

He shrugged. 'I'll get rid of my weapon, okay?'

She nodded, watching him carefully as he removed it from the holster, ejected the clip, put both down separately and slid them with his foot across the floor towards her.

'Raise your arms above your head and turn around,' she said.

He did as she asked, although it was more of a shuffle than a turn. She knelt down and picked up the clip and the gun. She emptied the clip and made sure the chamber was clear. When she was finished she asked him to turn back to face her.

A silence settled between them.

'You came to kill me?' she asked him.

He gave a nod, staring at her with the same sad eyes. 'Yes.'

At least he was honest, Rafaela thought. Stepping back, she motioned for Hector to move ahead of her. 'You're alone?' she asked, careful not to turn her back to him.

'That's how I work. It's better that way.'

She motioned for him to take a seat on the couch. She could hear it creak as he sank down into it, the cushions folding in under him. He looked up at her. 'What now?' The question drew a smile. 'You found me in your apartment, you know why I'm here. You have a badge. And a gun. You kill me, it would be accepted.'

'But you're a fellow officer,' she said.

'You know what I am,' he replied.

He tilted his head back and looked up at the ceiling. 'It's what I would do if I were you.'

'Is it that or is it that you don't want to live?'

His huge shoulders heaved. 'I live. I don't live. If I cared about my life how could I do these things? You're no different either. If you were, you would have left the city by now because you know that when I'm gone they'll send someone else and they'll keep sending them until you're gone, too.'

He didn't say it as though he was making a threat. There was no menace, no macho bravado. He spoke softly, his voice barely reaching a whisper. He was simply stating facts. He had raised a good question too. Why hadn't she left? With what she knew she could have made a deal with the Americans and been relocated in return for information. But then what? America wasn't her home. This was her home and, contrary to what the Americans believed, not every Mexican dreamed of a life across the border. Rafaela didn't want the American Dream, she simply wished to see an end to the Mexican nightmare. She wanted her country back, just like the majority of its people.

The problem wasn't simply the violence. It was the creeping acceptance that came with it. At first, as the cartels had become more extreme, there had been protest marches, and reporters, like her husband, along with other people had spoken out. Then they had begun to kill those who dared to remonstrate.

She crossed to the kitchen counter and picked up the thick blue binder that held the pictures of the dead girls. Her girls. Still holding the gun, she walked back to the man and tossed it towards him. He looked at it, confused.

'What's this?' he asked.

She dug a little handheld voice recorder from her bag and clicked on the record button, then placed it on the arm of the couch.

'I want you to tell me which ones you know about. And I want you to tell me everything.'

He opened the binder and caught sight of the first girl in her confirmation dress. In his eyes, she saw recognition. He glanced up at her and said softly, 'Do you believe in God?'

Rafaela nodded. 'I believe in the devil so, yes, I believe in God.'

'I'm lost, Detective,' he said, tears welling in his eyes. 'I am so lost.'

Sixty-nine

The road outside the shack grew quiet, the kids' soccer game finding its way gradually down the street. The last police patrol had passed more than an hour ago. Two cops had tried the door, which Lock had long since bolted from the inside, and a neighbor had come out to inform them that the lady who lived there was at work and the place was empty. They had moved on without making any further checks.

Mendez was sitting on the edge of the battered couch and rubbing his eyes, a man coming to terms with his new circumstances. Lock had dug some stale corn tortillas from a cupboard along with some overripe brown avocados. He split open the avocados with his Gerber knife, took out the stone in the centre, scooped out the browny-green flesh and mushed it over two tortillas, which he then rolled up into wraps. Beggars couldn't be choosers. He took one and handed the other to Mendez.

Mendez took the food without a word and a long moment passed as both men ate in silence, chewing as little as possible and swallowing as fast as they could. Lock opened a soda bottle that was half full of water, took a slug and passed it to Mendez. He gulped and passed it back.

After a few more moments had passed, Mendez finally looked up at him. 'You have a name, bounty hunter?'

'Nope,' said Lock.

'No name?'

'Okay.' Lock sighed. 'If it makes you feel any better, you can call me asshole.'

Mendez waved the stump of his rolled-up tortilla at him. 'You know what happened to the other guys who tried to take me back across the border, right, bounty hunter?'

Lock nodded. 'Sure do, but aren't you forgetting something?'

'What's that, bounty hunter?'

'Well, I'd say that, judging by the pot shots they were taking at you last night from that helicopter, you've just about worn out your welcome down here.'

Mendez's gaze fell to the bare floorboards. He took a final bite, chewed briefly, then swallowed. Last night, Lock had seen the terror in his eyes but it hadn't taken Charlie Mendez long to revert to the smug, self-satisfied moron that Lock had anticipated.

'That's true,' said Mendez. 'You've got me there.'

He was working his way up to something, Lock could feel it. His predatory little mind was turning over, the cogs clicking away.

'So, how much do you pick up when you hand me over?' Mendez asked him. 'Guy like you gets – what? Ten per cent? That's right, isn't it?'

Lock shrugged. 'Something like that.' In truth, he had no real idea how it worked. He wasn't even sure that someone in his position was able to collect part of the bond. And if he was entitled to the money, he had no interest in it. Money only interested him in as far as it allowed him to be his own man, not beholden to anyone. Other than that, he thought of it as merely a tool, a means to an end, and certainly not something that you accumulated as an end in itself. Having enough money could buy you freedom, but too much became its own prison. He had looked after enough wealthy people to know that.

Mendez, though, was warming to the topic. Unsurprisingly, for him money was clearly one way to manipulate people. 'You know, a couple of hundred grand is chicken feed compared to what you could make,' he said matter-of-factly.

Lock smiled. 'You mean if I don't hand you back to the authorities when we get you back home? If instead I smuggled you out of the country or let you go.'

Mendez returned a smile that showed he was used to having his way. 'That's right. So, what do you say, bounty hunter? You want to make some real money?'

'I'd say there's about as much chance of me helping you out as there is of the Iranian government legalizing gay marriage.'

'Come on, bounty hunter. Everyone has a price. Half a million bucks. That's got to be double what you'd get for handing me back.'

'Forget it,' said Lock. 'This isn't about money.'

Mendez's grin grew broader, as if what Lock had just said was utterly alien, which it probably was to a man like him. Lock didn't feel like explaining so he didn't add anything.

'This is personal to you?'

Lock stared.

Mendez leaned forward. 'I'm right, aren't I?'

Lock sensed where Mendez was about to take this and he didn't like it. This wasn't a conversation he wanted to have. It was all too raw. He could feel anger rising in him. If he allowed it to boil over, he would have no way of stopping it. He had promised Melissa to bring Mendez back alive. He wanted to keep his word and, by doing so, h o n o r her death. Also, he wanted Julia to have the chance to face the man who had drugged and molested her.

'I've had that look you're giving me now plenty,' Mendez went on. 'First I thought it was disgust, or pity, or both. But you know what I think it really is? I think you're all jealous because I go and do what most men would like to.'

'Jealous of a scumbag rapist? I don't think so,' Lock said, reaching down and clamping a hand around Mendez's throat tightly enough to stop him breathing. 'There have been sick assholes like you before now, there'll be sick assholes like you after, same as there'll be men like me to make sure they exit the gene pool. That's all there is to know about this little situation we find ourselves in.'

Mendez grasped at Lock's arm with both hands but his captor was too strong. His eyes bulged, and his face flushed as Lock squeezed harder.

Seventy

Eyes wet with tears, Hector's finger traced the outline of the girl's face. She had been seventeen when she had died. She had worked in a *maquiladora* owned by one of the businessmen Federico funded. She had been the prettiest girl in a place where there were many pretty girls. When Managua had made a campaign visit to the factory, she had caught his eye. A few days later, she had been held back after her shift ended, ostensibly to talk to the factory owner about a promotion. He had kept her so long that when she had left the bus that would have taken her home had gone. She had walked to catch a regular city bus, which had given Hector his opportunity. He had known she would miss her bus home.

He had done his job as best he could, reassuring her that everything would be okay. He had driven her to the ranch. There had been no American bounty hunters to stop him. After Managua and the others had finished, Hector had taken her to a plot of waste ground a half-mile from the factory and ended her life.

Then he had driven home and got so drunk that he had severed a tendon in his left arm: a shard of glass from the tequila bottle he had thrown at the wall ricocheted back towards him. Her name had been Maria Sanchez, and sometimes she visited him in his sleep. She was girl number seven in Rafaela's book of the dead, but girl number twelve of those he had either delivered, killed or disposed of. Rafaela's book was an abridged version of the complete story. There were others, some who hadn't had families to miss them, or whose families were in the south and didn't have the money to travel to the border to find out what had happened when the letters and the money stopped.

He had almost been here once before. A year ago, in a drunken state, he had lurched into a cathedral in Mexico City and crawled into confession. But he hadn't known where to start. He hadn't been to church since he was a boy. And he had been scared, as he was scared now of what was facing him. As the tears of contrition poured out of him, and his body heaved, he didn't know how to make them stop. It was as if his heart had merely been storing blood rather than circulating it through his body, so that when a valve was opened, it didn't flow in a stream so much as exploded outwards all in one, flooding through him.

As the red light of the recorder glowed, and Rafaela sat across from him and listened, Hector poured out his stories. They were all endings. Bad endings. Tragedies. When he finished each one, Rafaela turned off the recorder and gave him the beginnings and, where the women were a little older, some of the middle. Hector listened, and sometimes he wept. Rafaela didn't comfort him but neither did she tell him to stop crying. She didn't seem to take any pleasure from his distress but she didn't pity him either. It was what it was, a man recounting the terrible things he had done, and they both knew there was no way to excuse it.

The light outside began to change as the afternoon settled into evening, but Hector kept on talking until his throat was hoarse. Rafaela got him a glass of water. She took the gun with her, although they both knew they were past all that now. He wouldn't wait until she dropped her guard and attack her. That part of him was gone for ever. He had seen what he had done for what it was. He was finished. A *sicario* had to be able to do one thing and it had nothing to do with killing. He had to be able to close his mind to the consequences of his actions. That part was over for him.

He sipped the water and went on. As darkness fell he reached the final photograph and then he was done. He snapped the blue folder closed and placed it next to him on the couch. He rested his hand on top of it, and felt the spirits of the girls as he closed his eyes.

Rafaela reached over and turned off the recorder. When Hector opened his eyes, she was staring at him, as if to say, 'What now?'

Hector got up. She didn't raise the gun, or say anything, or make any attempt to stop him as he walked to the door of the apartment. He turned the locks and stopped. He shifted around. She still hadn't moved from her seat.

'I'm sorry for what I've done,' he said, and walked out, closing the door behind him.

He went slowly down the stairs, his legs so weak that he clung to the banister. Down he went, not stopping to look back. He was wrung out. Exhausted. Tired beyond any fatigue he had ever known.

On the ground floor, he pushed the door open and stepped out on to the street. There was a chill in the air. He had been inside for six or seven hours, long enough for them to realize that there had been a problem, that he had failed in his mission. Long enough to make other plans.

Rafaela's car was parked down the street. His car was parked around the corner, but it was her car he walked towards. When he reached it, he looked up at her balcony to see if she was watching, but it was empty and the doors leading out to it were closed, the curtains drawn. That was good.

He grasped the handle of the driver's door as hard as he could. Hard enough that he could feel the car's body move. It was enough. The blast lifted him off his feet and he was thrown high into the air, his eardrums bursting under the pressure as he left his body.

Looking down, he saw himself fall back to earth, his limbs interlaced with pieces of metal, his torso and head coming to rest at the far end of the empty street.

Curtains flapped through blast-shattered windows like black crows' wings but no one else screamed. He was gone. Everyone was safe. Safe now that he was no more. That thought, which seemed to come with his last breath, brought him peace.

Seventy-one

Hands tied behind his back and feet bound together, so that if he tried to get up he would fall flat on his face, Charlie Mendez glared at Lock as he jammed one of Mendez's own socks into his mouth and gaffer-taped it in place.

'Now, don't you look *purty*,' Lock told him, stepping back to admire his handiwork. 'All nice and wrapped up for the boys at Pelican Bay. And let me tell you, Charlie, they love them some good-looking sex offenders up at the Bay. You're really going to brighten up those long winter nights for some lucky guy.'

Lock walked to the rear of the shack where the back door led into a patch of badly fenced, overgrown, weedy lawn. Before he stepped outside, he looked around for signs of life in the neighboring backyards, but everything was quiet. People were at work and they put in long hours. To be dirt-poor on this side of the border meant going to work. The alternative was stark: stay home and starve.

He closed the back door behind him, dug out his cell phone,

powered it up and called Ty, who answered straight away, relief that Lock was alive evident in his voice.

After he had spent a few minutes bringing his partner up to speed, Ty said, 'There's a couple of things you need to know.'

For the next three minutes, Lock listened. Three times he interjected with a question. Finally he ended the call, and powered down the cell phone. He opened the back door, and glanced inside, making sure that Mendez hadn't moved. He hadn't. Lock stepped out again. What Ty had just told him had changed things.

He turned the new information over in his mind.

A plan took shape.

He powered his cell phone back up and made another call. Then he took a deep breath, and walked into the shack.

Mendez was where he had left him. Trussed up on the couch. He stared up at Lock, eyes burning with fear and resentment, a predator at someone else's mercy.

'Guess what, Charlie?'

Mendez mumbled something through the sock. Lock reached over and peeled away the tape at the edge of his mouth, pulled out the sock and held it up in front of Mendez between pinched finger and thumb.

'What?' Mendez asked.

'You know you were saying that I could do better than a few hundred thousand bucks? Well, it seems like your buddies down here agree. In fact, they just made me an offer. Five times my cut of the bond for bringing you back.'

'A million bucks? Bullshit,' Mendez said, his voice rising.

Lock held up an open palm and maintained eye contact. 'Asshole's honor.'

'You can't hand me over to them. They'll kill me.'

'There is that. It would definitely be a breach of my ethics. But I'd bet that a million bucks would take my mind off that. It's kind of a once-in-a-lifetime opportunity for a guy like me, don't you think?'

'So you can be bought, after all,' Mendez said.

Lock shrugged. 'I guess so. Looks like you were right.'

'Two!' Mendez hissed.

Lock cocked his head to one side. 'Two what?'

'Two million. My family will give you two million.'

'To let you go?'

Mendez nodded. 'That's double what they're offering.'

'True. But if I take a million from them, you'd be dead, not wandering around preying on other girls. My conscience would be clear. Pretty much clear, anyway. What you're suggesting is way different.'

'Three, then,' said Mendez, suddenly. 'In cash. Tax free. Account in the Cayman Islands. Switzerland. Wherever you like.'

'Forget it,' said Lock.

'Okay, five. Final offer. Take it or leave it.'

'You play pretty fast and loose with your family's money. A minute ago it was two million. Now it's five. You're a hell of a negotiator, buddy.'

'Who said it was my family's money?'

Lock took a step back. Bingo, he thought. There it was. Confirmation of what Ty had told him.

'Okay, back up there, Charlie. You're losing me. They want to give me a million to kill you. But your family can give me five million of the cartel's money to keep you safe. How does that work?'

Something flickered over Mendez's face that suggested he'd

shown Lock too much of his hand. 'What does it matter where the money comes from?'

'Well, when you're asking me to double-cross a major drugs cartel, I'd say it matters a lot. I want to be around to spend it, after all. Million in hand, with no reason to keep looking over my shoulder, sounds better than five and a bunch of ulcers.' Lock let the sock drop to the floor. 'If I'm getting into this, I'm going to need to know what I'm dealing with here. Why would you be able to access their funds?'

'I can't tell you that,' said Mendez.

Doesn't matter, Lock thought, you've already told me all I need to know.

'The final offer's five million,' said Mendez. 'Two when you get me across the border. The rest when I'm safely out of America.'

Lock studied the floor, apparently mulling over the offer, as the pieces clicked neatly into place. There had been one question to which he hadn't fathomed an answer: why would a cartel risk all this heat over a scumbag rapist like Charlie Mendez? Now he knew.

His chin sank to his chest. He thought of Melissa Warner. He thought of the other dead girls. He thought of Rafaela's indignation that two Americans, himself and Ty, would go to all this trouble over one dead and one kidnapped white girl without any concern for the legion of dead brown girls. Then, as the sun dropped towards the horizon and the room began to darken, he folded away his thoughts of the past.

'Three million up front and you have yourself a deal,' he said to Mendez.

Seventy-two

As dusk fell, Lock led an unbound Mendez out of the back of the shack, across the scrubby patch of grass, over a rickety wooden fence with missing slats and into a back alley. In an ideal world, they would have left later, but Lock had no way of knowing when the woman whose home it was would return. Even more crucially, his cell phone had been powered up: there had been half a dozen phone calls as Mendez had made the arrangements for the money to be transferred. Every minute they stayed conceivably brought them a minute closer to being found.

The scuff of sneakers at the end of the alley sent Lock's hand to the butt of his gun. A few seconds later a soccer ball rolled into view. It was followed by two teenage boys. They froze at the sight of the two men. Lock trapped the ball under his foot and waved them forward. He peeled off two five-dollar bills and handed one to each of them. 'You didn't see us,' he said, tapping the ball back to them.

They traded a look, shoved the money into the pockets of their baggy jeans and sloped off into the gloom. Lock tapped at Mendez's elbow and they moved off.

At the end of the alley Lock hunkered down in the dirt and checked their position on his GPS. Three hundred yards ahead lay a marshaling yard, used to store containers before they were hooked up to trucks and taken off for loading further south or north. When he had come across the yard on an earlier recon, he had thought about holing up in a container but decided against it. Right now they were less than a quarter-mile from the border, but the containers could end up anywhere. Cargo moved across the border came from as far away as China and went back that way too. Get in a container and you could die in there. It wasn't a chance he was willing to take, but if they could make it to the marshaling yard they could use that as cover and as a final staging post. Once they were inside and reached the north-eastern corner of the yard, all that would stand between them and America was a long sprint across open ground towards the river and the newly erected border fence.

Crouched in the dirt, he watched the moon rise, and they waited for a truck to roll towards the yard entrance. At last one did and they made their move, running in a low crouch behind it, and using its trailer as cover to take them inside the perimeter as a sleepy-eyed guard waved it through.

Safely inside, Lock found a narrow gap between two stacks of blue and red shipping containers, and Mendez sat down with his back to one. The yard's security was minimal – the guard on the gate and one more inside. No casual crew of thieves would touch any of the containers: it was all too likely that they would pick one being run by the cartels, and the price for that kind of mistake was death. No cop would be allowed inside to check the containers either, not without a warrant. There was too much risk that they would find something they shouldn't, something they couldn't turn a blind eye to.

In the near distance, Lock could see America through a gap in the newly erected border fence. But they weren't going anywhere. Not yet, anyway.

Seventy-three

An hour passed and the temperature dropped. Behind
the marshaling yard, armed police had massed at the edge of the
colonia, ready for one more sweep. Officers in riot gear were
positioned at fifty-yard intervals, one facing in, the next looking
out. Their vehicles were parked so close to the yard that Lock
could hear the ticking of engines cooling.

Maybe the woman whose home they had invaded had made a
report. Maybe the boys with the soccer ball had decided they
could make more than five bucks. Or maybe the cartel had
triangulated the position of the calls made from the cell phone.
The reason didn't matter. The cops knew he was close by. But they
didn't know where exactly. They must have assumed he was still in
the *colonia*. They would figure out he wasn't. The only question
remaining was how long it would take them.

With the police so close, Lock spent the time trying to estimate
their chance of surviving the dash from where they were to the
border fence. At most he believed that a hundred yards out from

their current position, they would likely be spotted. Fifty yards further they would probably begin to take fire. Keeping Mendez close to him would present the cops with double the regular body mass and double the target area.

It was possible that he and Mendez would get lucky. Shooting a man at range, or two men, was more difficult than it looked, especially given that the people shooting were cops rather than military. The ability to shoot to kill, more so than killing someone up close, was as much about switching off certain parts of the subconscious as it was about technical skill. Up close with a knife or your bare hands, millennia's worth of survival instincts kicked in, overwhelming your mind. Killing another human being from a distance took training, repetition and a readjustment of your mindset to get to the point where you could accurately and coolly shoot someone in the back.

So, some things were in their favor, but Lock figured it was a seventy-thirty split against. A thirty per cent chance that they would make it in one piece, and a seventy per cent chance that they would be shot, and those were odds he didn't like very much.

There was one other major barrier. A bad one. Bad because it didn't conform to logic. It was a political consideration. Even if a battalion of US Marines was standing on the other side of the border, they wouldn't be allowed to cross over to help him. They would have to stand and watch while he was killed. All kinds of US government agencies and operatives worked in Mexico with the tacit approval of the Mexican government. That wasn't the case here.

Here, the local authorities with the supposed approval of the Federal authorities, were engaged in the hunt for a convicted rapist, and the man they were probably by now claiming was his accomplice. In all likelihood, that was how it was being spun, and if it wasn't, it would be a variation on that theme. Whatever had changed behind the scenes, and the shots from the helicopter told Lock that something definitely had, they wanted Mendez dead – himself too, probably. It was classic spin-control for the cartels. If a situation gets out of hand, let the bodies pile up, shut things down and limit the number of those who can relate to the rest of the world what has gone down.

The land ahead was flat. No points of cover: it was exposed to the east, west and south. Not the kind of terrain you'd want to make a break over if your life depended upon it. Yet they would have to. But not now. They would need an edge and there was no better edge than the one he had in mind. The only snag was that his edge lay another sixty minutes in the future.

Seventy-four

Fifty-seven Minutes Later

Torch beams slashed their way across the darkness of the marshaling yard. A soundtrack of clanging metal accompanied the light show as containers were prised open, checked and slammed shut. Lock sat in the darkness next to Mendez and listened as the searchers worked their way methodically towards them. He rolled back the sleeve of his jacket to take another look at his watch, the seconds creeping slowly forward.

They still had a full three minutes before he'd planned on breaking cover. But in less than three minutes he could be staring down the beam of a flashlight, with a bullet slamming towards him on the exact same trajectory.

He surveyed the route to the barrier and reconfigured his plan. Crunching footsteps echoed through the narrow gap where he was hunkered down with Mendez. He needed at least another two minutes but he wasn't going to get them.

Shit happens. Deal with it, he told himself.

He brought the index finger of his right hand up to his mouth, a final caution to Mendez. He picked out his features in the gloom and saw that the gesture had been needless. The blood had drained totally from his face.

He tapped Mendez's shoulder then pointed forwards six feet to where he had already rolled up a section of chain-link fence, ready for them to crawl under. He started to duck-walk towards it, motioning for Mendez to follow him.

The back of his thighs burned. His every shuffled step sounded like an explosion as he inched his way to the perimeter. A babble of excited Spanish seemed to erupt almost directly behind them, but he kept the same careful pace. If they'd been seen, they were already dead. If they hadn't, a panicked burst of speed would seal their fate.

At the fence, he moved to the side, dipping his hand to indicate that he wanted Mendez to go first. He was treating Mendez as a principal now, a person whose life he was charged with protecting. It was the only way to make this work. His feelings were sealed away, as they always were when he was carrying out close-protection work.

He lifted the sheared strands of wire. Mendez snaked his way under, crawling on his belly, using his elbows and knees for forward momentum. The voices behind them grew louder. Close by, the boom of a container door being slammed made the hairs on the back of his neck shoot to attention.

The soles of Mendez's shoes cleared the last tendril of wire. He pulled himself clear of the fence, sat up, and turned to Lock, staring at him for a long beat, one side of his face bathed in light, the other lost to the darkness. He reached forward and held up the bottom of the fence so that Lock had room to crawl under it.

Lowering his head, Lock fell into a shallow dive, ass in the air, and keenly aware of his own vulnerability. His head cleared the gap under the fence. Then his shoulders. He stretched out his hands, fingers digging into the dirt to propel him forward.

Suddenly he felt Mendez's foot stamp hard on his right hand, crushing his fingers and sending a sharp jab of pain up his arm. He tried to twist it free but the pressure was too great. The next thing he knew, his weapon was plucked from his holster.

'What the hell are you doing?' Lock said.

'Saving myself five million bucks,' came the reply, as the pressure on his hand was released and Mendez took off.

Lock thrashed about, kicking against the ground on the other side of fence, trying to use his feet to thrust himself onwards. He wriggled forwards as hard as he could, a strand of fence wire raking his lower back as he pushed through.

As he cleared the fence, he raised his head in time to see Mendez's heels flicking up from the ground ahead of him as he made his break for freedom.

Pushing himself up and on to his feet, he took off after Mendez at a sprint, oblivious to the growing clamor of voices from the marshaling yard as the beam of a flashlight snapped across the break in the fence and a single voice, shrill with excitement, called out in Spanish.

Lock focused on the crunch of footfalls ahead of him as he powered after Mendez, rage driving him. Rage at Mendez for jeopardizing their chances of survival. Rage at himself for believing that he was smarter than he was and Mendez dumber.

Behind him, the shouts from the marshaling yard were louder. He didn't dare look back. Whatever happened next, happened. Knowing that death was on its way didn't stop it, not that he'd ever seen. You could brace yourself for a punch but not for a bullet.

The sweat that had beaded on his forehead started to trickle into his eyes. He blinked them clear. He could see Mendez approaching a dip in the ground and hurtled after him.

Mendez was slowing, and Lock, more used to pacing a foot race, was gaining. The gap closed. He was within twenty feet. Then twelve. Then ten. But Mendez was almost at the dip now. He would reach it before Lock, that much was certain.

Lock raced to estimate the countdown but time had fractured and spun away. *Was there a minute to go? More? Less?*

As he planted his left foot on the ground ahead, the answer came in the form of a sky-splitting clap of thunder to the east.

Lock dove for the ground, making himself as flat as he could. High above him, the sky lit up like the Fourth of July as a blaze of white light from a parachute flare obliterated the moon. He began to count.

Fifteen seconds later – the precise amount of time it took for the flare to explode and burn down, like a dying star – he raised his head.

Seventy-five

The flare had been set to go off a half-mile to the east of the yard, the idea being that any pursuers or searchers would read it as a signal that this was where the American rescue party was, and that they were signaling this as the point at which to cross. The Mexican cops would be drawn swiftly towards it, while Lock crossed the border with Mendez almost directly opposite the marshaling yard.

That had been the plan, anyway. And, from the sounds of men tearing out of the marshaling yard and the *colonia*, it was work- ing like a dream. The only problem was that Mendez was gone too.

Lifting his head clear of the ground, Lock watched the stream of excited men running hard in the direction of the flare. A couple of exploratory three-round bursts blew past him in the same direction, as a couple of trigger-happy cops let loose with automatic weapons.

Slowly he got to his feet as they moved off into the distance, his path ahead clear. He broke into a run, praying that Mendez hadn't doubled back on him. Within no time, he could see the great span of the corrugated-steel plate barrier looming ahead. There was more gunfire to his left. Then shouts in Spanish. A regular cluster fuck, as they chased each other's shadows.

He stopped and looked around, his eyes struggling to readjust to the gloom after the intense burst of light from the flare. Ahead, he heard something move in the darkness.

He dropped down, aware that Mendez had his weapon. Staying low, he moved forward, listening, his senses dialed up full. The sound came again. A person. Their movements slow and labored.

He stayed quiet and inched forward. He was coming to the dip in the ground before the barrier. He radared in on the sound. The person was below him. Except now he could see that it wasn't a natural hollow where the land fell away. It was a trench, ten feet deep and six feet wide – it had been dug out with heavy plant. A barrier before the barrier. An additional line of defense – perhaps to stop the people from the *colonia* taking a run at the border fence with a car.

Carefully, he leaned over the edge, his movement releasing a tumble of loose earth. There was a sudden break of movement to his right. Mendez was lying at the bottom of the trench, his left hand clasping a twisted right ankle. That was fine. It wasn't his left hand Lock was worried about. It was the right, which was coming up fast, holding the gun.

Lock dove back from the edge, a round sailing past where his head had been a split second before. *A lucky shot? Or did Mendez have some skill?*

Rushing him was out of the question. He'd probably take a

bullet before he was halfway down. And the shot was drawing some kind of chatter from the distracted posse running after the flare. Sooner or later they would come looking in this direction to check it out.

'Charlie?' Lock whispered into the darkness, being careful to stay out of sight. 'Charlie, you can't move and you can't stay there either. If we're both going to get out of this there has to be some trust on both sides.'

A voice came back from the darkness of the trench: 'Why should I trust you?'

'Because you don't have any choice. If I wanted you dead all I have to do now is get out of here and leave our *compadres* over there to deal with you. I lose the money, but if I don't care about the money it makes no difference to me. I should just get out of here.'

It was a hard sell and he didn't have time to make a winning case.

'So, go.'

He needed something else. A distraction. Something for Mendez to chew on, however briefly. Something to buy him the moment of doubt he needed. He patted down his jacket and something crinkled under the fabric. He reached inside and pulled out a wad of paper, waving it over the edge of the trench.

Mendez's voice came from the void. 'What's that?'

'Your mother gave it to me to give to you. It's a note. You want it?'

'What's it say?'

'How would I know? Look, do you want it or not?'

Lock edged forward until his head was back over the lip. He tensed, ready to spring back, but Mendez lowered the gun by a fraction.

'Throw it down.'

'Okay,' he said, shuffling forwards on his elbows.

He swung his legs over the lip so that he was sitting on the edge of the trench. 'I could bring it down to you,' he said.

'No,' said Mendez. 'I don't trust you.'

'Hey, you're the one with the gun but, okay, I'll throw it down.'

He folded it up, first into halves and then over again so there was a bit more weight to it. He reached down and tossed it towards Mendez. It fell about a foot from his reach. He looked up at Lock, eyes out on stalks, finger back on the trigger, waiting for him to try something. But Lock stayed perfectly still.

Mendez shuffled on his hands and knees towards the paper. Still Lock didn't move. Not a muscle.

Withdrawing his left hand from his ankle, Mendez grabbed the note, struggling to unfold it with one hand.

'Can you read it?' Lock asked.

Mendez screwed up his eyes as they tracked the white piece of paper, the gun loosening in his right hand.

Heels already dug into the side of the trench, Lock pushed off as hard as he could, launching himself into the air directly above Mendez, the air rushing around him, the ground and the barrel of the gun, which was coming up fast.

Mendez's body cushioned the landing. There was a shot, and a piercing scream as Lock's knee came down hard on Mendez's left ankle.

Lock knew better than to concern himself with whether he'd taken the stray round. You fought until your body stopped you. He threw a big, swooping right elbow at Mendez catching him high on the chest, just enough to send him off balance.

Mendez tried to twist his right hand around to get the angle for another shot but Lock dug the heel of his boot back into his ankle, drawing another shriek of pain. His hands grabbed at Mendez's shirt, and he crawled up the man's body so that they were face to face, so close that the gun was now redundant.

Lock head-butted him. It was enough to loosen the gun. He prised it from Mendez's fingers, clambered off him and stood up.

The shouts were getting closer, the flare a busted flush, the search party no doubt pivoting round and moving back towards them, realizing they'd been punked by what was known in the trade as a come-on – the oldest but most effective trick in the book.

Lock reached down, grabbed Mendez's hair and yanked him to his feet. Using sheer brute force, he began dragging him up the shallower side of the trench and towards the barrier. Now he could only trust that the coordinates he'd given Ty were accurate. If they weren't, there was no way he could manhandle a fully grown man with an injury over ten feet of sheer steel on his own.

He was almost there. He let go of Mendez's hair and instead threw a supportive arm around him. Mendez began to struggle.

Fuck it, thought Lock, as he half turned, planted his feet and unleashed a ferocious right hand to Mendez's head. Mendez folded like an old dollar bill and began to sink to the ground. Lock picked him up, slung him over his back and staggered towards the wall of cold metal as the first live rounds slammed into the ground behind them.

Half walking, half running, he stumbled onwards, his heart sinking with every step as he saw only sheet metal. He was already contemplating a dive back towards the trench when he heard the sweetest words: 'Yo! Over here,' Ty shouted, all six foot four of him materializing like a phantom from the darkness, falling into a crouch and letting loose a volley of covering fire towards the advancing search party.

Looking towards him, Lock saw the access door, three feet wide and a little over six feet tall, swing open. He ran for it as Ty moved in front of him, still firing. A round pinged off the steel barrier.

Barely through the door, he crouched and dumped Mendez unceremoniously on the bare ground. Mendez sprawled on his back, legs and arms flailing in the air, like a turtle's. Lock drew his leg back and kicked him hard in the side for good measure. 'Welcome home, asshole.'

Seventy-six

Ty drove the vehicle in which he had arrived at the RV point, the white Ford Ranger, as Lock sat in the back with a cuffed, shackled and subdued Charlie Mendez. Ahead of them lay a mile and a half of rutted farm track, not that anyone farmed cattle so close to the border. From here they would pick up a secondary road that would lead them eventually to the freeway. By Lock's calculations if they made it that far they would have slipped, at least temporarily, from the cartel's grasp. A set of headlights behind them, though, and they were done.

'I think you broke one of my ribs,' Mendez whined.

Lock glanced at him. 'If that's all that's broken you can count yourself lucky.'

'So, what now? What are you going to do with me?'

The question prompted Lock to trade a glance with Ty. Lock took a deep breath. 'That's down to you. And your family.'

Ty twisted around in his seat. 'Say what? We're handing him

over. Or have you forgot about that promise you made to the girl's momma?'

Lock checked the surprise that registered on Mendez's face. 'There's five million if we don't versus a couple of hundred grand if we do.'

Ty didn't seem appeased. 'And you think we can trust this piece of shit?'

Mendez seemed to forget his bruised ribs. He bounced forward in the seat. 'You can. I promise you.'

'Like your word counts?' growled Ty. 'Naw, Ryan. Hell, naw. We know the government will pay out, but this guy? Dude could peel a banana in his pocket and we wouldn't know about it.'

Lock eased back in the seat. 'That's why we're going to see the first three million in an offshore account by midnight tonight. Isn't that right, Charlie?'

Mendez's cheeks filled with air and he exhaled slowly. 'That's a lot of money to move all at once.'

Lock smiled, thinking back to their previous conversation about how the cartel had been paying to protect him. 'But some-one in your family must know how to get it done, right?'

Ty turned round to stare at him – badder cop to Lock's bad cop. 'Course, we could just drop you off with the Feds.'

'I'll make the call,' said Mendez.

They kept moving, at first tacking north to put more distance between them and any pursuing cartel members, then heading west.

Forty miles further along Interstate 10, they passed an Arizona State trooper parked on a crossway. His head swiveled as they passed. He pulled out, tucking in behind them for a few miles. It was no great surprise. This was a well-known drug route, and three males in the same vehicle were bound to attract attention. Ty stayed cool, keeping to the speed limit. After a few more miles the trooper grew bored and passed them, giving them a final sideways glance as he roared off into the distance.

'Here,' said Lock, handing Mendez his cell phone. 'Time you spoke to Mommy.'

They drove through the rest of the day. After some tense early calls, Mendez made the final arrangements for the initial transfer of funds. The money was scheduled to move at midnight. Ty would call the bank to confirm it had been lodged.

In the meantime, exhausted, they decided to take a break. They pulled into a motel parking lot a few miles shy of Phoenix. Lock got out first, leaving Ty in the car with Mendez, who had already fallen asleep, like he had in the shack: Lock had noticed then how he slept like a baby – not a care in a world. He guessed that was what money bought you: the knowledge that, no matter how bad things got or how far you screwed over other people or destroyed their lives, it would always get you out of a corner.

Lock pushed open the door of the motel office and walked inside. The carpet stuck to his feet. There was a Coke vending machine to one side and a long desk, behind which sat a young Hispanic man wearing blue jeans and a bowling shirt.

He smiled at Lock. 'How can I help you, sir?'

'I'd like two rooms. Adjoining if you have them.'

The hotel clerk rose from the stool he was perched on and walked over to check an old-fashioned ledger. His fingers traced over the paper. He looked up. 'I think we can accommodate you. Just the one night?'

'Yeah. One night,' said Lock. 'What time's check-out?'

'Eleven o'clock on the button. Not a moment later,' said the clerk. 'We like our guests to be punctual when it comes to checking out.'

'Got it,' said Lock, reaching over to take the single key fob.

With Ty babysitting Mendez in the room, Lock headed out to grab some food and supplies. In the parking lot of a nearby Walmart, he dug out his cell phone, powered it up and checked his messages. There was one from a man whose name he didn't recognize, but who obviously worked for Miriam Mendez, saying that matters had been taken care of and the money would be transferred at the designated time. Lock smiled to himself and punched in a Santa Maria number. He got a switchboard operator and asked to be transferred to Police Chief Gabriel Zapatero. He was informed that the chief was a busy man. Lock gave his name, asked to be put through to his secretary, if the chief wasn't available, and waited.

Less than twenty seconds later, Zapatero came on the line. Lock didn't waste time. He told him what he required for the return of the fugitive they were looking for.

'Of course, I could hand him straight to the US authorities myself, but it might look better coming from you,' he added, knowing that Charlie Mendez wouldn't make it back across the border, once he was handed over to the cartel. He gave a time at which he would call back and give a general area for the person collecting Mendez to wait in. Finally, he specified that the person had to be the chief and that he had to be accompanied by Detective Rafaela Carcharon, no one else.

'If I see anyone else with you, the deal's off and Mendez gets handed to the FBI,' Lock added.

After a few seconds' deliberation, Zapatero agreed to his terms with a grunt. Lock felt relieved. That meant Rafaela was probably still alive. He took down a cell-phone number where he could reach the chief the next morning and hung up.

He powered down the cell phone, removed the battery and walked into Walmart With his three-day stubble and a dead-eyed expression, he blended nicely with the local clientele as he cruised the aisles, scooping up what he needed and dumping it into his cart. He stopped off in the sports section to load up on fresh ammo.

Back in the motel room, Mendez was in the shower when Lock got back with dinner. After a few minutes, he came out with a towel wrapped around his waist. Ty and Lock did their best to ignore him. As he dressed, they ate. They watched some TV, then Mendez turned in for the night. Ty took first watch. The cartel would be out in force, checking motels like this one, which was why Lock had told Zapatero they were nearer Tucson than Phoenix. Still, they weren't about to take any chances.

Lock got into the bed opposite and, relying on a habit acquired with years of practice, and knowing tomorrow was a busy day, he was asleep within seconds of his head hitting the pillow.

Ty woke him a little after midnight. The transfer had been made by the Mendez family. Three million dollars into an off-shore account. They were millionaires. Lock told him to enjoy the feeling, rolled over and went back to sleep.

Lock slept until three in the morning, then took over guard duty while Ty got some rest. Mendez woke around eight, the sun already up outside, the day threatening to be unseasonably pleasant. Outside, a couple of cars came and went. Lock watched them through a slit in the curtains.

At nine o'clock he announced they were going out for breakfast. Mendez seemed spooked by the idea.

'Relax,' Ty told him. 'We're in the middle of nowhere.'

Lock opened the door and together the three men walked into the sunlight, got into the Ranger, and drove to a diner a half-mile down the road. They took a booth near the door, Lock sliding in one side so that he had a view of the entrance and the truck, Ty sitting opposite so that he had a view of the back door. Mendez was jittery, his nails dancing across the Formica table as he scanned the menu.

'You got the money?' he asked, after the waitress had taken their order and brought coffee.

Lock nodded. 'We're all good. You're getting collected at noon.'

'Who's picking me up?' Mendez asked.

Ty smiled. 'Mommy's coming in person.'

'Getting off her deathbed to see you. Guess blood really is thicker than water,' said Lock. 'I presume she'll have security with her and they have plans in place to get you out of the States.'

Mendez looked taken aback but didn't say anything.

Ty glanced at Lock. 'Man, must be nice to be a rich asshole who can fuck up other people's lives and walk away from it every single time.'

'Hey, have a little respect. That's what passes for the American Dream, these days. So don't be ragging on it, you hear me?' said Lock.

As Mendez glared at them, Ty saluted across the table. 'Sorry, boss.'

*

Two hours later, a black limousine pulled up in front of the motel and the crew-cut driver, a roll of neck fat bulging above the collar of his white shirt, got out and opened the rear passenger door. Clad in a suitably conservative blue pants suit, Miriam Mendez stepped from the limo. The driver walked alongside her as she headed for room twenty-seven. He knocked at the door and waited. Miriam took a step back and surveyed her surroundings with an air of distaste. The door opened.

'Mr Lock, it's good to see you again.'

Lock took her proffered hand and smiled. 'Likewise. Come on in,' he said, eyeing the driver and the bulge under his jacket. 'Wait in the car, buddy. We won't be long.'

The driver didn't move. Miriam turned. 'I'll call if I need you,' she said, dismissing him.

She walked past Lock, into the room, and the door closed.

Her son was sitting on the bed. He didn't look up as she entered and she made no acknowledgement that he was in the room.

'Was the transfer to your satisfaction, Mr Lock?' she asked.

He gave a curt nod. 'Received with thanks. And I'm glad to see you looking so well.'

She did her best to force a smile. 'A new treatment.' She cleared her throat. 'Well, if there's nothing further . . .'

Mendez got to his feet, still not making eye contact with his mother. Miriam Mendez started for the door but Lock moved to block her passage as Ty emerged from the bathroom, gun in hand. He crossed to the door that connected to the adjoining room.

'Before you go, Mrs Mendez,' said Lock, 'there's someone I'd like you to meet.'

Seventy-seven

Ty turned the handle, and opened the door. A middle-aged woman stepped into the room.

Lock made the introductions, his voice perfectly even. 'Mrs Mendez, this is Mrs Warner. Your son raped her daughter, and the cartel that was protecting him sent someone to kill her. I figured you'd have quite a lot to talk about.'

Mendez dove for the door, head down. Lock shifted his weight, using the turn of his hips to generate the power to send a crushing elbow into his face. He spun backwards, arms flailing, and landed on the bed. Lock drew a hand gun and pointed it at his head. Miriam Mendez gave a yelp and drew back her hand to strike Lock. Ty raised his weapon and l e v e l e d it at her face.

For a moment no one moved. Jan Warner took four steps towards Miriam Mendez and slapped her hard across the face. 'That's for Melissa.'

Miriam Mendez put a hand to her cheek, which flushed red. 'How dare you? I'm a sick woman.'

'You got that straight,' muttered Ty.

Mendez grabbed the edge of the bed and tried to haul himself to his feet. Lock pivoted and kicked him hard in the side. 'Stay where you are, Sparky. We have some more visitors on the way.' He turned to Jan Warner. 'You okay?'

She nodded. 'Yes, thank you.'

'You can hit her again if you like,' said Ty, generous to the last. 'I ain't gonna say anything.'

Jan shook her head, her eyes shifting back to Miriam Mendez. 'I just wanted you to know what you've done.'

Miriam ignored her. 'You can't keep us here,' she said to Lock. 'My driver will come back in a moment.'

'No, he won't. I guarantee you.' Lock waved to a seat in the corner of the room. 'Make yourself comfortable. A sick woman like you shouldn't be standing.'

Ty opened the interconnecting door and ushered Jan Warner back into the other room. She paused in the doorway, her eyes boring into Mendez before she glanced back to his mother. 'You might have money, Mrs Mendez, but that's all you have.'

Miriam Mendez sat down, glaring at Lock. He was beginning to see where her son had got his sullen demeanor from.

'This is kidnapping,' she said.

Lock exchanged a look with Ty as he walked back in, closing the door to the other bedroom behind him. 'You want to explain to Mrs Mendez what the word "irony" means, Tyrone, or shall I?'

Seventy-eight

Lock was standing by the motel-room window as a blue sedan pulled into the parking lot. Rafaela was driving. Police Chief Gabriel Zapatero sat next to her in the passenger seat. She pulled up and they both got out. They were in casual clothes. Rafaela was wearing brown boots, jeans and a sweater. Zapatero had on black loafers, sand-colored khakis, a black roll-neck and a dark blazer. There was no sign of any other vehicle. A red pick-up truck rolled past on the road outside but otherwise it was quiet.

Rafaela walked towards the room. Zapatero, ever cautious, stood next to the sedan. Lock opened the door wide as Rafaela approached. Zapatero looked pointedly in the opposite direction, as if he had no idea why he was there.

'What's going on?' she whispered to Lock.

Lock smiled. 'Trust me, okay?'

'Like I have a choice?' she said, taking in the balled-up figure of Charlie Mendez on the bed and the woman sitting rigid, with WASP-style fortitude, on a seat in the corner.

'You bring the money?' Lock asked.

She nodded back towards the sedan. 'It's in the trunk. But he wants me to make sure you have Mendez before he hands it over.'

Lock ushered her in with a wave of his hand. 'Not a problem. You get rid of your escort?'

She walked past him into the room. 'They're a half-mile back down the road waiting for us,' she said. Lock left the door open to allay Zapatero's paranoia.

'How many of them?' Lock asked her.

'Four in a red Dodge Charger with Texas plates.'

'You might suggest to Zapatero that they move up a little so that they can see you both. But they shouldn't get too close.'

Rafaela nodded.

Ty crossed to Charlie Mendez and lifted him to his feet. He smelt of stale urine and his eyes were wide as saucers. He flinched as Rafaela approached, and his mother started to get up, only to be calmed by a wave of Ty's gun. 'Sit down, bitch.'

'He's all yours,' said Lock. 'Soon as we have the money.'

Rafaela turned. Lock walked her to the door, keeping an eye out for any other vehicles making a last dash into the parking lot. Rafaela exchanged a few words with Zapatero. He produced a cell phone and made a call – no doubt passing on Rafaela's suggestion that the escort move in a little tighter. Then she followed him to the trunk.

The lid flipped open and Zapatero hauled out two large black canvas bags, similar to the ones Lock and Ty had used for their gear when they had crossed the border a few days previously. He handed the bags to Rafaela and grabbed two more. They stumbled forwards under the weight of the bags. Zapatero's jacket rode up to reveal a Glock tucked into a holster. Lock held the door open for them as they reached the room and walked in.

The police chief threw the bags on to the bed nearest the window, the frame creaking as they hit the mattress. Lock shut the door to hide the transaction from prying eyes.

Zapatero noticed Miriam Mendez and his eyebrows shot halfway up his forehead. 'What's she doing here?' he asked.

The question spoke volumes. Zapatero obviously knew exactly who she was. 'Deal of the week,' said Lock. 'Buy one, get one free.'

Rafaela ignored the exchange, dumping the other two bags on the floor before standing back, positioning herself at the far wall, away from the window.

Zapatero smiled. 'You're very thorough, Mr Lock. Perhaps you could assist my department again. We always need resourceful men such as yourself and your friend.'

'You can drop the act,' Lock said, with a nod to Rafaela. 'She knows you're in bed with Tibialis and the cartel. So do I. This is a one-off deal.'

Miriam Mendez started to her feet, and this time no gun was going to stop her as she advanced on Lock. 'You can't do this. They'll kill us both. I gave you three million dollars.'

Lock matched Zapatero's smile. 'Except it wasn't your money to give, was it, Mrs Mendez? It belonged to the cartel. To Chief Zapatero's friend Mr Tibialis. Isn't that right?'

The woman flushed. 'They weren't complaining. My family gave them what they wanted.'

'And what was that, Mrs Mendez?'

Her lips thinned with rage. Zapatero started towards her but Rafaela drew her weapon and pointed it at his head. 'Let her answer the question,' she said.

'What did they want from you, Mrs Mendez?' Lock pressed. 'It couldn't have been money. They were paying you.'

A darkness passed over Miriam Mendez's face. Her expression soured. She reminded Lock of the Santa Muerte skeletons he'd seen in Diablo. 'There are two types of money in this world, Mr Lock. Dirty and clean. They had the first kind and we could turn it into the second for them. Like lead into gold.'

'You mean you could launder it?' Lock said.

Zapatero was getting twitchy. 'Don't listen to her. She's a crazy old woman. She doesn't know what she's talking about. This is a law-enforcement matter,' he said, buying time as his hand inched towards the butt of his Glock.

Lock shook his head. 'Hey, Chief. Did no one ever tell you that you got to have equal numbers for a stand-off?'

His hand fell away from the holster.

'Now,' said Lock, 'Mrs Mendez, why don't you continue?'

Her lips thinned again. 'I've said all I'm prepared to say.'

'Oh, I highly doubt that,' said Lock, as the connecting door and main door burst open simultaneously and half a dozen men clad in black body armor, with POLICE emblazoned in blue lettering across their backs, rushed into the room.

'US Marshals! Keep your hands where we can see them,' they said, gun-facing everyone, Lock and Ty included.

Lock, Ty and Rafaela dropped their weapons, following the Marshals' instructions to the letter. Within sixty seconds, all six of the room's occupants were face down on the motel-room floor, hands cuffed behind their backs.

Either side of the motel room, doors opened to disgorge Arizona State Police and Federal agents who had been secreted inside, waiting for the go signal. Within minutes, the parking lot was bumper to bumper with law-enforcement vehicles.

Out on the highway, a red Dodge Charger, sporting Texas plates and with four Hispanic males inside, pulled a wide U-turn and sped off in the opposite direction. No one moved to stop it. The men inside would be allowed to go back across the border, where they would relay the news of Zapatero's arrest by the US authorities to the cartel.

Lock kissed moldy motel-room carpet as first Miriam and then Charlie Mendez were lifted to their feet and taken outside by the Marshals Arrest Response Team. Zapatero was next, his escort two clean-cut FBI agents, who looked fresh out of the box at Quantico. Lock, Ty and Rafaela were relieved of their weapons, uncuffed and helped to their feet as the motel's Hispanic front-desk clerk strode into the room and extended a hand to Lock.

'Armando Hernandez, US State Department.'

Lock shook his hand. 'You boys get everything you need?'

'We had a lot of it worked out already, but nothing beats hearing it from the horse's mouth. You all okay?' Hernandez asked.

A couple of Federal agents squeezed past him, picking up the holdalls with the ransom money, tagging them and taking pictures with a small digital camera before hauling them into the other room. Ty watched the bags with the expression of a kid who'd just been told that Santa Claus doesn't exist.

'We're good. Don't worry about Tyrone,' Lock said, placing a hand on his partner's shoulder. 'He's just a little emotional right now.'

'That's for damn straight,' said Ty.

As soon as the area outside the motel was secured, they emerged into the midday sunlight, Lock, Ty and Rafaela. Rafaela walked out into the middle of the parking lot and, cupping her hand over her eyes, looked out over the open countryside beyond the road that fronted the motel. Lock stood next to her.

'He came to kill me,' she said.

Lock followed her gaze out over the desert. The landscape here didn't look all that different from what he'd seen on the other side of the border. The people hadn't been that different either. Most of them, anyway. The silent majority who wanted to raise their families in peace.

'Who came?' he asked her, as behind them Ty, still pissed at having to sacrifice the money, tapped his foot against the rear wheel of an Arizona State Police cruiser.

'The bodyguard,' Rafaela said. 'Hector.'

'Didn't do much of a job,' said Lock.

'I showed him the same pictures of the girls that I showed you.'

'What did he say?'

Rafaela lapsed into silence. Her eyes narrowed. 'I think he understood the pain. He felt it too.'

'Maybe that's all any of us can do,' said Lock, as across the parking lot Charlie Mendez was bundled into the back of a police cruiser for the long drive north to his new home at Pelican Bay Supermax.

Epilogue

Two Months Later

Lock's fiancée, Carrie Delaney, had been buried close to her parents' house in Connecticut. After her death, while they were making arrangements for the funeral, they had asked Lock for his thoughts on her final resting-place. Because his work involved so much travel, he had thought it best that she stayed close to them. What meagre roots he had lay with her, and she was gone. She had been his home.

This was his first visit to her grave in a little more than four months. He suspected that, however good anyone's intentions, lengthening intervals between such visits were the reality.

He had brought a small bunch of white lilies with him. Falling on to one knee, and feeling the poignancy of that motion, he laid them gently against her gravestone, next to some other flowers placed there by her mother a few days before.

He had visited her parents earlier that morning. They were, as they had been since her death, warm and welcoming. He wasn't sure that he would have felt the same way. It had been his mistake that had led to her death in California, but they graciously saw it as just that – a mistake, a cruel intervention of Fate.

While he had sat in their living room drinking coffee, he had told them about events in Mexico. The story had splashed big on both sides of the border, although the Justice Department, for reasons of their own, had managed to downplay his involvement. He and Ty had helped them out by spending the past few months very firmly off-the-radar.

Since the trap that they had helped set for Miriam Mendez and Police Chief Zapatero in the motel room outside Phoenix, events had moved fast. Charlie Mendez was now inside the Secure Housing Unit at Pelican Bay. For his own safety, he would remain there indefinitely, alone in a single cell, allowed out for a solitary hour of exercise once a day. It was, as far as Lock saw it, a fate worse than death. More importantly, he was where he could do no harm to any other young woman. Despite the white-hot rush of anger he had felt when he'd pursued him, Lock had realized that Melissa's wish to see him returned to serve the sentence handed down by the court had been right and proper. It would have been easy for Lock to put a bullet in Mendez's brain. It would also have been wrong.

In what some might have seen as a righteous act of karma, Miriam Mendez wasn't going to make it to trial, never mind a jail cell. Her cancer had returned, for real this time, and she was, according to his contacts in Santa Barbara, deteriorating fast. Death's hand on her shoulder must have woken something in her conscience because she had handed the US government all of the details of the family's deal with the cartel. In return for her son's protection, the cartel had used the family's varied business interests as a way of laundering their drug money – at a nice profit for both sides. Police Chief Zapatero, knowing that his arrest by the US authorities was as good as a death sentence, had, in return for immunity from prosecution, confirmed her story.

On the other side of the border Manuel Managua, the politician, had been arrested. Federico Tibialis could not be found. There was a ten-million-dollar price on his head but he had more money than either God or Santa Muerte, and would likely stay on the run for longer than Charlie Mendez had managed. Despite Ty's best efforts to convince him to reprise their new career, Lock had decided that their temporary detour into bounty hunting was best left at that.

Like her boss, Rafaela had also been offered protection by the US government – albeit under terms dictated by the fact that she was wholly innocent of any wrongdoing. At first she had turned down their offer of Federal protection, until a long, exhausting talk with Lock had persuaded her that she was more useful to everyone alive. She was staying at a secret location somewhere in the United States and helping both governments piece together what had happened to the young women she thought of as her girls. Depressingly for everyone, the vile activities of the three men, Managua, Tibialis and Zapatero, still accounted for only a fraction of the deaths. There were other predators out there in the borderlands. The killings were an epidemic.

Julia was slowly coming to terms with her ordeal, and receiving private counseling, paid for by Lock when her parents had been told by their private insurance company that their policy didn't cover the treatment she needed. Julia might never be the same person, but she would come to terms with what had happened and, he prayed, be able to move on with her life. He had long since realized that was as good as it got. You made your peace with events. You didn't forget, but if you took one day at a time then slowly you found that life went on.

Lock stood in front of Carrie's grave for a while longer until his eyes were wet and his bones chilled. After an hour, he turned around and walked back towards the cemetery gates. Ty was waiting for him with Angel, the Labrador he had adopted with Carrie and who had been staying with friends of Ty while he and Lock worked.

The dog danced excitedly at Lock's feet, and he reached down to scratch behind its ears. Finally Ty said, 'Dumb question, I know, but you okay, brother?'

With no artifice between the two men, Lock shook his head. 'Still hurts, Ty. Hurts like hell.'

His friend placed a massive hand on Lock's shoulder. 'Wouldn't mean nothing if it didn't.'

Acknowledgements

Thanks to:

Marta and Caitlin. I love you both.

My agents Scott Miller of Trident Media in New York, Luke Speed at Marjacq in London, and Jon Cassir at CAA in Los Angeles for their advice and guidance.

Maddee James and Jen Forbus for running my website.

As always I'm very appreciative of the support of friends and family on both sides of the Atlantic. A special shout-out to steely-eyed dealers of death Kestrel Carroll, Chris Garfield, Ed G., Mark Greaney, Gregg Hurwitz, Scott Mackenzie, Lynda and Richard Murphy, Becky Treppas, and Selina Walker for sponsoring my participation in the 'A Run Down Hero Highway' event in New York City. I finished bleeding – but I finished.

A very special namecheck for Sara, sister of my friend, Andy Carmichael. Both of them are brave individuals, who are in my thoughts more than they know.

Finally, to the most important people in the entire process, my readers. I hope you enjoy this latest installment in Ryan and Ty's adventures.

About the Author

To research the Ryan Lock series of thrillers, **Sean Black** has trained as a bodyguard with former members of the Royal Military Police's specialist close protection unit, spent time inside America's most dangerous maximum security prison, Pelican Bay Supermax in California, and ventured into the tunnels under Las Vegas. A graduate of Columbia University in New York, he lives with his wife and daughter in Los Angeles.

For more information on Sean Black and his books, see his website at www.seanblackbooks.com or follow him on Facebook: www.facebook.com/seanblackthrillers

Made in the USA
Monee, IL
26 September 2021